Modern Elementary Geography

This edition published 2026
by Living Book Press

ISBN: 978-1-76153-875-9 (hardcover)
         978-1-76153-822-3 (softcover)

Modern Elementary Geography

by

Jo Lloyd

Contents

Introduction

It was almost 150 years ago that English educator Charlotte Mason wrote *Elementary Geography*. The first book in a series of geography titles for use in school rooms and homeschools across England and the British Empire, the focus of this book was physical geography. It served to teach readers about topics such as the form and motion of the Earth, directions, and the meaning, purpose, and use of maps. Grounded in fundamental geographical concepts, part of its value was that it taught children about place, encouraging them to look around their own local neighbourhood through a geographer's lens.

With the sustained interest in her philosophy and method of education, while first printed in the 1880's, this book continues to be popular today. However, even with the revised edition published in 1925, there are many aspects of contemporary geography, discoveries, and research that is simply not reflected in Charlotte's original text. While some components of her book are still applicable today, there is so much more that can, and should, be included in a modern course of geography.

A lot has changed since *Elementary Geography* was first published. At that time only 39 states were officially admitted to the union of the United States and large parts of the interior of Africa were unknown. The Greenwich Meridian had just been selected for 0° longitude and the National Geographic Society was newly founded. The world map of Charlotte's time was dominated by empires, not smaller independent nations, and World War I and II were yet to shape the world, let alone other significant events of the 20th and 21st Centuries.

There have been significant developments in science and technology, including changes and innovations that have altered the way geography is understood and taught. During Charlotte's era the approach was to describe places and people. Today we seek to analyse and understand these spatial processes and patterns, using some powerful insights from extensive data. Charlotte's original text cannot account for our expanding view of the universe, man landing on the moon, space technology and the advent of Global Positioning Systems, or the evolution of digital maps.

Charlotte Mason was interested in new research and encouraged fresh approaches to knowledge and teaching, qualities I also embrace. With many years of experience in homeschooling and a degree in geography, I am pleased to support students and parents in learning about geography. This book stays true to Charlotte's original vision of engaging learners but highlights contemporary knowledge and advances in physical and social geography.

While bringing Charlotte's work into the modern era, the original framework of her 41 chapters has been retained, allowing readers to exchange the old for new with ease. Likewise, I've kept Charlotte's approach of including poetry within the lessons. However, these are now folded into the lessons and the poems reflect the diversity of people worldwide, showcasing a range of voices and perspectives.

The hallmarks of Charlotte's approach to progressive assessment and map work have been preserved in this book. The original format of questions for students makes it easy to check on their progress and all the answers are provided too. Given geography is learned chiefly from maps, map questions are given. This includes modern approaches to mapping, such as online map options, satellite imagery, and bathymetry.

Those embracing the Charlotte Mason method can expect the same engaging approach with written text that draws the reader in and is suitable for narrations. This isn't a dry textbook. It has a literary quality to teach children foundational geography. As a home educator, I know how important it is to harness the attention of little ones. I know how we long to make these lessons and topics come alive in our children's hearts and minds. We want the goodness and beauty that comes from a Charlotte Mason education, but need the truth evident from modern research.

I hope you find joy in exploring the countless wonders of our world. It is my delight to offer this book and share my wisdom and knowledge so you can teach this subject with confidence and flair. May this be just the beginning of a lifelong journey of reading, learning, discovering, and experiencing the people and places of the world around us.

A Warm Welcome to the Children

As you open this book, you may wonder what geography is all about.

Geographers study places and people. It is a subject perfect for people who are naturally curious. It is for anyone who ever looked down a road or river and wondered where it goes. Geography is for those people who sit on the train or bus watching houses and shops pass by and ponder who lives in those houses and what they buy from those shops. This is a subject that helps us understand our world.

So, to study geography is to be an explorer of the world, and geography is a subject that we all live every day.

Modern Elementary Geography showcases a range of places in our beautiful world. Some places you may have seen with your own eyes. They may be a part of where you live. For example, you might live within a mountainous area and when you read the chapters about hills, mountains, and valleys you can look out your window and see these in the landscape around you. Others you may not have seen just yet; so, you might read about fjords and glaciers, imagining what they look like, and want to explore them in the future.

I enjoy learning about our world and exploring it. I have studied geography extensively and have learned from some enthusiastic teachers. I've read many books, articles, research papers, pored over maps and statistical data, and trekked through landscapes doing fieldwork to explore and understand our world. I understand that reading good books about this topic is exciting and I am thrilled to share this book with you. Perhaps it will capture your imagination and help you to see the world around you in new ways.

This book is a starting point for studying geography. It will help you understand parts of our world including oceans, continents, landscapes, and the places people live. My hope is that this book will be just one of many geography books you enjoy in your life as you become an intrepid explorer.

CHAPTER 1

Our Solar System

To begin a study of geography it is useful to consider our place in the universe. When we ponder the wonders of our world we can sometimes forget that our planet is just one of many. A good way to remember just how big our universe is, is simply to look up. Have you ever looked up at the stars and just gazed at the night sky? If you live in the city it can be hard to notice many stars; but stand outside in a nature reserve, national park, or out on a farm, where there is little artificial light, you can look up at night and see a whole sky full of stars. There are so many stars in our universe it is impossible to count them all and many children are taught the popular nursery rhyme about stars in the sky:

Twinkle, twinkle, little star; how I wonder what you are!

Enjoying the night sky, a stargazer will notice that some lights do seem to be bigger and brighter than the rest; they don't seem to twinkle like other stars do, or how it is described in the song. Rather, their light stays constant. This is because they are not twinkling stars at all. They are distant planets of our solar system. While stars generate their own light, making them twinkle, planets do not produce light. Instead, they reflect the light from the sun. This is why they look different to the stars when you gaze up at them at night.

In our solar system there are eight planets. These are Mercury, Venus, Earth, Mars, Jupiter, Saturn, Uranus, and Neptune. Mercury is the planet closest to the sun while Neptune is the furthest away. We live on planet Earth. It is the third planet from the sun. Venus is the second planet from the sun, sitting between Earth and Mercury. Moving away from the sun, the fourth planet is Mars. The first four planets – Mercury, Venus, Earth, and Mars – are all terrestrial planets. They are all relatively small and solid, with rocky surfaces.

Each of the eight planets in our solar system orbit around the sun, as do asteroids and comets. Some planets orbit the sun much quicker than others given the distance they need to travel. It takes Earth 365 ¼ days – one year – to make a trip around the sun. The shape the planets travel in is called an ellipse, which is like a flattened circle or oval shape. To complete the orbit within this time, Earth travels at nearly 30 kilometres (18.5 miles) per second. In comparison, it only takes Mercury 88 days to orbit the sun. It has a shorter path because it is so close to the sun and the sun's gravity pulls on it, making it move faster. However, Neptune is the planet furthest away from the sun and so takes a lot longer to make its orbit: 164.8 years!

Beyond the four inner terrestrial planets lies the main asteroid belt. This is a part of our solar system where asteroids revolve around the sun. There are millions of asteroids, ranging in size from small to over 1 kilometre (0.6 miles) in length. Scientists monitor the movement of asteroids, using telescopes and radar to watch for any coming close to Earth's orbit and presenting possible danger. Past the main asteroid belt are the four other planets of our solar system: Jupiter, Saturn, Uranus, and Neptune. Jupiter and Saturn are giant ice planets, while Uranus and Neptune are gas giants.

No matter how far away, what the planet is made of, or how quickly it moves, all the planets are centred around the sun. It is the heart of our solar system. The sun is a massive star and the only one in our solar system. The sun is so big that one million planets the size of Earth could fit inside it. Gravity from the sun keeps all the planets, asteroids, and even the smallest piece of space debris, in its orbit. Energy from the sun is what enables us to have life as we know it here on Earth. The connection between the sun and Earth is what creates our seasons, ocean currents, weather, climate, and the beautiful, coloured lights in the night sky, auroras. Yet, while it is the centre of our solar system, it is only one of billions of such massive stars that are dispersed across the Milky Way galaxy.

We see the sun in our sky during the day and enjoy the light and heat it provides. The way the Earth orbits around it defines our years, and the rotation of the Earth is what creates day and night. To visualise this, it can be useful to think about Earth as having a "day side" and a "night side". This is because, while our sun is massive, it still only illuminates half of our Earth at any time: the "day side". The "night side" is in the dark, away from the light of the sun. Likely, it is daytime while you are reading this. This means you are in the "day side" of Earth that is facing towards the light of the sun. You experience the sunlight and enjoy the daytime. However, the other side – the "night side" – is facing away from it, making it dark there. This means it is night-time and people are sleeping and resting. When the Earth rotates to face the sun their day will begin and yours will turn to night.

Along with the sun, the other main light in our skies is the moon. Unlike the sun, the moon can be seen both at night and during the day. Most planets have a moon and some asteroids even have moons. Saturn and Jupiter have many moons, with Saturn having 146! Here on Earth, we have only one moon. That one moon orbits our planet, just as the Earth orbits around the sun. Like planets, the moon doesn't generate its own light. The light the moon gives is light reflected from the sun. It is reflected off the surface of the moon, creating the moonlight we see. Over the course of a month, you will notice that the shape of the moon changes. Depending on what phase of its orbit the moon is in, you may see the whole moon, called "the full moon", and it might be quite bright in the sky, reflecting the light from the sun from its full surface. Other times you may just see part of our moon, or barely be able to see much of it at all. At times it is like a small crescent hanging in the sky.

Just as Earth has a "day side" and "night side", the moon has a "near side" and a "far side". Both sides experience day and night, but the far side is always looking away from Earth. From Earth we always see the near side of the moon, no matter where you live in the world. Whether you are in Australia or North America, everyone sees the same side of the moon: the near side. While we cannot see the far side of the moon from Earth, it still experiences night and day depending on whether the sun is shining on it or not.

You may have heard someone refer to a "dark side" of the moon and wonder how this relates to having "near" and "far" sides. The idea of having a dark side comes from the fact that the moon doesn't generate its own light but also from a time when space communications equipment wouldn't work beyond a certain point. It was called the "dark side" because communications would be lost, leaving spacecraft in the dark. There isn't really a dark side of the moon as such, but years ago people associated it with the far side. Because we cannot see it from Earth it was shrouded in mystery and darkness.

Many scientists devote their skills to helping us understand more about the moon, planets, stars, and other aspects of our solar system. There is much to learn and space science is a really exciting area. But it isn't just scientists that are captivated by what we can see in our skies. Artists have created beautiful paintings celebrating the beauty and wonder of our vast solar system. Explorers would navigate their journeys using the night sky, following the alignment of planets and stars to plot and track their journey, and the Bible tells how a bright star appeared in the sky to herald the birth of Jesus Christ. Poets and lyricists capture the wonder of the night sky or the glory of the bright sun. Some even give clues about spotting the planets among the stars, such as in the beginning two stanzas of this poem by Henry Wadsworth Longfellow:

<u>*The Light of Stars*</u>

The night is come, but not too soon;
And sinking silently,
All silently, the little moon
Drops down behind the sky.

There is no light in earth or heaven
But the cold light of stars;
And the first watch of night is given
To the red planet Mars.

by Henry Wadsworth Longfellow

CHAPTER 2

Planet Earth

Earth is the fifth largest planet in our solar system and the only planet where there is life and liquid water. Earth has incredible biodiversity, one key feature that distinguishes it from other planets. It has teeming coral reefs swimming with fish, vast grasslands, and rainforests vibrant with many different plants and animals. Space scientists are yet to find another planet that has the array of species of life that Earth holds. Being one of four terrestrial planets, Earth is made up of rocks and metals. These form five major layers, three of which are solid, one is liquid, and one is quite mysterious.

Our Earth is dynamic, which can be hard to capture in diagrams. Cross-sections usually show four rather distinct layers of our planet, but this suggests they are quite separate and doesn't show all the layers. The depths of each layer aren't as strict and uniform as the simple lines of a picture can show. Just as space scientists research aspects of astronomy and planets, geologists are the scientists who study our planet Earth. Geologists examine the history of our physical planet and the materials that make up our world, like rocks and minerals. They make new discoveries about how our planet works. The work of space scientists and geologists inform geographers. Geography looks at where things are on Earth, why they are there, and how they are changing over time. This means that geographers need to understand the geology of our physical planet.

Back in 1864 novelist Jules Verne imagined the centre of the Earth as holding a sprawling subterranean sea, giant crystals, and even a lost cavern of dinosaurs. However, the truth is quite different to his book, *Journey to the Center of the Earth*. Rather than being a place where dinosaurs roam, it is almost like a different planet within our own. The inner

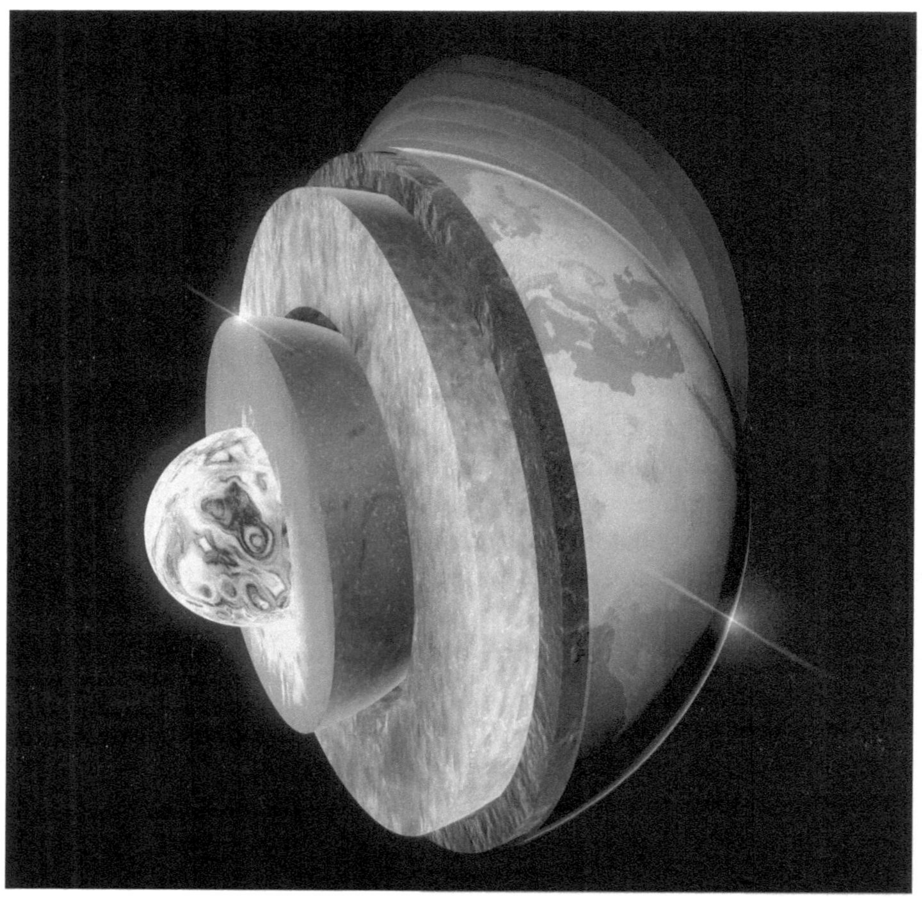

The layers of the earth

core of planet Earth is solid iron and nickel and nearly 2,500 kilometres (1,500 miles) thick. It is also extraordinarily hot. It is a scorching ball which is almost as big as Earth's moon, yet, still today we know more about other planets in our solar system than we do about this part of the Earth. While many older books show the inner core as just one layer, scientists now believe it is made up of two. In the innermost depths of the inner core a smaller core exists, much like a tiny pip can be found inside an apple core. While somewhat elusive, making it difficult to map, scientists using supercomputers have pieced together elements of data to get a picture of this innermost core.

The second layer, called the outer core, surrounds the inner core with iron, nickel, and sulphur. Like the inner core, this has exceedingly high temperatures. However, different to the inner core – which stays as a solid, dense iron ball due to the intense pressure – this is a fiery liquid layer. Given we are so used to seeing rocks as thick, solid parts of our world, it can be hard to think of rocks so hot that they are molten. However, for the rocks in this layer of our planet, the heat and pressure are just so intense that the rocks cannot stay in their solid state. This outer core is around 2,300 kilometres (1,400 miles) thick. By way of comparison, this is about the same distance between Perth and Adelaide in Australia, New York City and Houston, Texas in America, and a little further than travelling between Beijing and Guangzhou in China. It is this outer core that creates Earth's magnetic field. The magnetic field is vital for life. Its strength helps to maintain water in liquid form, making our planet habitable. Without it, plants, animals, and humans would not survive on Earth.

The third layer of our planet is called the mantle. This layer is around 2,900 kilometres (1,800 miles) thick and is the largest of the four layers. Being so thick, it varies in temperature. Some parts can be very hot, around 3,700°C (6692°F), while others are around 700°C (1300°F). Overall, compared with the blazing inner layers of the planet, this one is relatively cooler. This is a large part of the planet, with the Earth's mantle making up 84% of the Earth's total volume. It is made up mostly of dense rock. Iron, potassium, sodium, calcium, and aluminium are just some of the elements found in the mantle. The materials and heat within the mantle help shape the landscapes we see on Earth.

The uppermost part of the mantle is called the lithosphere. This is a solid part of the planet and is a part of the outer two layers. Spanning the top 100 kilometres (62 miles) of Earth, the lithosphere is in the upper part of the mantle and within the fifth and final layer, the crust. This is where the tectonic plates lie. The countries of the Earth lie on these massive, rigid slabs of rock, called tectonic plates, and these move within the mantle. When you read about earthquakes, volcanic eruptions, and the formation of mountains you are learning about geological activity caused by tectonic plates moving and interacting in the lithosphere.

It is the fifth, and final, layer of Earth that is the thinnest. Called the crust, just like the crust on a loaf of baked bread, it is the outermost layer of the planet. The crust represents just 1% of the total volume of our planet but sustains the diversity of life that we see in the world around us. The crust is only about 5 kilometres (3 miles) thick under parts of the ocean and around 70 kilometres (43 miles) under the continents. The distance from the crust to the centre of the Earth is 6,000 kilometres (miles), through solid and molten rock.

Scientists divide Earth's crust into two types:

> the continental crust, which forms the continents; and
>
> the oceanic crust, which makes up the ocean floors.

Both are shaped by plate tectonics and are composed of different rocks and minerals. Of the two, the continental crust is thicker, extending from 30 to 70 kilometres thick (19-44 miles), deep into the mantle. The oceanic crust is thinner but can reach great depths, this dark volcanic rock plunging into deep, cold ocean trenches. However, this part of our planet isn't just rock and scientists are making new discoveries about life hundreds of metres within the crust.

The thin and light layer of Earth's crust is a crucial zone. It is here that coal and clay, diamonds and dirt, and other precious resources and valuable minerals are found. Powerful geological forces continually shape this part of our planet. It is in the crust that features like the Mariana Trench and Mount Everest were created. The Earth's crust is where mining activities take place. Its rich resources are extracted for human use. For instance, South Africa's gold mines, some of the deepest in the world, go as far as 4 kilometres (2.4 miles) tapping into the lucrative shallow parts of the crust. However, there is a hole in Russia that is believed to be the deepest anyone has ever drilled. Thought to be welded shut now, it was constructed during the Cold War when scientists thought they would take a "shortcut" to the mantle by drilling into the ocean floor, because this is where the crust is thinnest. Here the crust is only about 6 kilometres deep (nearly 4 miles) and this tunnel leads halfway to the boundary of the mantle, over 12 kilometres (7 miles) underground.

From the Earth's thin crust to its scorching core, understanding the structure of our unique planet and its position in the solar system is vital for beginning a study of geography. While it is fanciful to think of journeying to the centre of the Earth, the reality is that scientists use computers and data to gain a better understanding of what is actually within the Earth's core. This is work that is important to geography because geography is all about place. Knowing where our planet's place in space, along with its composition, provides the foundation for physical geography. The work of geologists, astronomers, and other scientists plays a key role in shaping the research conducted by geographers. Geographers explore the physical aspects of our world to try to solve problems affecting both people and places which means they must first understand the structure of our physical world.

Earth, the blue marble

Questions on Chapters 1 and 2

For answers see page 199

1. Which planet is closest to the sun?
2. Which planet is furthest from the sun?
3. How many planets are there in our solar system?
4. Why do planets shine rather than twinkling like stars?
5. What is the name of the path that planets take around the sun?
6. How many days does it take Earth to orbit the sun?
7. What are the five layers of the Earth called?
8. Is the inner core solid or liquid?
9. What is the study of rocks and the form of our Earth called?

An open coal mine

CHAPTER 3
Earth's Atmosphere — Part 1

Winds blow the open grassy places bleak;
But where this old wall burns a sunny cheek,
Then eddy over it too toppling weak
To blow the earth or anything self-clear;
Moisture and color and odor thicken here.
The hours of daylight gather atmosphere.

By Robert Frost

Surrounding Earth are layers of gases which act like a protective blanket for the planet. Just as you might snuggle under a blanket on a cool night to keep warm, this layer of gases provides a covering over our planet. The curtain of gases that wrap around Earth are called the atmosphere. Gases are substances which have no fixed shape or volume. They aren't like water that freezes solid into ice, or liquid you see when you pour milk or juice into a glass. Instead, gases will expand to fill any available space and, in most cases, are invisible.

To understand gases better, it is useful to imagine an inflated balloon. The gas inside fills the balloon, expanding to fit the available space inside. Once inflated, the balloon is no longer small and limp. It is full and firm due to the gas inside. Just as air or helium fill a balloon, the gases in our atmosphere spread and expand to fill the space around the world. These gases are our atmosphere and while invisible, they form a crucial layer that blankets our planet.

All the planets in our solar system have an atmosphere. Some planets and moons have atmospheres that are quite different to Earth's. This is part of what makes each planet unique. For example, Mercury has a particularly thin and wispy atmosphere, while Venus and Jupiter are covered by ample thick blankets of atmosphere. Nearly all of Earth's atmosphere is oxygen and nitrogen. This is life-giving and demonstrates the strong link between life on a planet and the type of atmosphere it has. There is also water vapor, dust, and a small amount of trace gases in Earth's atmosphere.

Our atmosphere gives us the oxygen we need to live and protects us from harmful radiation from ultraviolet rays. Like a blanket, the atmosphere regulates the temperatures necessary for life on Earth. This insulates the planet, keeping it warm and helps to prevent extreme temperature fluctuations between day and night. Earth is the only planet to have liquid water and the atmosphere plays an important role in this. The way the atmosphere envelopes around Earth creates pressure and without this we wouldn't have water, an essential for all life.

Our atmosphere also plays a crucial role in generating the weather. As the atmosphere insulates the whole planet, it traps heat. Our weather patterns are created as this heat and water moves around the Earth. The sun's heat on gases within the atmosphere causes the air to move around the planet as it becomes warmer or colder. Warm air is less dense and contains more energy than cold air, so it rises. As the air moves, it creates shifts in the atmosphere. These shifts are what lead to different weather systems moving around the planet. They may bring warm, sunny days, or rain and inclement weather. Understanding the atmosphere is key to predicting weather because the interaction between elements within our atmosphere, such as temperature, humidity, air pressure, and wind, create our weather.

The wind that moves around the land is also created by our atmosphere. Wind is the movement of air due to different air pressures within the atmosphere that shift across the surface of the Earth. Two terms are commonly used to describe these shifts: high-pressure and low-pressure systems. These terms describe where the weather system is in the atmosphere, with a high-pressure system describing a weather system higher up in the atmosphere and a low-pressure system being closer to land. Each system is characterised by dominant weather conditions.

High-pressure systems generally bring clear skies and cooler temperatures because air is moving from a higher pressure point in the atmosphere to a lower one. The air descends and spreads outwards. On the other hand, low-pressure systems have lower atmospheric pressure compared to the air surrounding them, so the air is rising. This can often bring unsettled and warmer weather. As the air from high-pressure areas moves into areas of low-pressure, winds develop. A gentle breeze will dance and sway if there is little difference between the two systems. There will be massive gusts if there is a large difference, created as the air moves quickly between the two.

While it plays a critical role in establishing what life is like on Earth and creating our weather patterns, the atmosphere is only a very thin layer. This thin layer is incredibly significant though. Just as the inside of the Earth is layered, there are different layers in the atmosphere. The nitrogen, oxygen, and smaller trace gases of our atmosphere, such as argon, carbon dioxide, helium, and neon, are found in the following layers:

troposphere
stratosphere
mesosphere
ionosphere
thermosphere
exosphere.

The troposphere is the thickest and lowest part of Earth's atmosphere. It extends from the ground up, continuing for around 12 kilometres (7 miles). Nearly all of our weather is formed in this part of the atmosphere, being the layer where water vapor is found. Compared to other layers of the atmosphere, the troposphere is more humid given this water vapour. However, moving vertically up through the troposphere, the air becomes thinner. This is why climbers ascending Mount Everest rely on oxygen tanks. As they gain altitude there is less oxygen in the air. As it thins, the temperature drops. Higher up in the troposphere it is colder and there is less pressure and less oxygen. Most commercial airplanes fly within the troposphere and so need to be able to withstand the cold temperatures of this altitude and the turbulent conditions that moving air pressure systems can create. In the upper boundary of the troposphere there are jet-streams. These are fast moving winds in the thinner, upper layer and commercial aircraft climb to higher altitudes to use these jet-streams. This allows them to move through the air quicker and save fuel by travelling along these streams of rapidly moving air.

Beyond the troposphere is the stratosphere. With little water vapour, this layer of the atmosphere is very dry, so clouds are rare. If they do form, they are very wispy and thin. The stratosphere extends to about 50 kilometres (31 miles) above Earth's surface and this layer is crucial to all life on Earth. This is because the ozone layer is part of the stratosphere. Like the oxygen and nitrogen, ozone is a gas. Forming a layer in the stratosphere, ozone absorbs harmful ultraviolet (UV) radiation from the sun that would otherwise reach the Earth's surface. Absorbing these most dangerous types of UV radiation, the ozone layer acts like Earth's sunscreen and makes life possible.

Today scientists are concerned about the effects of ozone depletion in this part of the atmosphere. Ozone concentrations happen naturally within our atmosphere and the ozone layer is uneven, being thinner near the north and south poles. However, it has become evident that the ozone shield is depleting and an annual ozone "hole" over Antarctica has been present each spring for many decades. Scientists from various research institutes and universities continue to monitor this. The ozone layer serves as a protective shield for both humans and ecosystems and helps to regulate the climate, safeguarding life on Earth as we know it, so this is important work.

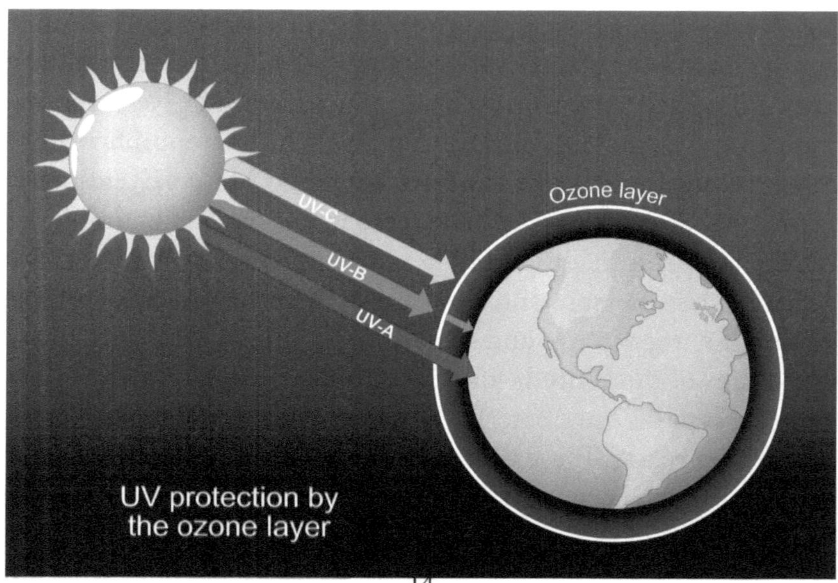

Earth's Atmosphere — Part 2

The atmosphere is divided into layers that vary in temperature. The troposphere is the lowest part and the part of the atmosphere that we live in. Most of our weather is contained here, as is around three-quarters of our air and almost all of our rain. The boundary layer is the lowest part of the troposphere and where the winds blow. The next layer is the stratosphere, which is a lot hotter because of the absorption of ultraviolet radiation from the sun. The ozone layer in the stratosphere serves to protect us from harmful radiation and is important for the health of our whole planet. Beyond these two layers are four more, including the place where some of the coldest temperatures of our Earth have been recorded.

The region above the stratosphere is the mesosphere. It is within the mesosphere that shooting stars are found. Known as meteors, these are debris of rock that enter Earth's atmosphere from outer space. When you watch the night sky you can sometimes see what are commonly called "shooting stars". They are recognisable from their fire tail which burns as they briefly race through the atmosphere. Compared with other atmospheric layers, less is know about the mesosphere. This is because this layer of the atmosphere is too high to use weather balloons or aircraft for research, but too low for spacecraft.

The ionosphere is above this layer, sitting within the bottom of the thermosphere. Notice how the word "ion" is included in its name and this gives a clue. Ions are atoms with an electric charge and the ionosphere is charged with ions. This layer of the atmosphere conducts electricity and reflects radio waves. The energy from solar radiation helps us to listen to our favourite radio stations and also causes the spectacular auroras in the skies of the northern and southern hemispheres. The ionosphere is a vital layer for both light and sound.

Sometimes called "the Northern Lights" and "the Southern Lights", bands of coloured light move through the night sky in areas far north and south within this layer of the atmosphere. These are auroras. The aurora in the northern hemisphere is called the aurora borealis, and in the southern hemisphere it is the aurora australis. The lights are often swathes of green, purple, or yellow, but can even be pink, red, or blue. This beautiful phenomenon is created within the ionosphere as the solar wind interacts with the charged particles in the atmosphere within the Earth's magnetic field. The light almost seems to dance as billions of tiny flashes fill the dark sky. The colours of the auroras are determined by the composition of gases in the atmosphere and its density, the energy involved, as well as the altitude. This is why auroras can be so different around the world. Astronauts have watched the polar lights from the International Space Station, viewing these particles of light waltz in the sky, and depending on where you live, you may see them one night too. Residents of Hobart in southern Australia have witnessed some spectacular colours across the sky and many tourists travel to Norway, Sweden, or Iceland just to see this amazing sky show.

24 hours a day, 7 days a week, the Hubble Space Telescope explores the universe. Launched in 1990, it was the first major optical telescope in space. It has changed the way we see and understand space because we have a better view of planets, stars, and galaxies. The Hubble Space Telescope gives an unobstructed view because it orbits in the thermosphere, high above clouds and light pollution. The thermosphere extends between 80 and 700 kilometres (50 to 440 miles) above Earth's surface. This is the thickest layer of the atmosphere and, like the ionosphere, the name hints at its characteristics. "Thermo" is a term that relates to heat and warmth. It is in the word "thermometer", being an instrument used to take a temperature. The thermosphere is a very hot layer of the atmosphere because it absorbs so much heat from the sun. While no clouds or water vapour are found here, like the Hubble Space Telescope, the International Space Station orbits within the thermosphere.

The region beyond the thermosphere is the exosphere. This is where the Earth's atmosphere meets space. It can be an explosive part of Earth's atmosphere with intense solar storms. No weather is found here, but sometimes auroras are seen in the lower parts of the exosphere. Due

The Aurora Borealis

to volatility, satellites used for geographical information, including the Global Positioning System (GPS), orbit the Earth much higher to avoid the dangers and potential collisions, transmitting the information and data they collect back to Earth.

There isn't really a clear boundary where our atmosphere ends and outer space begins, but the region of space surrounding Earth is the magnetosphere. It is formed by Earth's magnetic field interacting with solar wind and is constantly in motion. Of all the four rocky planets, ours has the strongest magnetic field and this is generated because of the powerful forces deep within the centre of the Earth. Our magnetosphere plays a key role in Earth being habitable because it effectively shields our planet. It repels unwanted solar and cosmic particle radiation and erosion from solar wind. This is a complex area of space science and there are many space craft in the magnetosphere to help researchers better understand this part of our amazing Earth and how it protects us.

Earth's atmosphere helps to support life. Just like the thick rind of a watermelon protects the soft fruit inside, the atmosphere serves to protect us from harmful solar and space conditions and conserve the elements we need on Earth. The gases surrounding Earth provide a stable atmosphere with just the right chemical ingredients we require. Without the multilayers of our atmosphere, life on Earth would not be possible.

<u>*Aurora*</u>

Of bronze and blaze
The north, to-night!
So adequate its forms,
So preconcerted with itself,
So distant to alarms, —
An unconcern so sovereign
To universe, or me,
It paints my simple spirit
With tints of majesty,
Till I take vaster attitudes,
And strut upon my stem,
Disdaining men and oxygen,
For arrogance of them.

My splendors are menagerie;
But their competeless show
Will entertain the centuries
When I am, long ago,
An island in dishonored grass,
Whom none but daisies know.

by Emily Dickinson

CHAPTER 5
Air and Weather

Nearly all of our weather forms in the lowest layer of Earth's atmosphere: the troposphere. The fog we see on colder days, the thunderhead clouds that loom on the horizon, or the wispy high cirrus clouds that stretch across the sky, all are made here as winds within the troposphere move air masses. An air mass is a large volume of air which generally has both the same temperature and amount of moisture. The amount of moisture in the air is called humidity. Those who live in tropical areas will know just how humid it can get in some times of the year as the air holds more and more moisture. The way these air masses move up and down within the troposphere creates our weather.

As it rises, air expands, and it loses temperature. Becoming cooler higher up in the atmosphere, it also sheds moisture. This means that clouds dissipate because water droplets evaporate. As the moisture drops, cloud droplets, rain, snow, or hail forms and when air masses sink, they are compressed. Falling closer to the surface of the Earth, the air then warms again, allowing it to again carry more moisture, and the cycle continues. Air is constantly moving around us and this happens even if you don't always notice it. The wind that we feel on our faces (and that blows our hair about) are caused by the shifting weight of air. Winds are caused by air moving and the pressure being exerted on the air masses.

Air might seem light, but it does push down upon the Earth's surface. This is what we call air pressure. At sea level there is a lot of air pressure but move higher up into the mountains, and there is less. If you have ever felt your ears pop while taking off or landing in an aircraft, taking a high-speed elevator, or driving up or down a mountain, you have experienced this change in air pressure. Air masses are categorised as being high-pressure or low-pressure systems to describe the effects of this.

A high-pressure system occurs when the air mass exerts a higher pressure or force because it is more dense than the air surrounding it. This pushes and spirals down from the atmosphere to the Earth's surface. High-pressure systems are what bring hot weather during the summer months and tend to bring dry, clear weather. Columns of air are compressed by the weight of air above and as it warms, the clouds evaporate, bringing sunny conditions. In the Northern Hemisphere high-pressure systems rotate clockwise, while in the Southern Hemisphere they move in a counterclockwise direction.

Low-pressure systems work in the opposite way. Within a low-pressure system, air is pulled and dragged upwards from the Earth's surface to the atmosphere. Forced up, it then cools. Any water within the air condenses to form clouds. In winter, low-pressure systems can mean snow, and in summer they can produce cyclones as the upward air moves across warm water, taking in more moisture. Low-pressure systems rotate clockwise in the Southern Hemisphere but counterclockwise in the Northern. This is caused by the air rising and converging towards the centre because it is lower than the surrounding air pressure. The movement of these high- and low-pressure systems creates the daily weather changes we experience. Wind distributes moisture and heat across our planet, which is why a range of weather conditions are experienced around our world in any one day.

Air is constantly moving due to its weight and the rotation of the Earth. Flowing in certain directions, how winds interact is key to weather. If there are differences between two meeting pressure systems, then strong winds will prevail. However, if the atmospheric pressure is similar then their meeting will cause only a slight breeze. Whether it is sunny with clear skies, a dull day full of rain, or a cold day bringing snow, these conditions are created in Earth's atmosphere as the air masses flow across the planet.

A meteorologist will forecast weather conditions by considering a range of factors and this is important work. They can predict whether it is likely to rain, snow, bring strong winds, or sunny skies. Knowing what type of weather to expect in the days or weeks ahead can help us be prepared. If there is a high chance of rain, we can wear wet weather gear or grab an umbrella, and if a harsh snowstorm is predicted we might choose to stay safe at home. To make these forecasts meteorologists examine the movement of the high- and low-pressure systems. They watch how air masses move from one location to another across the Earth, carrying their weather conditions to a new region. Meteorologists examine the current air mass in that region to see if it might collide with one incoming, creating storm conditions. This is because when air masses meet, they form boundaries. These are called "fronts" and are often categorised like this:

a stationary front: where the two air masses don't move

a warm front: where a warmer air mass replaces a cooler one

a cold front: where a colder air mass replaces a warmer one.

Fronts can bring substantial changes in weather as different air masses meet and interact. When one air mass displaces another the weather can change dramatically.

You may have heard meteorologists talk about air pressure in their weather forecasts and wondered how this is measured. In 1643, an Italian physicist, Evangelista Torricelli, invented the barometer. This is the instrument that measures air pressure. Meteorologists still use them today, although now they are digital devices and much smaller and more compact than Torricelli's invention, one of which was 10 metres (35 feet) high! A barometer will show a drop or rise in air pressure. Meteorologists examine this shift as they predict short-term weather changes. A rapid drop in air pressure will herald the arrival of a low-pressure system, which brings wind, cloud, and often rain. However, when the barometer shows high-pressure systems, you can expect clear skies and dry air.

Air pressure, temperature, humidity, wind speed, and direction are just some the factors that determine our weather. Meteorologists examine these to forecast what the weather will be like. They use computer programs and mathematics to create maps, graphics, videos, and charts to report on their predictions. These maps show how the air masses are moving across regions, putting the weather into your local geography. You can check the forecast when making plans for your day. The weather forecast helps you to see how warm or cool it will be, and whether you may need a warm jacket or raincoat.

Importantly, the work of meteorologists can help us prepare for severe weather events. In 1974 Darwin, Australia was struck by Cyclone Tracy

A barometer

on Christmas Eve. Over 70 people lost their lives, many were injured, and thousands evacuated as most of this northern Australian city was destroyed. With winds of deadly speeds and pouring rain, nearly three-quarters of the homes in Darwin could not be lived in anymore. Proving the resilience and determination of people in "the Top End", the city was rebuilt within a few years despite it being one of Australia's worst natural disasters. However, after Cyclone Tracy, changes were made to the way the weather bureau predicts severe weather events. This cyclone showed just how tough instruments and technology need to be for this job. The anemometer at Darwin Airport measuring wind speed and direction broke because the winds were just too strong. Today, better technology is available for weather forecasting so people can be more accurately warned about dangerous weather conditions like this and make arrangements for safety. Modern rain radars can even show exactly where it is raining and how intense it is.

While weather is forecast for the short-term and technology can show just how quickly weather conditions may be changing, it is important to think about climate too. Climate is the type of conditions expected in a place during different seasons over a longer period of time. It tells us what the weather might be like during the seasons of the year. For the people of Darwin, this means to expect a warm dry season in the middle of the year and that tropical cyclones can occur during the wet season. Climate information is prepared using weather data and helps to predict trends in the future. Scientists specialising in the study of climate are called climatologists. Climatologists study weather patterns and the atmosphere over a long period of time, including how it may be changing.

Questions on Chapters 3, 4 and 5

For answers see page 199

1. What are the main components of our atmosphere?
2. What is the first layer of Earth's atmosphere called?
3. In which layer of the atmosphere is the ozone layer found?
4. List some of the colours of auroras.
5. What does a barometer measure?
6. What type of weather does a low-pressure system bring?
7. Clear skies, warmer and drier conditions are associated with what type of atmospheric pressure system?
8. What is the name of the instrument that measures wind speed?
9. Describe what a weather forecaster or meteorologist does?

CHAPTER 6

The Equator

"A sparkling blue and white jewel" is how American astronaut Edgar Mitchell described Earth after gazing at it from space. While not many people can view Earth firsthand from space, we can all enjoy the photographs and images made during space missions and from man-made satellites, showing our planet and its place in the solar system. Satellites help us to observe Earth and to gain a perspective on our world that we simply cannot see from our own homes and backyards. Look at a satellite image of Earth and you can see the blue of the oceans, the green, brown, and gold of our lands, and white and grey clouds circling around above. Along with photographs and a variety of maps, geographers use satellite images for their work.

Studying geography involves maps. Maps are pictures of a place. Big or small, they show the shape, size, and features of an area and are full of information. Showing what is on the ground on a piece of paper, cloth, or a screen, maps have been used by many different cultures and societies since the Stone Age. Each map shares facts about our large, three-dimensional world on a smaller, two-dimensional scale. This helps us to learn more about places both close by and further afield.

Rather than putting such information onto a flat piece of paper or a screen, globes are a model of what Earth looks like as a whole, round planet. They are spherical, offering a picture on a much smaller scale, so we can literally hold the world in our own hands. Many globes show terrestrial information; meaning they show the natural features of Earth, such as mountains, deserts, forests, and grasslands. Some even offer this in a tactile way and map readers can feel the mountain ranges on the map rising higher than the plains. Other globes focus on the political themes of our world, showing the geographical boundaries of countries in an array of colours so map readers can differentiate between the many countries of the world. Countries may even be vividly coloured pink, yellow, lilac, or red, vastly different to a terrestrial globe which shows what it would look like to view the Earth from space.

Look at a globe or a map of the world and you will often see a black line running through the middle of it, crossing Earth horizontally. This is an imaginary line and not something a satellite image would show, nor could you see it as you crossed by in a ship or airplane. This is the equator. It effectively divides our planet into two halves: the Northern Hemisphere and the Southern Hemisphere. The equator runs through three oceans: the Pacific, Atlantic, and Indian Oceans. It also runs through more than ten countries. In Africa this includes Kenya, Uganda, Somalia, and the Democratic Republic of Congo. Within South America the equator passes through Brazil, Ecuador, and Colombia, while in the Asia-Pacific region it crosses the countries of Indonesia, Maldives, and Kiribati. Such countries are said to be "equatorial regions" because they are at, or near to, the equator.

The word 'hemisphere' means half of a ball. This is because in ancient Greek the word "hēmi" meant half and in Latin the word "sphere" refers to a ball or globe. Used together, they reflect the fact that our planet is shaped like a huge ball and can be divided into two halves: the northern

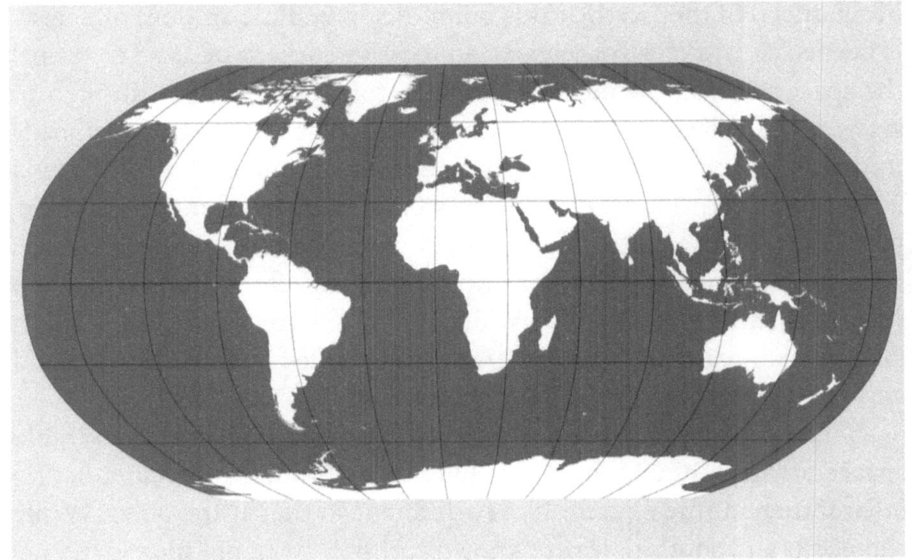

hemisphere and the southern hemisphere with the equator dividing the two. Yet, Earth is not perfectly round; it is not a true sphere. Rather, it has what is called "the equatorial bulge", meaning it is bigger across its centre and slightly squashed at the North and South Poles. Isaac Newton first proposed that Earth was this shape – calling it an oblate spheroid – back in 1687 and he was correct. While poetically we refer to the world as being a round sphere, it really is squashed a bit at the two poles, and more swollen at the equator.

Being halfway between the north and south poles, the equator runs at 0° latitude, Earth's widest point. If you travelled around Earth on the equator you would travel on the equatorial circumstance of Earth and it would take 40,075 kilometres (24,900 miles) to go all the way around. This is a greater distance than if you travelled around the Earth at the North or South Poles because our planet is flatter at the poles. Despite all the images we see of a perfectly round world, Isaac Newton's 17th Century description was accurate.

The planet's rotation causes the equatorial bulge. Earth rotates faster at the equator than it does at the north and south poles. This increased rotational speed at the equator means that the gravitational pull of Earth is slightly weaker at the equator compared to the poles. This is why many space launches occur from places close to the equator, taking advantage of the speed of the Earth at this point. An incredible amount of energy is needed to launch a spacecraft and massive rockets are used to propel the spacecraft as they move directly up, forcing their path through to space. To launch close to the equator means that the spacecraft is already moving a higher speed, offering an important advantage. French Guiana in South America is where Europe's Guiana Space Centre is located, just 5° above the equator. There are also launch options in the southern hemisphere, with the Arnhem Space Centre offering an Australian spaceport in the Northern Territory. This is a state-of-the-art modern facility, where satellites and rockets are surrounded by tropical woodland and the characteristic red dirt of the region.

Yet, equatorial regions are defined by more than just favourable spacecraft launching conditions. Due to its location, the climate and environment at the equator is very different to that at the poles. While the north and south poles are known for their freezing, snowy, and icy conditions all year round, at the equator most cultures recognise just two seasons: the wet and the dry. This is because it is hot all year round, but for some of the year it is hot and wet, while other months it is hot and dry. The wet season brings heavy, frequent rainfall while during the dry season there is little rain, just hot weather. This heat and seasonal rain pattern supports diverse and vibrant ecosystems, meaning that some unique plants and animals are found in the equatorial regions of our world.

The Maldives is an equatorial country. It has a tropical climate so is hot and often humid, but has distinct wet and dry seasons. More than 1,100 coral islands make up this island nation. Formed by natural atolls, it lies to the southwest of Sri Lanka and India. The dry season is enjoyed between December and April: this is when the rainfall is at its lowest. The wet season lasts from May to November, sometimes bringing heavy rains. This is a part of the world known for its beautiful beaches and clear, sparkling emerald, green ocean waters. Male is the national capital of Maldives, but most tourists come to stay on the resorts scattered across the 200 inhabited islands. Taking a seaplane or boat transfer, tourists reach their resorts, where they can stay in waterfront villas, swim with the whale sharks, walk along the sandy beaches, and snorkel along the ocean reefs, looking at the tropical fish and manta rays that live in the waters. Sitting in the horizontal middle of our Earth, this is a beautiful part of the world.

The Equator – A Haiku

Halfway between poles,
Broadest girth of planet Earth
At zero degrees.

by Jo Lloyd

CHAPTER 7

Latitude and Longitude

Just as you couldn't point out the equator while crossing over it on a plane or ship, there are other lines only seen on maps. These are the lines of latitude and longitude. While we cannot see these lines intersecting our planet on the ground, they help us to know exact locations which is why they are featured on so many maps.

The equator is the horizontal centre line of Earth's surface. From this centre, lines of latitude are measured in equal horizontal intervals all the way to the North and South Poles. These lines are used to measure how far north or south of the equator a place is. Sometimes they are called "parallels" because these lines run parallel to each other. Starting at 0° from the equator, locations are given in degrees north or south of that centre line. A smaller number shows a place is relatively close to the equator, while a higher number shows a location is further away. There are 180 lines of latitude with 90 parallels in the northern hemisphere and another 90 in the southern hemisphere. Around 111 kilometres (69 miles) lies between each line of latitude and the Poles are located at the extremes. The North Pole lies at 90° North while the South Pole is found at 90° South, the southernmost point of our world.

Latitude measurements pinpoint how far a place is from the equator. Being very close to the equator and known for its heat and humidity, Singapore sits just over 1° North of the equator (1°N). With its cold winters and mild summers, London, England, is much further away, at about 51° North (51°N). The largest research station in Antarctica, McMurdo station, is located at 77° South (77°S). This measurement shows it is 77 degrees away from the equator in the southern hemisphere and not too far from the South Pole. However, this measurement of degrees can be broken down into even smaller units to give greater precision to a location. Minutes and seconds can be added as each degree is divided into 60 minutes and each of those 60 minutes can be further split into 60 seconds. This finer subdivision allows geographers to identify a location within a 30 metre (100 feet) radius by using degrees, minutes, and seconds.

There is a special method for writing measurements of latitude, showing the degrees, minutes, and seconds. The degrees are given first, using a ° symbol. Next, the minutes are given with a ' symbol. Finally, the seconds are offered through the " symbol. For example, Cape Town, South Africa lies at 33 degrees and 56 minutes south of the equator. The latitude measurement for Cape Town is given as 33° 56' S. Mount Fuji is located in the northern hemisphere, within the country of Japan, at 35 degrees, 21 minutes, and just under 49 seconds north of the equator. The measurement for its latitude is given as 35° 21' 48.9" N. Giving the precise location of places like Cape Town and Mount Fuji means that Global Positioning Systems can zero into these places with great accuracy on a map.

While latitude measures the distance north and south from the equator using 180 parallels, longitude describes a location in relation to how far east or west it is. Just as latitude parallels take their 0° starting point from the equator, the 0° starting point for lines of longitude is the Prime Meridian. The Prime Meridian passes through Greenwich, England and is the geographical line from which time zones around the world are based upon. Lines of longitude begin at the Prime Meridian and places are described as being anywhere from 0 to 180° east or west. This effectively covers the whole Earth from this vertical starting point in England. Using this system of geographic measurement, Tokyo, Japan is 139° East (139°E), while Dublin, Ireland sits at just 6° West (6°W). In the same way that lines of latitude are called parallels, these invisible lines of equal longitude are called meridians.

When used together, lines of latitude and longitude offer an exact location to show where a place is in relation to being north or south of the equator and how far east or west of the Prime Meridian. In this way, latitude and longitude effectively act as a network of gridlines across our planet. The degrees, minutes, and seconds provide coordinates to tell the exact location of all places, no matter where you are on Earth.

The horizontal measurement is always given first; meaning latitude comes first and then longitude (the vertical). To find a place, you first determine its distance north or south of the equator (its latitude), and then its distance east or west of the Prime Meridian (longitude).

While there are different ways of providing these geographical locations, the most common is known as Degrees, Minutes, Seconds, or shortened to DMS. When giving coordinates in DMS, the latitude then the longitude are provided, both in degrees, minutes, and seconds, like this:

Sydney Opera House, Australia: 33°51'22" S, 151°12'54" E

Central Park, New York City, United States of America: 40°47'6" N, 73°58'5" W

Along with the equator, there are four other lines of latitude often shown on maps. Two of these define the Earth's tropical zone and two define the coldest zones on the planet, the polar regions. The tropical zone extends from the Tropic of Capricorn through to the Tropic of Cancer, close to the equator. There are polar regions in both the northern and hemispheres and these are far from the equator, extending from 66.5° to the pole at 90°.

The North Pole lies within the Arctic Circle. The Arctic Circle is located between the 66th and 67th parallels in the northern hemisphere. This is the place to spot Arctic foxes, polar bears, Arctic hares, terns, narwhals, snowy owls, and other animals that can survive the intense cold conditions. Eight countries lie within the Arctic Circle, including large swathes of Russia, Greenland, Canada, and parts of Norway, Finland,

Sydney Opera House, Australia: 33°51'22" S, 151°12'54" E

Sweden, Iceland, and the United States of America. Likewise, in the southern hemisphere, lying between the 66th and 67th parallels south of the equator lies the Antarctic Circle. Within the continent of Antarctica, this is the coldest region on Earth. Antarctica is covered by a very thick ice cap and surrounded by the sea ice of the Southern Ocean, making it colder than the Arctic Circle. This means the animal life is different at the South Pole. While Arctic foxes and wolves are not found within the Antarctic Circle, there are different species of penguins, seals, and whales. The Antarctic and Arctic Circles are parallels of latitude defining very cold temperatures. These are the horizontal extremes of our planet.

In comparison to the poles, the other two key lines of latitude are all about lots of sunshine all year round. The Tropic of Cancer and the Tropic of Capricorn lie at equal distances from the equator, one in the northern hemisphere and the other in the south. Both were named around 2,000 years ago. Their names were chosen because of the constellations that could be seen in the night sky at the time. In ancient times explorers and travellers would navigate by the skies and so the Tropic of Cancer and the Tropic of Capricorn served as crucial lines of demarcation, found by the stars. The two parallels are both 23.5° from equator; with the Tropic of Capricorn located at 23.5° South and the Tropic of Cancer at 23.5°North. The area between the two Tropics is called the tropical zone. Generally shortened to "the tropics", some older geography texts call it the "Torrid zone", following Greek philosopher Aristotle's classification. This area includes all the countries and regions that lie on the equator and extend as far north as the Tropic of Cancer

Central Park, New York City, United States of America: 40°47'6" N, 73°58'5" W

and as far south as the Tropic of Capricorn. Unlike the North and South Poles which see no sun during the winter, within this region the sun is directly overhead for the whole year.

Around one-third of the world's population lives within the tropics. This is spread across the continents of North America, South America, Africa, Asia, and Australia. In the southern hemisphere, the Tropic of Capricorn runs through many countries, including Madagascar, Chile, Argentina, French Polynesia, and Botswana. The Tropic of Cancer passes through sixteen countries, including Algeria, Saudi Arabia, Oman, and Mali. These are places where it is warm all year round and many tropical locations are known for their lush, green vegetation and hot weather.

Questions on Chapters 6 and 7

For answers see page 200

1. What geographic line marks the horizontal centre of the surface of Earth?
2. Do you live in the southern or the northern hemisphere?
3. What are lines of latitude often called?
4. What are lines of longitude called?
5. What is the line of longitude at 0° called?
6. Name three countries that the Tropic of Capricorn passes through.
7. Is the Antarctic Circle located in the northern or southern hemisphere?
8. The Tropic of Cancer is 23.5° North of the equator. How many degrees north is the North Pole?

CHAPTER 8

Cardinal Points of a Compass

"Never Eat Soggy Waffles" and "Nobody Ever Swallows Whales" are just some of the mnemonics used to remember the four points of a compass: North, East, South, West. Also called cardinal directions, these are the four main points you see on a compass. Knowing these directions is important because it can help to describe the relative location of places and natural features of a landscape. They are key to navigation too. Look at a map and you will often see a compass rose showing at least those four cardinal points, or perhaps just a North Point. This is simply an arrow pointing north. The Global Positioning System (GPS) in cars or on smartphones generally show at least a North Point to help travellers head in the correct direction so they can reach their desired destination.

In Geography using terms like "left" or "right" or "forward" or "behind" can lead to confusion. This is because they are all relative to where you are standing and the direction in which you are facing. So, north, south, east, and west are used instead. No matter where you are on Earth, or what direction you are facing, you know that the Arctic Circle is north of the equator and the Antarctic Circle is south of it. There can be no confusion about where they are located. Similarly, no matter which way you turn, San Francisco and Los Angeles remain on the west coast of the United States of America. At home you might refer to your doors as the "front" and "back" to describe where they are located; but to be more accurate geographically you could use the four cardinal points. If you enjoy watching the sunrise from your front door each morning, chances are it faces east to give you such a glorious sight to start every new day. Why not check this with a compass?

Cardinal directions can be used to accurately describe locations on a map. For example, Botswana is a country in the southern part of the

African continent, while the countries of Algeria, Morocco, and Egypt are located in the north. Kenya, Somalia, and Uganda are in the east, while Gambia and Senegal are some of Africa's western-most countries. Referring to these nations as being in the north, south, east, or west helps to ensures all map readers can easily locate them. It is more precise than describing them as being at the "top" or "bottom" of the continent.

In addition to the cardinal directions of north, south, east and west, there are ordinal directions that offer more specific bearings. These directions are derived from the cardinal points and combine them to give four further directions:

North east (NE)
South east (SE)
South west (SW)
North west (NW)

These are often called "intercardinal directions". This is because *inter* in Latin means "between" and these are between the four cardinal points. Using the four cardinal and four ordinal directions, geographers can describe the location of places more accurately. We can describe Kenya as laying to both the north and east of Botswana, that is, Kenya is northeast from Botswana. Cameroon is northwest from Botswana, as is Gabon and Angola. Geographic directions are relative to each location and the cardinal and ordinal points provide the tools for describing this.

To give even more directional detail, further intercardinal points can also be given through the eight secondary intercardinal points:

North-northeast
East-northeast
East-southeast
South-southeast
South-southwest
West-southwest
West-northwest
North-northwest

This means that, when used together with the cardinal and ordinal points, there are sixteen points that can be used to describe a location. This gives greater detail to geographers and anyone needing location details. A pilot of a plane or ship captain relies on such directions, as does a bus or taxi driver. A park ranger might describe the location of a particular natural feature in a national park as being in the north-northwest of the park, or that a river flows to the southeast border. There are many different ways these locational details can be used.

Hikers and explorers often use such directions when going out on their adventures. They use detailed maps which give them plenty of information about the terrain they are heading into. This can include the types of vegetation they will find at that place, how high mountains will be, and where they can find shelter and sources of fresh water. This is crucial information so they can find their way safely and avoid dangers. Along with such maps, they will take other equipment, including a compass so they can check their relative location and orientation against the information on the map. Although you can get smartphone apps, hand-held compasses are generally more reliable in these situations because mobile (cell) phone reception isn't always possible in remote areas. A manual, pocket-sized compass is more practical.

A compass is a navigational tool. It is an important instrument that helps you determine your location in relation to the two magnetic poles of the Earth: the magnetic North Pole and the magnetic South Pole. The magnetised needle within the compass will align with the Earth's magnetic field which is generated deep within the core of the Earth.

A compass

This movement means a user can work out their location using cardinal and ordinal directions. The needle pivots around until it aligns with the Earth's magnetic field, at which point the users of the compass can orient themselves to know which direction they are facing. Surveyors, military personnel, and aviation and mining industries regularly use compasses for their work, but anyone can use one. Learning how to use a compass is an important skill and, by using one, you just may discover that your front door lays due North, or that your local park is southeast, while the shops downtown are to the northwest of where you live.

To use a compass hold it securely in your hand. You can rest it in your open palm, or you may find it more comfortable to hold it with both hands. In that case, pinch it between your thumbs and index fingers, keeping it steady. Then, watch the needle. Observe how it swings around. You may need to move the compass slightly and often it is easiest to move your whole body, not just the compass, turning to the direction that it falls to: North. Then, to see how the compass works, turn to face the East and notice how the needle moves in the opposite direction. Return it to true North again and you might like to then turn the opposite way, to the west, again watching how the needle moves as well. With each turning movement you make, the needle will shift, always seeking to point North. To test this, walk in a straight line while facing North and you will see that the needle only quivers a little because you remain pointed in the same direction while stepping forward.

The needle moves this way due to the strong magnetic forces of our Earth. It is easiest to see this movement as you turn slowly. So, try it by turning full circle, watching the needle adjust. You will see it move northeast, east, southeast, south, and so on.

Your compass may also include tiny lines, not just the cardinal and ordinal points. These lines show degrees. Since a circle has 360 degrees in total, these cardinal points divide the circle into quarters. North is at 0 degrees (0°), East at 90 (90°), South lies at 180 (180°), and west is at 270 degrees (270°). This allows you to describe your location in terms of degrees and is more exacting than just referring to cardinal and intercardinal points. A compass can be a very handy tool when walking and exploring!

CHAPTER 9

Global Positioning System

Most often shortened simply to "GPS", Global Positioning System is a navigation system that helps locate places on Earth. Operated through a network of satellites orbiting the planet and a range of receiving devices on the ground, GPS is a powerful tracking tool. It is widely used across a number of fields. Geographers rely on it, as does the aviation industry, maritime businesses, military operations, emergency services, transport and logistics companies, and surveyors. It is highly probable that you and your family have used it too because GPS is the system that powers smartphone and car navigational systems.

To deliver this crucial service, a minimum of two dozen GPS satellites continuously orbit Earth within the exosphere. They circle the planet twice a day in one of six distinct orbital patterns. This ensures constant and uninterrupted global coverage. As they orbit, the satellites broadcast radio signals. These radio signals travel through space at the speed of light and relay geographical information to monitors and receivers located on the ground at various points around the world. This data is then used to calculate exact coordinates and positions, enabling precise location tracking. With a GPS receiver or a GPS-enabled phone, users can rely on the network to determine their location. Some GPS receivers are so advanced that they can pinpoint exact locations to within 2 centimetres (¾ inch) using this intricate global monitoring network.

Just as aircraft, ships, trains, and submarines all use GPS, a driver might use it to cross town or head further afield too. It is a straightforward system: simply enter your desired destination into the GPS and allow the system to plot the potential routes using satellite data. You can then select which route you wish to take and even note how long the journey is likely to take. Some hikers use handheld GPS receivers as a precaution, particularly when traversing unmarked trails. These devices allow them to navigate tracks and terrain with greater accuracy. Additionally, GPS receivers enhance personal safety because location information can be critical in a rescue situation.

GPS technology is used in many fields of science. For instance, GPS devices are used by scientists to monitor the migration of animals and to detect earthquake activity too. There are also active tagging programs for sharks. One of the world's largest shark tagging programs is run by the state government of New South Wales in Australia, using GPS technology to watch the movement of sharks. Fitting acoustic satellite tags to sharks enables monitoring through a network of listening stations along the coast. This provides the locations of sharks when they surface, offering an additional level of information to help keep beachgoers safe. Downloading an app allows users to receive alerts about sharks in particular locations or at specific times.

While there are many uses and application of GPS technology, there can be places where GPS receivers don't work so well. You may have experienced this when using a system on a smartphone or in the car. This is because satellite radio signals can be distorted by the Earth's atmosphere. Buildings and trees can also block radio waves, making it difficult to receive data from the satellites. However, sophisticated computer systems in the GPS network can apply corrections before sending them to GPS receivers to help with this problem. Mathematical models were instrumental in developing GPS, applying mathematics to land surveying to develop this amazing system. The satellites, Control Segments, receivers, and the math-based software are what ensures that GPS is accurate and why it is so widely relied upon.

Often story books about pirates feature a plot line of seeking lost treasure, complete with a map where X marks the spot. It is exciting to read the twists and turns to learn who finds the treasure, generally an old wooden chest filled with gold and precious jewels. Yet, in our modern age, these constellations of GPS satellites help people all around the world to find many different treasures. What we seek is more likely to be knowing where a place or a person is, rather than the chests of gold that pirates are searching for in these swash buckling tales. It is GPS that can assist people to track their fitness, determine when a parcel will be delivered to their doorstep, support their next geocaching adventure, or help them to navigate driving to a new place. So, the next time you use a smartphone or car navigational system for directions, remember the complex network of satellites orbiting our atmosphere and mathematical models that are working behind the scenes to provide this vital geographical information.

Questions on Chapters 8 and 9

For answers see page 200

1. Name the four cardinal points you would see on a compass rose.
2. Name the four ordinal points.
3. Using four simple compass arrows on a piece of paper, draw the four cardinal points.
4. Please point to the east.
5. Please point to the west.
6. What does GPS stand for?
7. Describe one way that you might use GPS technology.

A satellite orbiting the earth

CHAPTER 10

Sunrises, Sunsets and Seasons

While we tend to talk of sunrises and sunsets, the sun doesn't actually move its position in our solar system to rise or set. While the sun rotates on its own axis around every 27 days, it does not move from its position. It is the planets that orbit around the sun, which is the centre of our solar system. The movement of the Earth in relation to the sun not only determines just how long one year is, but also creates sunrises and sunsets, and establishes the length of our day. Even though we don't feel it, our Earth is always rotating as it orbits around the sun. Just as one year is created by the Earth orbiting around the sun, one day is created by the rotation of the Earth.

As the Earth moves, half of the planet is always in the light, facing towards the sun, while the other half is facing away, experiencing darkness and night. The half facing towards the sun, receiving its light, is experiencing day but as the Earth continues to rotate, day shifts to night. This means that while you enjoy your midday lunch, those on the opposite side of our planet are in the dark at night-time. As the Earth continues to rotate and you draw nearer to the end of your day, they are headed towards the sunrise and start of theirs. This continuous movement of the Earth means that as different parts of the world move in and out of sunlight, spectacular sunrises and sunsets are created. While it may seem that the sun rises in the east and sets in the west – and indeed, we use these terms to describe the movement – it is our planet that moves, not the sun. The cycle from day to night, then night into day, continues as the Earth spins. It never stops.

The rotation of Earth gives equatorial regions around twelve hours of daylight and twelve of darkness. Day and night are about equal. However, in other places days and night can be much longer or shorter, depending on what season of the year it is. For these countries, summer days mean more hours of daylight but also more darkness through the winter months. The winter days can feel short because there are fewer hours of sunlight and the light in winter is not as intense because it is further away.

This shift in the amount of sunlight is due to the axis or tilt of the Earth. Like the lines of latitude and longitude we see on maps and globes, the Earth's axis is another invisible line. Globes show this with the rod that passes through the centre line of the sphere, allowing you to spin the globe just as our Earth spins. Generally, the rod comes out where you would find the North and South Poles, giving Earth a tilt of about 23.5°. Diagrams show it as an imaginary line that passes through the core of our planet. Regardless of how it is shown, just like every planet in the solar system, the Earth spins upon this axis, just as a turning wheel spins on an axle.

This axial tilt of the Earth means that, throughout the year, the sun shines on our planet at different angles. This creates the seasons. For some months of the year the sun's light just doesn't reach parts of our world. Regions of our planet are tilted away from the sun, while others are bathed in light. In Glasgow, Scotland, it gets dark by 4pm during winter months, but during the summer the sun sets after 9pm. This is quite different to Singapore. Being close to the equator, daylight begins around 7am and nighttime will start around 7pm every single day of the year. There is little seasonal variation in the amount of daylight received.

At the extremes of the planet, both the North and South Poles are associated with pole stars that are aligned with the axis of the Earth. There is a North Pole star in the northern hemisphere, called *Polaris*. In the southern hemisphere lies the *Polaris Australis*, which aligns with the South Pole. Under the light of the auroras and the pole stars, winter at both Poles means long winter nights. Sunlight doesn't reach the poles in the depths of winter as this part of our planet is tilted away from the sun's light during that time of the year. This means, whether it is day or night, it is dark through winter because the sun's rays are hitting a different part of our Earth and don't reach the poles. However, in the summertime this changes. During the summer months, one Pole is tilted towards the sun and the sun still remains overhead throughout the night hours. The sun doesn't set. This makes for very long days and because there is so much sunlight it can be hard to sleep since it is still so light outside despite being nighttime. Just as equatorial regions are accustomed to regular amounts of daylight and night hours, polar regions expect a huge variation between the amount of light over the course of the seasons.

Depending on where you live, you might experience the traditional four seasons of winter, spring, summer, and autumn (fall), or it might be quite different. In the tropical zone there are often just two seasons: the wet and the dry. The varying amount of sunshine a place receives over a year is what creates the seasons. It also means that the seasons on one side of the Earth can be very different to the other. When it is summer we enjoy going to the beach and eating ice cream, appreciating the glorious weather. However, at that same time, people in the opposite hemisphere might be preparing to go ice skating, skiing, or just enjoying a hot chocolate in their colder weather. This is why Australians might have their Christmas celebrations on the beach, while in the United Kingdom it is winter and a white Christmas is likely.

Many Indigenous cultures acknowledge seasons specific to their traditional lands, reflecting more subtle changes as the year passes. For

A mountainside in winter and summer

example, the Aboriginal people in Kakadu National Park in northern Australia recognise six seasons in their year. In Antarctica there are really only two seasons: summer and winter. Tilting towards the sun during the summer gives twenty-four hours of sunlight which is why it is sometimes called "the land of the midnight sun". The sun is up at midnight! Yet, during winter, the South Pole tilts away from the sun so there is continuous darkness in the depths of winter. There is no sunrise or sunset to be seen.

CHAPTER 11

Solstice and Equinox

Have you ever noticed that some days feel longer than others? When we are having fun, time seems to fly by, yet other days seem to drag on and on. Children often find that Christmas Eve seems drawn out as they eagerly anticipate joyous Christmas celebrations. Despite these feelings, every day is twenty-four hours long, however, there are two days each year that are celebrated as being longer or shorter. These special days are called solstices.

A few days before Christmas Day those living in southern hemisphere experience the summer solstice, their longest day of the year. While this doesn't mean the day is longer than twenty-four hours, it is the one day in the year with the most sunlight. This is due to the Earth's orientation in relation to the sun. On Summer Solstice, which can land between 21- 23 December, the southern hemisphere is at its fullest tilt towards the sun which gifts the longest amount of time between sunrise and sunset. On this day Sydneysiders can expect around 14½ hours of sunlight and a hot summer to follow.

At the same time, those in the northern hemisphere experience their longest night of the year and the Winter Solstice. This is when they have the shortest amount of daylight. The North Pole is at its fullest tilt away from the sun and cloaked in darkness. At this time of the year people revel in the famous Christmas markets in Germany, Austria, and other European countries. With the scent of cinnamon and hot chocolate in the air, there are plenty of beautiful gifts to choose from and delicious foods to eat. Market-goers enjoy hot pretzels with mustard, fried sausages, fruitcakes, gingerbread, and roasted chestnuts as they browse the pretty stalls. Within these shorter days and longer nights, twinkling lights fill the market squares and celebrations overflow.

Just like the seasons, solstice is due to the 23.5° axial tilt of the Earth. This tilt means that parts of our planet enjoy more or less sunlight as the Earth orbits the sun. While the Winter Solstice in the northern hemisphere sees that part of the world at the furthest point away from the sun, the southern hemisphere is at its fullest tilt and closest point to the sun. This is why those in the northern hemisphere experience their Summer Solstice in June, when the southern hemisphere is marking the Winter Solstice, often gathered around a bonfire under the night sky.

Summer Solstice is celebrated in different ways around the world. In Sweden it is called Midsommar and is an important holiday. Traditional costumes are worn, games played, dances and feasts enjoyed. A typical Midsommar feast will feature new potatoes with dill and chives, cured salmon, and pickled herring alongside rye bread and often served outside. Dessert may be a luscious cake with sweet summer strawberries. These are all seasonal summer foods. With an array of summer flowers blooming in gardens, floral garlands will adorn the heads of women and children in celebration of the season. Many Midsommar celebrations include dancing around the maypole. Dancers hold long, wide ribbons of various colours and the dances they perform create beautiful designs as the ribbons overlap and intertwine to prettily decorate the maypole. The Swedish flag of blue and yellow is proudly flown too.

On the Summer Solstice in England many people flock to Stonehenge, a famous site that is an arrangement of massive stones. This ancient monument is shrouded in mystery with many questioning how it was built and why it was placed on this specific site on the Salisbury Plain. While details remain unknown, we do understand that Stonehenge holds an important and close connection to the sun. The huge stones were meticulously positioned to align with the movement of the sun throughout the year. During Summer Solstice the alignment is striking and so visitors come to witness this. On this day of the year the sun sets in perfect alignment with the stones, celebrating the long hours of sunlight. Many visitors will stay all night, waiting to see the sun rise again the next morning in perfect alignment with this ancient rock formation.

While many calendars will include the dates for the Summer and Winter Solstices, the exact timing of these is determined with remarkable precision by scientists. This is because the solstice represents the exact moment when the Earth's axial tilt reaches its maximum angle toward, or away from, the sun. It is at that moment when the cheers are the loudest at Stonehenge because the northern hemisphere is tilted closest to the sun, creating the longest day of the year.

Along with marking the longest and shortest days of the year with the Summer and Winter Solstices, there are two other important days of the astronomical seasons. These are the equinoxes. While the solstice indicates more or less sunlight for a day, showing the extremes, the equinoxes are all about balance. These are two days when the amount of sunlight and darkness are equal around the world. The equinoxes are pivotal moments that signal the transition between seasons, occurring around mid-March and mid-September. After that one day of equal distribution of daylight and darkness for all regions of the Earth, the balance of night and day shifts. The equinoxes set the stage for gradual changes towards the extremes of summer and winter.

When you draw an equals sign on a piece of paper as you complete your mathematics you make two horizontal lines of equal length. These

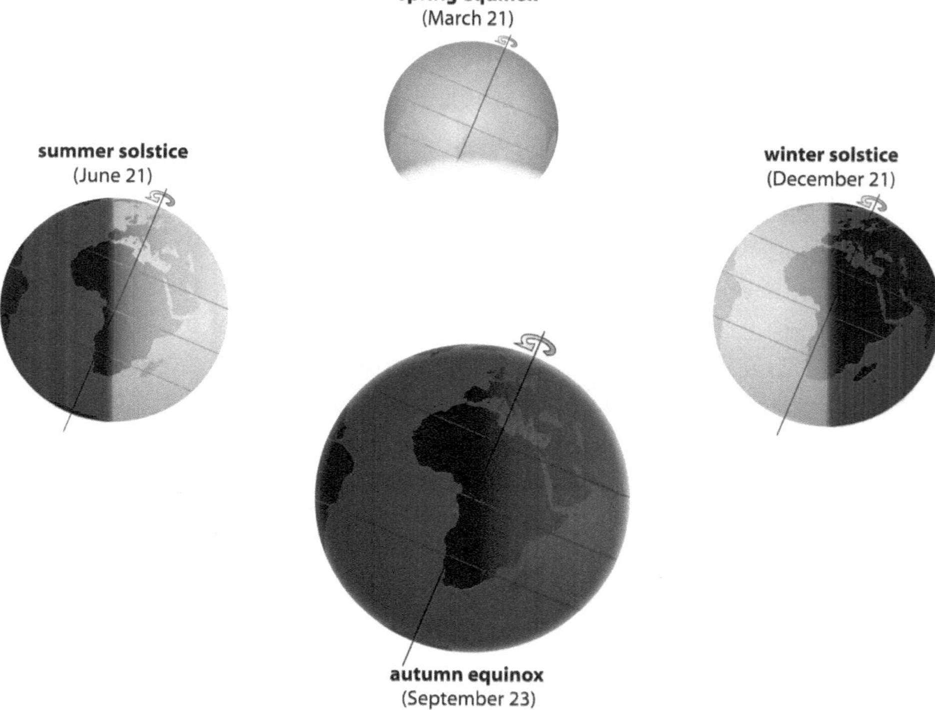

two lines run parallel to each other. They are exactly the same length and exactly the same distance from each other all the way along the line. The very symbol is all about equality. You will notice that the word equinox features the same root word as equals, and that reflects what an equinox is about: it is about things being equal.

Just as there is a Summer and a Winter Solstice, there is a Spring and an Autumn Equinox. One hemisphere celebrates the Spring Equinox (sometimes called the "Vernal Equinox"), while the other marks the Autumn (Fall) Equinox. The two mark the days on our calendar when both hemispheres experience nearly equal amounts of sunlight and night-time. This happens because the Earth's axis is neither tilted away from, nor towards, the sun. Both hemispheres have about the same amount of light. Most places on Earth experience twelve hours of daylight and twelve hours of night. Like an equals sign in mathematics, there is balance between the two.

In many places the Spring Equinox signals the time to start planting seeds for a summer harvest. It is also associated with spring cleaning, freshening homes after the winter months and preparing to welcome the warmer weather. People gather to celebrate these days too. Thousands descend on Chichén Itzá in Mexico. Once the centre of the ancient civilisation of the Mayans, the Temple of Kukulkán – "El Castillo" – is a gathering place to witness and celebrate the equinox. People come to see "the serpent of light". As the equinox sun sets, shadow and light makes it appear as though a diamond-backed serpent is moving down the pyramid-shaped temple. In other places the Autumn Equinox is a time to celebrate the harvest, as crops are brought in for the year, the balance of sunlight and bright moonlight enabling farmers to work later to bring the harvest in before the cold of winter.

Questions on Chapters 10 and 11

For answers see page 201

1. What is the Earth's axis?

2. Why don't countries along the equator experience seasonal differences in the amount of sunlight?

3. If it is summertime at the North Pole, what season would it be at the South Pole?

4. What is the North Pole Star called?

5. What is the longest day of the year called?

6. When people in the southern hemisphere are celebrating the Summer Solstice, what day is marked in the northern hemisphere?

7. On what two days of the year is there roughly equal amounts of both sunlight and darkness over the whole Earth?

Sunrise at stonehenge

CHAPTER 12

Climatic Zones

Latitude tells how far north or south a location is from the equator. This is important because proximity to the equator helps define climatic zones around the world. The closer a place is to the equator, the warmer its temperatures tend to be. Locations nearer to the North and South Poles are much colder due to their greater distance from the equator, which affects their climate.

While climate and weather are related, they are different in timescale. Weather is the conditions in our atmosphere each day around the world. When we discuss the weather, we tend to talk about how hot or cold the temperature will be, whether it is expected to rain, or be windy. It is what is happening in the short-term. In contrast, climate refers to long-term patterns and trends. Climate is about the average weather conditions for a place. For a particular area, climate summarises the average, maximum, and minimum temperatures and the amount of rainfall received over an extended period. So, if you are planning a holiday and want know the best time of year to travel to that destination, you would research the climate. That would tell you, for example, just how hot it gets during summer and if it generally snows over the winter.

There are broad climatic zones that have been mapped across our planet. A climate zone map helps us to understand what the climatic conditions are like in various countries. There are many regions of Australia that are hot and dry, while parts of Canada and Russia are some of the coldest places to visit during the winter. These maps give a summary of the climatic conditions.

Geographers and scientists classify climatic zones in different ways but the most common is the Köppen Classification, also called the Köppen-Geiger system. This system categorises the whole world into five different climatic zones. Each one is defined by the predominant vegetation because Vladimir Köppen established the system to show the close linkages between the native vegetation and climatic conditions. Tropical climates have lush, green plants because of the hot and humid climate, which is vastly different to what is found in a polar region. This method of describing climate centres on vegetation because the temperatures and amount of rainfall a place receives affects what trees, shrubs, grasses, and other plants can grow and thrive in that area. Using this information, the Köppen Classification uses the following five broad climatic zones:

     the tropical zone
     the arid zone
     the temperate zone
     the continental zone
     the polar zone.

The climatic region around the equator, between the two tropics, is the tropical zone. It is referred to as Zone A. Given the constant amount of sunshine received in this area, the climate is warm all year round. Places in Zone A don't experience cold winters, but it can get quite humid. This climatic zone is defined by its abundant plant life, with luxuriant green

Sahara

tropical vegetation. Holidaymakers often favour tropical destinations like Bali in Indonesia, Cancun in Mexico, Fiji, or the Seychelles.

Beyond the Tropical Zone is the arid zone. On maps this is usually shown in shades of red, orange, or pink. These arid climates don't receive much rainfall. They are dry areas. This may be a dry heat, like deserts, but also includes cold dry regions, like the Eurasian Steppe. Spreading across parts of Russia, Mongolia, and China, winters in the Eurasian Steppe are chilly, often falling below freezing temperatures. While there are some shrubs and small trees, the steppe is covered with grasslands because grasses can thrive in these conditions. A lot of Australia is included within the arid zone, being a hot, dry climate, along with the Sahara Desert and parts of the Arabian Peninsula.

Compared with the dry grasslands of the arid zone, shades of green are commonly used on maps to show the areas within the temperate zone. Many regions of the Earth fall within this zone. New Zealand, parts of the eastern Australian seaboard, the western coast of the United States of America and Great Britain all form part of the temperate zone. France, Paraguay, Japan, China, and southern regions of the African continent are also within this zone. Some of these places experience mild temperatures all year round while others have hot, humid summers and cool winters. Many productive agricultural regions are included within this zone.

The conditions experienced in the continental zone are quite different. Here, winters are cold, often bringing snow. Summers might be

Antarctica

cool, warm, or even hot, but all have long cold winters. Parts of Canada, Russia, and Mongolia fall within the continental zone, along with regions of China and western Europe. Sometimes called boreal or taiga forests, this is the world's largest land biome. Lying within the subarctic areas of the northern hemisphere, taiga forests are swathes of thick coniferous (pine) forests. Generally covered in snow during the winter months, these trees can withstand freezing conditions. Canada, Scandinavia, Siberia, and Alaska all have taiga forests and the largest forested area stretches from the Ural Mountains in Europe through to the Pacific Ocean.

The fifth and final climatic zone is the polar zone. On maps it is usually shown in light shades of grey, almost white. It includes regions that are under icecaps, including Greenland and Antarctica. These are places where some of the harshest conditions on our planet are felt. Extensive icesheets run for kilometres, deep in the Earth. The polar zone also includes the tundra areas a little south of the North Pole. Tundra is a dry, treeless plain. There is little vegetation to be found within these areas because the summer temperatures are just too low to support much vegetation growth. With little rainfall and permafrost – the name given to soils that are permanently frozen – these conditions mean that only hardy grasses and shrubs can survive in this harsh landscape.

Questions on Chapter 12
For answers see page 201

1. Why does latitude help define climatic zones?
2. Name two of the five Köppen climate classifications.
3. Looking at a map, name the climatic zone you live in.
4. What type of trees are found within the boreal or taiga forest?
5. In which Köppen Classification zone is the Sahara Desert located?
6. In which Köppen Classification zone is the South Pole located?
7. Looking at a map, name three countries that lie within the tropical zone.

CHAPTER 13

Continents and Countries

Geographically, we classify the world into five oceans and seven continents to better organise and understand the diverse landscapes of our planet. Dividing landscapes in this way also helps us to understand their similarities and differences. This book was written in Australia, which is both a country and a continent. The seven continents are:

> Australia, also called Oceania
> Asia
> Europe
> Africa
> South America
> North America
> Antarctica.

Continents are very large landmasses. Most continents are much larger than countries and include many countries. There are over fifty countries in Africa, the world's second largest continent. This includes the northern countries of Tunisia, Egypt, and Libya, and in the south, Botswana and Madagascar. Of all seven continents, Asia is the largest, spanning from the Mediterranean Sea over to the Pacific Ocean, while Australia is the smallest.

The creation of continents is explained through plate tectonics. Scientists understand that the lithosphere – Earth's outermost layer of crust and uppermost mantle – is made up of large, rocky plates. These plates fit together like a jigsaw puzzle, covering the Earth's surface, and are constantly moving, albeit rather slowly. There are seven major plates and other minor ones. The major plates are the Australian, Eurasian, Pacific, African, Antarctic, and North and South American plates. The movement and interaction of these plates is responsible for a lot of geological activity, including volcanic eruptions and earthquakes. The movement of these plates also formed the continents and features like the Himalayan Mountain range across Asia. Tectonic activity creates physical characteristics of our world across every continent.

Tectonic plate movement created the San Andreas Fault in the United States of America. A famous geological feature of our world, the San Andreas Fault is where the Pacific tectonic plate meets the North American plate. It stretches over 1,200 kilometres (750 miles). In parts of the landscape of the American state of California the effects of this activity can be seen. Some parts look like they just don't line up. The movement of the tectonic plates created fault scarps, which are steep banks or cliffs. There are also valleys and depressions in the ground where it has pulled apart. This reveals the tectonic activity occurring under our continents.

The continents are the largest landmasses but there are also many separate islands. So, when defining the continents, geographers include the islands associated with it. They identify the outlying islands of each continental region. For example, Japan is made up of many different islands within the Pacific Ocean and is part of the Asian continent. Given all continents border at least one ocean, the islands within the boundaries of those waters are considered to be part of the continent too.

Across the seven continents of Earth there are nearly 200 countries. These are smaller land units. While continents are geologically defined by their large landmasses, a country is both a geographical concept and

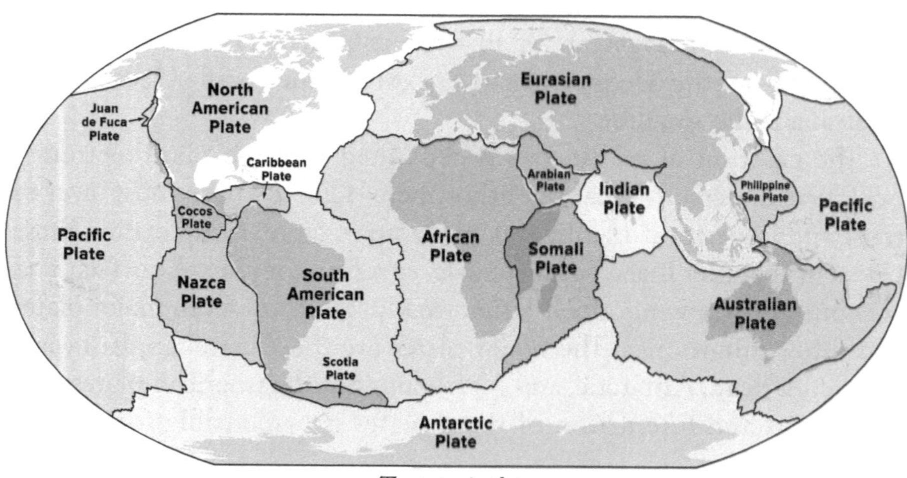

The tectonic plates

a political one. Countries have clearly defined boundaries, as seen on maps. These are created through history, culture, conflicts, and political agreements, which means they vary greatly in size. China, Russia, Brazil, Canada, and the United States of America are the largest countries on Earth. The smallest country in the world is found on the European continent. Covering an area of less than 2.6 square kilometres (1 square mile), Vatican City is a country surrounded by Rome, the national capital of Italy. Its population is less than 1,000 and is made up of the Pope, cardinals, and priests.

Along with having a defined boundary, countries are places which are governed by their own political and administrative system. The population that lives within the borders is subject to the government that runs the country. Each country makes its own laws and decisions. They choose how to use their resources and care for their people. Most also have a defence force to defend their borders in times of war. These aspects define a country.

While continental boundaries are not usually subject to change, country boundaries do shift and can do so relatively quickly. If you look at a map from the last century you would see some country names and borders that no longer exist. A modern map will not include Yugoslavia, Czechoslovakia, the Union of Soviet Socialist Republics (the USSR), East and West Germany, Persia, or Ceylon. These country names and boundaries have changed through political events and history. Sri Lanka, a country and island in the Indian Ocean, was once called Ceylon. The cooler temperatures, humidity, and rainfall of the central highlands of the island produce high-quality tea. While the name of the island changed when the country became an independent nation, Sri Lanka is still known for producing and exporting delicious Ceylon tea.

While the island Sri Lanka is one island and one nation, some islands host multiple countries across their shores. This means the name of the island is different to the countries found there. For example, the island of Borneo is the third largest island in the world. It is located in southeast Asia. This one island represents three different nations: Malaysia, Indonesia, and the Sultanate of Brunei. The name Borneo refers to the island itself, not to a particular country. Similarly, the island of Hispaniola lies within the Caribbean Sea. It is divided between the nations of the Republic of Haiti and the Dominican Republic. Each of these countries has their own distinct government, legal system, and economic structure, which are recognised by other nations around the world, but they share the one island.

Regardless of whether a country is within a large continental landmass or part of a small island, all countries are important political units. While continents are large geographic regions, the countries within these can engage in diplomatic relations, form alliances with other nations, or enter into treaties to work together. Representatives of nations can be involved in decision making that affects the whole planet. What excites geographers is the great diversity across the continents and nations of our world physically and socially. From the glaciers and volcanoes of Vatnajökull National Park in Iceland to the wilderness region of the Arabian Peninsula, there is much to discover and learn about our world.

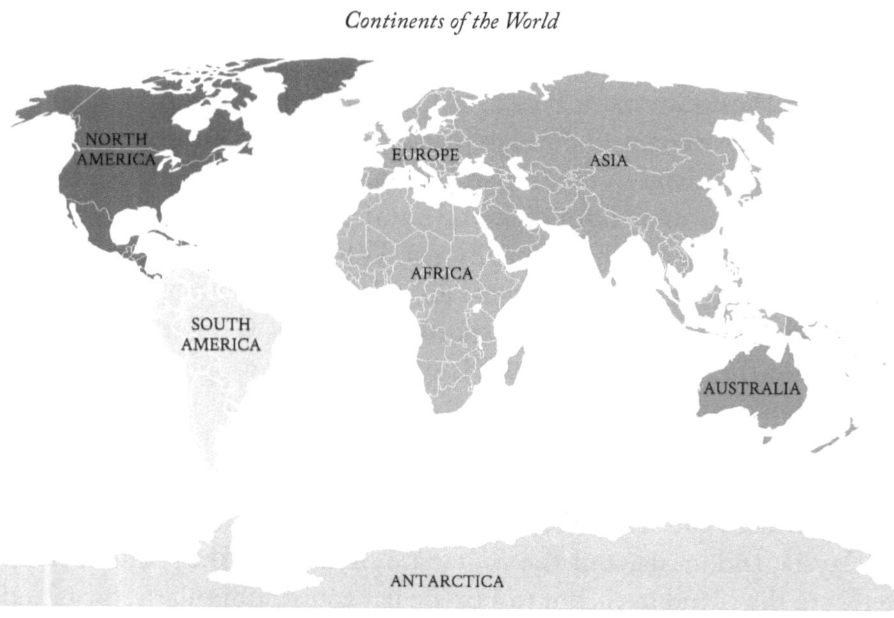
Continents of the World

CHAPTER 14

Antarctica

Earth's southern-most continent is Antarctica. It is our coldest desert, located within the polar climatic zone and is known for being the driest, windiest, and coldest place on Earth. The lowest temperatures ever recorded on Earth were at Vostok Station in Antarctica at around -90°C (-130°F). Ice covers 95% of this vast continent and can be nearly 5 kilometres (3 miles) thick. The frozen ice of the South Pole represents the largest store of freshwater on our planet. The most remote continent on Earth, Antarctica is surrounded by the Southern Ocean. This is a cold ocean, so cold that over half of it freezes over during winter. When the Southern Ocean freezes it creates a virtually impenetrable barrier of sea ice. It is impossible to reach the continent by boat in winter because of this ice.

Despite challenges accessing this part of the world, a lot of scientific research is undertaken in Antarctica. Many scientists investigate aspects of marine biology because the Southern Ocean is teeming with marine life! While you won't find polar bears in Antarctica, there are a diverse range of whales and seals, including blue, humpback, and minke whales, as well as sea birds, krill, and phytoplankton. Within the coastal areas of Antarctica there are many species of penguins, standing tall against the ice in their distinctive black and white.

Every continent in the world has mountain ranges. Antarctica has many mountain summits, including the Transantarctic Mountains. Mount Vinson is the highest peak in Antarctica and is part of the Ellsworth Mountains, which were named after Lincoln Ellsworth, an American aviator. He first spotted the mountain range from the air in 1935, though it wasn't until 1967 that a mountaineering team reached the summit of Mount Vinson. Mount Vinson was named after another American,

Carl Vinson, who was an American politician and strong supporter of exploring this continent. Along with the mountain, an aircraft carrier of the US Navy was also named after this man who served many terms in the US Congress.

Perhaps surprisingly, given how cold it is and how far south it is located, along with mountains, Antarctica is also home to several volcanoes. This includes a couple of active volcanoes. The southernmost active volcano on Earth is Mount Erebus. After Mount Vinson, Mount Erebus is the most prominent peak on the continent and the American Antarctic base, McMurdo research station, sits near it. Mount Erebus is just one of several volcanoes on Ross Island, off the coast of west Antarctica. Within the snow and ice at the top of Mount Erebus lies a lava lake. Puffs of steam and spewing lava show how active the volcano is. Infrared cameras and monitoring equipment capture the changes in the volcano, with many scientists observing how the lava lake churns, huffs, and smokes all year round.

With its freezing conditions and isolated location, there are no native peoples in Antarctica. While the frozen continent has lured many explorers, even 100 years ago very little of the continent had been explored or mapped. However, with recent exploration and satellite imagery we have a fuller picture of this place. This is a land for science and discovery, so Antarctica is governed very differently to the other six continents. The land of Antarctica doesn't belong to any one nation. Instead, a number of countries hold territorial claims to the continent. A territorial map of Antarctica is cut up like a pizza, with the claims of countries showing they want to explore it further. Many just undertake summer research but a handful of countries operate year-round scientific research stations on this intriguing international continent.

To care for this continent, the Antarctic Treaty was first signed in 1959, during the Cold War era. This was a time when many nations and groups were concerned that the continent could be used for the development of nuclear weapons and they wanted to prevent this. Twelve nations gathered together and signed the Treaty, agreeing on the best way to manage this unique continent. Representatives from Argentina, Australia, Belgium, Chile, France, Great Britain, Japan, New Zealand, Norway, South Africa, the United States of America, and the then USSR all signed the Treaty. It was clear that this southern-most continent was different to all the others and being able to research it was important to the whole world, so these nations gathered to determine how to care for it. The Antarctic Treaty is still an international agreement today and designates Antarctica as a place of peace and science.

Governed by this treaty, Antarctica is very different to a country. There is no government of Antarctica and no permanent population. A person cannot become a citizen of Antarctica. Instead, it has a transient population of scientists, researchers, and support personnel who have permission to work there for a short period of time. Antarctica doesn't have a president or prime minister; nor does it have a police force, legal system, or defence force. Instead, it is governed by a set of international agreements. Some of these seek to conserve the environment, including the fauna and flora, and others protect the marine ecosystems. Those who visit Antarctica include geographers, marine biologists, glaciologists, seabird and krill ecologists, meteorologists, and astronomers. They travel far south to carry out important research. Some scientists and support staff simply travel down for the summer months, while others will stay there longer, overwintering on the continent. In the summer months there are also tourists. Many sea voyages leave from the southern tip of South America with keen sightseers on board, ready with cameras as the boat pushes through sea ice, which melts through the summer. Some tourists even take a flight directly to the Antarctic Peninsula.

Tourists like to visit the islands within Antarctic waters, including the South Orkney, South Shetland, and South Sandwich Islands. These islands are external territories of various countries, meaning they are part of that nation despite being located far away. Many like to stop at South Georgia Island to learn more about the history of the whaling industry, visit Sir Ernest Shackleton's grave, see the snow-capped mountains, and the elephant seals and king penguins in Fortuna Bay. Some tourists comment that it is perhaps the wildest place you can visit on Earth and is the trip of a lifetime. However, visiting this part of the world requires careful planning, a generous budget, and permission from an Antarctic Treaty member country. It also has its risks. The reward is experiencing the spectacle of huge icebergs, active volcanoes, massive penguin colonies, and vibrant sea life amid an ice-swept land.

CHAPTER 15

Africa

Unlike Antarctica which has no permanent residents or distinct countries, the continent of Africa has a population of over 1.4 billion people and is home to more than fifty countries. It is bordered on the east coast by the Indian Ocean and the Red Sea, to the west is the Atlantic Ocean. The Mediterranean Sea lies to the north. Africa is the only continent that three key lines of latitude run through. The Equator, the Tropic of Capricorn, and the Tropic of Cancer all pass within African countries and the Equator almost neatly halves the continent. This is a continent with a range of climate zones and astounding geographical features. With diverse cultures, dense rainforests, desert regions, extensive grasslands, and even snow-capped mountains, there is much to explore and discover in Africa.

The Sahara Desert is the world's largest hot desert and dominates the northern part of the African continent. It covers around one-quarter of the continental landmass, covering ten countries, including Chad, Mali, Morocco, and Tunisia. While the Sahara Desert is about the same size as the country of Brazil, the geography is very different. Here you will find some remarkable land features, including oases, ergs, regs, and hamadas.

An oasis is a body of water in the desert, which seems contradictory. It may be centred around a natural spring, well, or irrigation system and offers relief from the harsh climate. In the hot, dry Sahara Desert date palms, olive trees, small shrubs, and grasses all grow close to oases, and pygmy crocodiles and cobras may be found here. An oasis gives welcome refreshment to animals and people.

While it is tempting to imagine deserts as just being sand with a few oases, they are far more than just that. The Sahara Desert in Africa contains various distinctive desert features, including ergs. Ergs are large

An oasis in the desert

sand dunes. They are the postcard image of the Sahara. These stretch for hundreds of kilometres and can reach 300 metres (1,000 feet) high. Ergs are valuable in parts of the Sahara, being used for the mining of salt. Around one-fifth of the Sahara Desert is covered by ergs and this is the landscape most people expect in this part of Africa, ever-changing areas of loose sand, swept by the wind.

However, walk a few hours and the view is no longer of sand dunes, but the soft, flat surfaces of regs. Regs are desert plains, made up of a mixture of sand and gravel, and make up a large part of the Sahara Desert. They are often red in colour, but can also be black or white. Flat compared to the sandy dunes of ergs, regs are known as desert pavements. They are sometimes referred to as stony deserts because they are large, flat open spaces within the desert, full of hardened sand. There is very little plant life in these areas and they are hostile to human life. Rodents are the few animals you see.

Along with these desert landforms, there are also rocky plateaus in the Sahara Desert. These are called hamadas. The Atlas Mountains, that stretch through the northwest corner of Africa, from Morocco to Tunisia, are hamadas, as are the Tibesti Mountains in central Sahara.

Hewn by the erosion of softer rock leaving solid rock, hamadas create dramatic landscapes, standing tall against ergs and regs. These are harsh landscapes. Like the sand dunes and rocky pavements, this part of the desert has strong winds, aridity, and extreme temperatures, with hot summer days and cold winter nights.

While rainfall and water are scarce in the Sahara Desert, there are aquifers, seasonal lakes, and two rivers within this region: the famous Nile River and the Niger River. This means that vegetation and animals can still survive in many areas. Camels are found here, along with gazelles, addaxes, snakes, lizards, scarab and dung beetles, scorpions, wild dogs, and over 300 species of birds. Precious water helps to support the wildlife. The Nile is the longest river in the world and has supported civilisations from ancient times. Although it is most commonly associated with Egypt, where it meets the Mediterranean Sea, it runs through ten other African countries, including Uganda, Rwanda, and Kenya.

The Niger River sustains life in the Sahara Desert and the Sahel region, which is located south of the Sahara Desert. In contrast to the dry desert landscape, during the rainy season the Sahel region shines with fertile green vegetation, offering farmers fodder to harvest between June and September. The seasonal rainfall transforms this semi-arid grassland. Stretching from Senegal and Mauritania in the west, over to Eretria in the east, the Sahel is a transition zone between the Sahara Desert and the more fertile, tropical regions further south. The rainfall is welcomed in what is otherwise a barren region.

South of the Sahel is the savanna of Africa. These grasslands cover around half of Africa, mainly central Africa. While there are different grasslands in this region, the Serengeti is the most well-known. It is a vast area and home to the highest number of large mammal species on the continent. These grasslands are the stage for the cyclical migration of elephants, giraffes, lions, hyena, wildebeest, and zebras. During the summer months it rains and so the rivers freely flow. In turn, the vegetation becomes green and lush, providing plenty of food for the animals. Winter brings a dry season and as the grasses dry off, the animals migrate to other areas to find food, returning again in the spring.

Along with deserts and grasslands, the continent of Africa also boasts some spectacular coastal environments, stunning rainforests and mountains. It also has a Great Lakes region. Within the Great Rift Valley there are seven major African Great Lakes, including the largest lake in Africa, Lake Victoria, which is the southern source of the Nile River. These lakes support an array of fish species, water birds, and other aquatic life. They also offer feeding grounds for larger animals like wildebeest and hippopotami. The four countries that make up the Great Lakes region are Uganda, Rwanda, Burundi, and the Democratic Republic of the Congo. In this region lies the second largest tropical rainforest in the world, where there are slender and quick chimpanzees, as well as the greatest of the apes, gorillas.

Each year tourists flock to game reserves and national parks in southern Africa to see some of most famous animal and bird species of the continent. Sometimes it is so crowded that you have to wait in line to see the animals. As the northern part of the continent is dominated by the Sahara Desert, many visitors travel to the southern regions of Africa, hoping to spot giraffes, lions, cheetahs, elephants, rhinoceros, leopards, and the black and white stripes of zebras. The reserves and national parks of South Africa are very different to the deserts of the north, with lush sub-tropical vegetation, wooded grasslands, and forests extending to the coast.

From the savanna plains where animals roam and feed, to the snow-capped tops of Mount Kilimanjaro and Mount Kenya, the huge continent of Africa is a land of contrasts. The scenic coastlines are breathtaking, as are the extensive coffee plantations of Ethiopia, the African country considered to be the birthplace of coffee. There are many impressive landscapes and places to experience, including small traditional villages where ancient practices continue, but also modern world cities, making the great geographical diversity of this huge continent perhaps its most defining feature.

Questions on Chapters 13, 14 and 15

For answers see page 202

1. What is the largest continent on Earth?
2. In which ocean would you find Sri Lanka?
3. Which three countries are represented on the island of Borneo?
4. What ocean surrounds Antarctica?
5. Name the seas and oceans surrounding Africa.
6. The world's longest river is in Africa. Which river is it?
7. Describe what an oasis is.
8. What are some animals you might see in the grasslands of Africa?
9. What is the largest lake in Africa?

Map Questions on Chapters 13, 14 and 15

For answers see page 203

1. Name the oceans and seas bordering the continent of Africa.
2. Name the two continents located south of Asia.
3. The equator passes through thirteen countries, including seven in Africa. Name the African countries that the equator passes through.
4. Find the South Orkney, South Shetland, and South Georgia Islands on a map of Antarctic waters.
5. Find and name two of the four main seas surrounding Antarctica.

Mount Kilimanjaro

CHAPTER 16
South America

For nearly 50,000 kilometres (31,100 miles) the Pan-American Highway stretches from the northern-most tip of North America in Alaska, through the United States of America, Central America, and South America, all the way to the southern-most point of South America. It is the longest road in the world but has one gap. This is the Darién Gap on the continent of South America. Travellers arriving at Yaviza, Panama continue by crossing the Gulf of Uraba by ferry, landing in Turbo, Colombia. There the Pan-American Highway continues all the way to Tierra del Fuego. The Darién Gap is a wild, tropical jungle with crocodiles, jaguars, many invertebrates, poisonous snakes, and exotic species of reptiles, insects and birds.

South America is a continent of spectacular features and contrasts. There are tropical islands and glaciers, deserts and rainforest, mountains and plains, dire poverty and extravagant wealth. It is the fourth largest continent in the world and the Atlantic Ocean washes along its east coast and the Pacific Ocean on the west. Like Africa, the Equator runs through the continent of South America. It passes through the countries of Brazil, Ecuador, and Columbia, meaning parts of South America are equatorial zones. Fans of Paddington books will know South America as the continent where Aunty Lucy lives, in the Home for Retired Bears in Lima. After all, Paddington was from "deepest, darkest Peru", a long way across the Atlantic Ocean and the tea and marmalade sandwiches of London, England.

The highest city in the world is found on the South American continent. La Paz in Bolivia sits at 3,869 metres (11,940 feet) above sea level, making it a little higher than Mount Fuji in Japan. Clinging to the Andes Mountains and sprawling down the canyon, cable cars transport people around parts of the city, straddling the impressive drops and rises in altitude. You can ride the cable cars and explore the city, enjoying the colourful multi-storey buildings, or see the Vallee de la Luna ("Moon Valley"). This is a stunning geological formation where clay spires jut out of the eroded mountain top. You may like to just stop and watch the locals, listen to their conversations in Spanish, and eat empanadas, a delicious pastry with all sorts of tasty fillings. However, while visiting, many tourists need to take precautions to avoid altitude sickness given La Paz is located so high up in the Andes.

The Andes Mountains are a massive mountain system which extends through the western part of South America. From north to south, the Andes Mountains pass through seven countries: Venezuela, Colombia, Ecuador, Peru, Bolivia, Chile, and Argentina. The same plate tectonic processes that formed the Rocky Mountains created the Andes. The Amazon and many of the other major rivers in South America originate in the Andes and some of the largest volcanoes on Earth can be found here. These mountains are so high that, despite being close to the equator and in a tropical region, peaks like Mount Cotopaxi in Ecuador are snow-capped.

Another amazing part of South America is the Atacama Desert in northern Chile. A plateau to the west of the Andes, close to the Pacific Ocean, it is one of the driest regions of this continent. In some parts of the desert no rainfall has been recorded for the last 400 years. Lying in the rain shadow of the Andes and between the Chilean Coast Range, it is one of the driest spots on our planet because the two mountain ranges shield it from rainfall. This blockage of moisture leads some geographers to call it a "death zone" for vegetation. Because of the unique conditions of the area, the Atacama Desert serves as an important testing site for NASA. Soil samples from this region are similar to those from the planet Mars and so instruments are tested for missions to Mars. Some space themed movies have been filmed here too, as the landscape looks like something beyond planet Earth.

However, the natural feature for which South America is perhaps most famous for is the world's largest tropical rainforest. Lying east of the Atacama Desert and covering around one-third of the continent, is the Amazon Basin. The Amazon Rainforest is located mainly within

Brazil, but also extends to the countries of Columbia, Venezuela, Ecuador, Bolivia, Guyana, Suriname, and French Guiana. It covers nearly 7 million square kilometres (over 2.3 million square miles), meaning it is about twice the size of India. This is one of the world's wettest rainforests and features many different plant, insect, bird, fish, mammal, reptile, and amphibian species. It is estimated that there are 400 billion trees in the Amazon Rainforest. These trees have a huge influence on the rain cycles of South America as each tree releases water into the air every day, giving a lot of moisture to sustain the rainforest. These forests also provide a home for a substantial population, with over 47 million people living within the Amazon Rainforest.

While many people know about the Amazon Rainforest, some of the lesser known parts are the Amazon Cloud Forests along the coastal mountains of Peru and Ecuador. A cloud forest is a place where tall trees swirl with clouds. These forests have a very high humidity, being at, or close to, 100%. This amount of moisture in the air, being released from the trees, sees the forest cloaked in cloud-like fog, creating the cloud forest. In South America highland tropical rainforest covers the slopes of the Andes and the moist air from the ocean is at a such a high elevation that clouds condense on the plants. This process generates these stunning cloud forests. The moisture in the air allows different plants to grow, including epiphytes, which are called "air plants" because they seem to just grow in the air. Trees of the Amazon Cloud Forests are covered with lichens, mosses, epiphytes, and flowering orchids, all plants which capture water from the air because of the ever-present clouds. An array of insects, mammals, and frogs thrive in these cloud forests too, along with the Andean bear and more than 300 species of birds. The humid air that supports this range of flora and fauna comes from the lowland Amazon Rainforest, moves west and up the slopes of the Andes Mountains, to form the Amazon Cloud Forests.

Along with the main continent, there are some famous islands within South America, including the Galápagos Islands and the Falkland Islands (known as the Malvanias by Argentinians). The Galápagos Islands are an archipelago in the Pacific Ocean. Located around 1,000 kilometres (620 miles) offshore, their isolation has resulted in the development of some unusual animal life, including giant tortoises and land iguanas. Far south in the Atlantic Ocean other South American islands are found. Famous for a geopolitical conflict, both the United Kingdom and Argentina claim the Falkland Islands as part of their territory. There are more than 700 islands in the archipelago, from islands with stunning white sandy beaches to others with rugged and craggy coastal cliffs. Each summer around one million penguins nest on the Falkland Islands. This includes the majestic King penguins and the Rockhopper penguins with their energetic behaviour and distinctive "rock star" look.

South America extends from the Caribbean Sea in the north to its southern-most tip at Ushuaia where ships depart for Antarctica. Capturing around one-eighth of the land surface of Earth, this is a continent of high mountains, impressive waterfalls, ice fields, glaciers, and extensive rainforest areas. Known for ancient sites like Machu Picchu in Peru, there are also many large cities, including the megacities of Mexico City, São Paulo, and Buenos Aires. The sandy beaches and carnival atmosphere during festival time of Rio de Janeiro in Brazil along with the famous Copacabana Beach are known to tourists and residents alike, while Bogotá, the capital of Columbia, is a wonderful mix of old colonial heritage and modern opportunities. Rich cultures, ancient history, and diverse landscapes define this continent.

CHAPTER 17

North America

The North American continent stretches from Panama at the northern tip of South America, right up to the Arctic Circle. It is surrounded on three sides by ocean: the Pacific Ocean on the west coast, the Atlantic Ocean along the east coast, and the Arctic Ocean to the north. The world's largest island, Greenland, forms part of the North American continent, along with many other smaller islands. With such a large landmass, on this continent there are icy glaciers, sweeping plains, desert landscapes, white sandy beaches, impressive canyons, and rugged mountain ranges through the Appalachians, Rocky Mountains, and the Pacific Mountain System. On the international boundary between the United States of America and Canada you can see Niagara Falls where over 3,000 tonnes of water flows every second, dropping nearly 60 metres in height.

More than twenty nations are represented within the continent of North America. These include Costa Rica, Honduras, El Salvador, and Nicaragua in the south, and the United States of America and Canada in the north. Islands within the Atlantic Ocean, including Hispaniola, Jamaica, Puerto Rico, and the Bahamas, famous for crystal-clear turquoise waters, white sandy beaches, and vibrant coral reefs, form part of the American continent. More than 700 islands and 2,000 cays make up the Bahamas. Cays are small sand islands that form on the surface of coral reefs. These are created as ocean currents deposit sediment like grains of sand, on a part of the coral reef. Over time this builds up, creating a small, low island, fringed by coral reefs, seemingly in the middle of nowhere. Cays within the Bahamas are a popular destination for holiday makers. These are the idyllic tropical retreats of picturesque postcards and screensavers.

After Asia and Africa, North America is the third largest continent in the world. While Canada and the United States of America form a large part of that landmass, there are cold islands to the north. This includes the challenging Arctic climate in parts of northern Canada and Greenland, the lands of the Inuit people. A unique and fragile part of the world, glaciers, tundra, and ice landscapes dominate, with long, cold winters and short, cool summers. Synonymous with ice and snow, Greenland is the world's largest island. A Danish territory close to the North Pole, about 80% of the country is covered by the Greenland Ice Sheet. Climate scientists regularly travel to this island for research, studying the impact of climate change on sea levels and melting ice. Tourists also like to visit, particularly along the west coast of Greenland where the Ilulissat Icefjord is located. The Icefjord is the sea mouth of one of the world's fastest and most active glaciers and offers a massive collection of icebergs calved from Sermeq Kujalleq, the fastest moving glacier in the Northern Hemisphere. Hustling into boats, tourists sail near the icebergs, some of which can be as big as a city skyscraper.

Along with these cold, dry regions of the north, further south there are dry, hot deserts, closer to the equator. Receiving little rain, these areas are classified as semi-arid. The three major deserts of North America are in the southwest: the Mojave, Chihuahuan, and Sonoran Deserts. Like the Atacama Desert in South America, these deserts lie in the rain shadows of nearby mountains. Due to their height, the mountains block the rain and trap the heat, which creates hot, dry winds. Because of this, only a few types of plants and animals can survive here. The roadrunner and rattlesnake are unique creatures in these desert regions, as are plants like cactus and the Joshua tree.

Beyond the deserts are the wide, open plains of the prairie. These grasslands extend from the Canadian province of Saskatchewan in the north, through Alberta and Manitoba, and continue through the states of North Dakota, South Dakota, Nebraska, Kansas, Oklahoma, and Texas in the south of the United States of America. With fewer trees and rich soils, large areas have been converted to livestock grazing and crops, but there are areas important to tribal and wildlife communities too. Referred to as the Great Plains, it can be tempting to visualise this part of North America as a featureless, flat plain, but that isn't the case. One of the largest grassland areas in the world, the Great Plains feature low, gently rolling hills and valleys. It is productive land and prized for its value to agriculture.

On the western border of these plains lie the Rocky Mountains. Often simply called "The Rockies", these are made up of several tall, rugged mountain ranges. Starting in the northwestern state of Alaska, these mountains run through Canada, the United States, and down to Mexico. In Mexico the mountains are called the Sierra Madre, and through Central America they are the Central Highlands, yet it is the same mountain range, despite the name change. The Great Continental Divide runs through the Rocky Mountains and this is an important geological feature of the North American continent.

A Continental Divide is a physical boundary that creates a division in the land. Continental Divides are found on each continent on Earth. They are a key part of the landscape when examining how the rivers flow from the mountains. This is because each river feeds into a specific bay, sea, or ocean basin and the Continental Divide determines where the river will flow. In North America, the Great Continental Divide separates the waters that will flow between the two bordering oceans. Water flowing east will drain into the Atlantic Ocean, while water making its way west will reach the Pacific Ocean because of the naturally occurring ridge between the various river systems.

Along with The Rocky Mountains, another important mountain range on this continent is the Alaska Range. These mountains run in an arc from the Alaska-Canada border, over 965 kilometres (600 miles) to the Alaskan Peninsula. Denali (also called Mount McKinley) is located within the Alaska Range and is the highest peak in North America. Perhaps what is most striking about this mountain is its height from base to peak. While Mount Everest is the highest peak in the world, Denali has the largest vertical rise of any mountain in the world. Climbers attempting Denali have to face this vertical rise of over 5,500 metres (18,000 feet), well beyond that of Mount Everest. Unlike Everest, the base of Denali doesn't have foothills, meaning climbers can stand at the base of the mountain and see its full, glory and sheer height. The structure, vertical rise, and conditions of the mountain makes it a challenging climb. The north face of Denali, named the Wickersham Wall, is covered with snow all year round. Ice and glaciers sit at its base and the mountain is so massive that it even generates its own weather system.

Along with these natural features of North America's deserts, mountains, plains, and icy terrain, there are many well-known human engineered landscapes and structures too. The American cities of San Francisco, Los Angeles, New York City, and the national capital, Washington DC, have all been depicted in various books, television shows, and movies, sharing stories of America's social geography. Many are familiar with the Empire State Building in New York City or the celebrations heralding the beginning of a new calendar year in Time Square. Other landmarks many are familiar with include:

> the Golden Gate Bridge in San Francisco,
> the White House in Washington DC, serving as the official residence of President of the United States of America;
> the Statue of Liberty, World Trade Center Memorial, and Central Park in New York City;
> Mount Rushmore National Memorial in South Dakota, featuring Presidents Washington, Jefferson, Roosevelt, and Lincoln; and
> the Pearl Harbor Historical Site in Hawai'i.

Also on the North American continent, Canada has many notable social and cultural sites too, such as the World Heritage Site of Old Quebec. An urban area, it showcases the French history of this part of Canada, holding the stories of more than four centuries. Like all our continents, when studying the geography of North America, there is a lot to enjoy. Along with natural landscapes, there are the many different places where people live, learn, work, and play.

Questions on Chapters 16 and 17

For answers see page 203

1. The equator passes through which three South American countries?
2. Name two of the seven countries the Andes Mountains pass through.
3. What is the highest city in the world?
4. Which highway passes through both North and South America?
5. What are the two largest countries in North America?
6. Describe what a cay is and how it is formed.
7. What is the tallest peak in North America?
8. What is the north face of Denali called?
9. What is a Continental Divide?

Map Questions on Chapters 16 and 17

For answers see page 204

1. Darien Gap covers 96 kilometres (60 miles) of treacherous land between the countries of Panama and Columbia, with dense rainforest, high, steep mountains, and swampy ground. The southwest coast of Darien Gap is the Pacific Ocean and the Gulf of Uraba is to the northeast. Please find both water features on a map.
2. The equator passes through the countries of Brazil, Ecuador, and Columbia. Find the capital cities of each nation.
3. Find the Andes Mountains on a map and name the seven countries they pass through.
4. The Galápagos Islands are an archipelago of islands in the Pacific Ocean and a part of Ecuador. In which direction do they lie from the South American continent?
5. Find the national capital of Greenland.
6. San Francisco, New York City, and Chicago are some of the biggest cities in the United States of America. Find each city and note which state it is located in.
7. Nassau is the national capital of the Bahamas, a country made up of more than 3,000 islands and cays. Which country lies directly south of the Bahamas?
8. The Pacific Ocean washes against the eastern shores of the United States of America while the Atlantic Ocean borders the west. Name three states on the west coast.

CHAPTER 18

Australia and Oceania

In 1908, a poem then titled *Core of my Heart* by Australian Dorothea Mackellar was published in the *London Spectator Magazine*. Known now as *My Country*, this poem remains popular in Australia. It shares details of Dorothea's homeland: the sweeping plains, forests, mountain ranges, climate, weather, natural disasters, and the farming life of Australia. Mackellar's words captured the unique beauty of this continent of the southern hemisphere, the smallest continent in the world. Located within the geographical region of Oceania, Australia is just one of thousands of islands within the waters of the Pacific Ocean, which is the largest and deepest on Earth.

Over 11 million people live in the Pacific Islands, a physically and culturally diverse area which holds the world's largest tropical and sub-tropical coral reef habitat. Spanning 88 million square kilometres (34 million square miles) from the west coast of Ecuador to Papua New Guinea in the east, there are hundreds of species of coral, thousands of different types of fish, molluscs, crustaceans (crabs and prawns), starfish, and sea urchins, many of which are not found in any other place. It is a vast part of the world.

Being the only continent in Oceania, the landmass of Australia dominates this region. The country of Australia is made up of a mainland and the southern state of Tasmania, an island that lies across the Bass Strait. There are other smaller islands that surround the coastline of Australia, but Tasmania is the largest. While the heart of mainland Australia are sandy and stony deserts, Tasmania is cooler and greener, and known both for its wilderness and as the birthplace of Queen Mary of Denmark. While Canberra is the national capital, Australia is perhaps most famous for the city of Sydney. It is known for its stunning beaches, the iconic steel arched Sydney Harbour Bridge, the curves of the Sydney Opera House, and the colourful sails of many yachts enjoying this pretty part of the city.

The country of Australia lies completely in the Southern Hemisphere. If you head south from Australia the next continent is Antarctica. Australia's isolation means there are a range of plant and animal species only found here, so many international visitors are keen to see a koala munching on eucalyptus leaves, a kangaroo with a joey in its pouch, a wombat, or an echidna nosing around for ants. They are surprised to hear the laugh of a kookaburra or see the pink and grey feathers of galahs. Tourists wish to see the colourful Great Barrier Reef, the extensive Blue Mountains, or the Wet Tropics of Queensland, where lush rainforest meets the sea.

While Australia is the largest country in Oceania, there are others. The nation of New Zealand, located to the east of Australia, and Papua New Guinea, a country on the western half of the island of New Guinea, are the two other major landmasses in the Pacific Ocean. As the Pacific Ocean is so vast, the numerous small islands are grouped into three smaller subregions: Polynesia, Micronesia, and Melanesia. These are based on cultural connections and the region's history.

Samoa, Tonga, Tuvalu, the Cook Islands, French Polynesia, the Pitcairn Islands, and Hawai'i are just some of the islands that make up the subregion of Polynesia. Sometimes known as the Polynesian Triangle, Hawai'i tops the triangle in the north, while New Zealand | Aotearoa is the westernmost point and Rapa Nui (Easter Island) marks the eastern part. Many Polynesian islands are small islands, created through volcanic hotspots in the Pacific Ocean. Though they come from a diverse range of islands within the region, the indigenous people of Polynesia share many similarities, including their shared reliance on the ocean. Being superb mariners, skills in shipbuilding, fishing, and navigation are highly prized. The people from Polynesia include Samoans, Tongans, Cook Islands Māori, New Zealand Māori, Hawaiian Māoli, and Tahitian Māohi.

Tahiti is a well-known Polynesian island. Technically it is just one island within French Polynesia but generally all 118 islands in the area are referred to as "the islands of Tahiti". Tahiti is a popular tourist destination, with many travellers wanting to explore this archipelago and the atolls too. This is a territory of France, so French is the language spoken in Tahiti. It is a tropical region, experiencing a dry season and wet season each year, with the wet season bringing the risk of tropical cyclones.

Further on from Tahiti, at the eastern edge of the region of Polynesia, closest to the American coast, lies Rapa Nui. An island known for its large stone carved statues, called Moai, it is one of the world's most isolated inhabited islands. Hawai'i also lies within Polynesia. Given it is part of the United States of America it is associated with the North American continent, but this chain of volcanic islands actually marks the northern-most part of Polynesia.

The tall, rugged volcanic islands of French Polynesia and Hawai'i are quite different to the low-lying atolls found in Micronesia, many of which are barely above sea level. This region lies in the northeastern part of the Pacific Ocean, between the Philippines and Hawai'i. It is made up of over 2,000 islands. This includes the Marshall Islands, the Federated States of Micronesia, Guam (a territory of the United States of America), Palau, Nauru, and Kiribati. There are individual islands in Micronesia, however, like Polynesia, there are also archipelagos. Sometimes called island chains, archipelagos are groups of islands close together, found in oceans, lakes, and rivers. The Bahamas, Bermuda, the Philippines, Indonesia, the Canary Islands, and Hawai'i are all archipelagos. There are even human constructed archipelagos off the coast of Dubai in the United Arab Emirates. However, the many archipelagos in the Pacific Ocean formed due to the volcanic activity of the Ring of Fire.

Along with islands and archipelagos, there are many low-lying atolls within Micronesia. An atoll is fringed by coral reefs, being formed when coral rings around an undersea volcano. Over time the coral builds up and the volcano recedes into the ocean, until just the circular coral reef remains, a lagoon forming in the centre when the volcano falls into the sea floor. With a fringe of land around a vivid azure-blue lagoon, these atolls are prized by some holiday makers seeking sapphire waters for swimming and sunbathing. Yet, given the way they are formed, atolls are not everyone's idea of a picture-perfect paradise. Easily hidden by ocean waves, they can present danger to unsuspecting sailors.

Melanesia is the subregion to the south of Micronesia. It stretches from Papua New Guinea in the west to Fiji in the east. Vanuatu, the

Palau islands from the air

Solomon Islands, and the French islands of New Caledonia are all within Melanesia. Affected by volcanic activity, the landscapes of many nations in this region are punctuated by high cliffs and old volcanoes. Today Melanesia is an important biodiversity region, with unique species found in the rainforests, cloud forests, mangroves, and marine environments. There are some amazing coral reefs in this subregion too. The Coral Triangle extends from Malaysia to the Solomon Islands, and across to the Philippines. Three-quarters of the world's coral species are found within this Triangle, along with over 2,000 types of reef fish and turtles. Around the world there are just seven species of ocean turtles and six of those visit the Coral Triangle in Melanesia.

Australia and the islands of the Pacific Ocean make up Oceania. The Pacific Ocean borders the eastern coast of Australia, while the waters of the Indian Ocean crash upon its western coastline. As Dorothea Mackellar's poem shares, between the oceans lies a nation of ragged mountain ranges, sweeping plains, exquisite forests, wide flowing rivers, and alpine regions with snow in winter and blankets of wildflowers in summer.

CHAPTER 19

Asia

A Farmhouse on the Wei River

In the slant of the sun on the country-side,
Cattle and sheep trail home along the lane;
And a rugged old man in a thatch door
Leans on a staff and thinks of his son, the herdboy.
There are whirring pheasants, full wheat-ears,
Silk-worms asleep, pared mulberry-leaves.
And the farmers, returning with hoes on their shoulders,
Hail one another familiarly.
…No wonder I long for the simple life
And am sighing the old song, *Oh, to go Back Again!*

By Wang Wei (translated by Witter Bynner)

Eurasia is the largest continent on Earth and so is divided into two continents: Europe and Asia. Europe lies west of the Ural Mountains and Black Sea, spreading over to the Mediterranean Sea and Atlantic Ocean. Asia is located to the east and is sometimes referred to as "the Orient" because *oriens* in Latin means "rising" and "eastern". This is a big landmass, representing nearly fifty countries, thousands of islands within the Indian and Pacific Oceans, and 30% of the total land area of Earth. There are nine island nations in Asia, including Japan, the Philippines, and Indonesia. Around 60% of the world's population live in Asia, representing a diverse group of biomes, climates, and cultures. Given the size and diversity of Asia, geographers typically divide it into six geographic regions: Southeast Asia, Southern Asia, the Middle East, Central Asia, Northern Asia, and Eastern Asia.

Southeast Asia is located to the north of the Australian continent. It is

bordered by China in the north, India to the west, and the Pacific Ocean
to the east. Located within the equatorial tropical zone, it is warm to hot
all year round in Southeast Asia. The continental landmass within Southeast Asia includes the countries of Vietnam, Laos, Cambodia, Myanmar,
and Thailand and many islands within the Malay Archipelago form part
of this region too. This includes the islands of Singapore, Indonesia, and
the Philippines. This area spreads across the Indian Ocean, the South
China Sea, and the Pacific Ocean and is one of the most diverse areas
of the world, with thousands of native languages spoken.

The other southern region of Asia is Southern Asia, sometimes
referred to as the Indian Subcontinent. This area is west of Southeast Asia.
Sri Lanka, the Maldives, Pakistan, and Bangladesh are just some of the
nations within this region which is dominated by the highest mountain
range in the world: the Himalayas. The Ganges and the Indus Rivers
are the great rivers of this region and the source for these is the melt of
ice and snow within the Himalayas. This tall mountain range affects the
weather experienced within this part of Asia, with the sheer height of
the Himalayas blocking the flow of air creating very hot temperatures
during the monsoonal season.

West of Southern Asia is the Middle East. Close to Europe, this is
the western-most part of Asia. Nearly twenty countries make up the
Middle East, including Israel, Iraq, Iran, Syria, Türkiye, Oman, and the
United Arab Emirates. While the Mediterranean, Aegean, Caspian,
Black, Red, and Arabian Seas are found here, it is within this region that
some of the driest and hottest places within Asia are found. This includes
the Arabian Desert, which is a very different climate to the abounding
tropical rainforest enjoyed in Southeast Asia. The Arabian Desert spans
across much of the Arabian Peninsula, the largest peninsula in the world.
This includes the Rub' al Khali, the "Empty Quarter", which is one of
the most inhospitable regions on Earth. It features high sand dunes,
soaringly hot temperatures during the day, and winter nights which can
dip below freezing. While this region has been a part of trade routes for
thousands of years, today its economic value is within the reserves of oil
and natural gas held beneath the sands.

Adjoining the Middle East is Central Asia, including the countries
of Tajikistan, Uzbekistan, and Mongolia, with its short grasses of the

Steppes. Many ethnic groups are represented in Central Asia, with different languages and dialects spoken. The area is largely arid, with jagged mountain peaks and desiccated areas, yet, in a land of contrasts, the world's largest inland body of water, the Caspian Sea, lies within this region, bordering Kazakhstan and Turkmenistan. There are also vast glacial regions within the Hindu Kush Mountain range. Parts of this region were crucial to the ancient Silk Road, the network of trading routes which allowed the economic and cultural exchange between the Far East and the western parts of the world such as Europe and Africa. This geographical link between east and west had a profound impact on commerce, culture, and history.

Sometimes called "Asian Russia", Northern Asia is the region at the northern most part of the continent, bordering the Arctic Ocean at the north. With plains, plateaus, tundra, and the extensive taiga forest of conifers, this area includes Siberia. A part of Russia known for its frozen landscapes, Siberia stretches all the way from the Ural Mountains to the Pacific Ocean in the east. Rich in resources, there are fields of natural gas, gold, and oil within this remote area of Earth. It remains sparsely populated, due in part to the climate, which plunges down to -40°C (-40°F) during winters and only reaches around 10°C (50°F) during the heat of a summer day. Yet, the cold, snowy winters and the mild, humid summers make the conifer trees of the taiga forest thrive. These forests are evergreen and are found on the slopes of the Himalayas, through Korea, China, and Japan. They are a distinctive feature of this part of Asia.

While dozens of countries are represented within the Asian continent, one nation exerts its dominance in this region, and indeed, the world: China. China is one of the largest countries in the world. Similar in land size to the United States of America, China is a global leader in manufacturing and exports and holds numerous natural resources across its vast land area. Lifestyles in northern rural China are very different to how people live within the megacities of Shanghai and Beijing, where rapid advancements in technology are made. China is one country within the region of Asia called Eastern Asia, which also includes the nations of North Korea, South Korea, Taiwan, and Japan. Eastern Asia is a major economic powerhouse in the global economy. Like China, Japan and South Korea are countries known for their advanced technology and manufacturing, exporting a range of high-quality goods around the world. It is likely that there are many items in your home that have been made in Eastern Asia, including electrical appliances, clothing, household items, or perhaps your family car.

The huge continent of Asia is one of contrasts. It has the highest point on Earth (from sea level), with Mount Everest, but also has a sea which is nearly 500 metres below sea level (1640 feet), the Dead Sea in the Jordan Rift Valley. Given the fertile river valleys of the Ganges, Yangtze, Yellow, and Mekong Rivers have supported civilisations living in this part of this world for centuries, it also has a cultural richness. From the vast desert regions of the Gobi and Arabian Deserts to the biodiverse tropical rainforests of Southeast Asia, the people and places of Asia are a fascinating topic.

Thai lantern festival

Questions on Chapters 18 and 19

For answers see page 205

1. What are the three regions of the Pacific Ocean?
2. Name four islands found in Polynesia.
3. What is the national capital of Australia?
4. Which ocean borders the west coast of Australia?
5. Which ocean borders the east coast of Australia?
6. What is the southern-most state of Australia?
7. Name two of the six regions of the Asian continent.
8. Singapore, Indonesia, the Philippines, Vietnam, Laos, Cambodia, and Thailand are part of which region of Asia?
9. Name one sea found in the Middle East.
10. Name one river found in Asia.
11. What is the highest point on Earth?

Map Questions on Chapters 18 and 19

For answers see page 205

1. Which key line of latitude passes through Australia?
2. Name the water body that lies between the mainland of Australia and the state of Tasmania.
3. Tahiti is part of French Polynesia and is located east of the Cook Islands. Name two main islands that lie to the west of the Cook Islands.
4. What is the national capital of New Zealand | Aotearoa?
5. Thailand is located in Southeast Asia. Which countries border Thailand?
6. Kazakhstan is the ninth largest country in the world and home to the Baykonur Cosmodrome spaceport. Which country borders Kazakhstan to the north?
7. The national capital of Turkmenistan boasts the honour of being the only place to have an indoor ferris wheel. Name the capital of Turkmenistan.
8. Name the seven countries that make up the Arabian Peninsula.
9. Shanghai and Beijing are two megacities in China. Find them on a map and name which is the national capital.

CHAPTER 20

Europe

Often geographers highlight the largest countries, the tallest mountains, the longest rivers, and the biggest lakes and oceans. Yet, to focus only on these when exploring Europe means you may miss some of the special highlights. Vatican City, Monaco, Liechtenstein, Luxembourg, and Malta are rather tiny nations found in the European continent. In a composition of contrasts, the smallest country in the world, Vatican City, is home to largest church in the world, St Peter's Basilica. Whether you visit the Sistine Chapel to see the stunning ceilings painted by Michelangelo, marvel at the treasures in the Vatican Museums, stroll along St Peter's Square, or walk through the gardens, Vatican City is the only country to be entirely designated as a UNESCO World Heritage site. It is also the only country in the world to offer automated teller machines (ATMs) in Latin, the official language of Vatican City. While its population is less than 1,000, thousands of people travel to this tiny country each day, proving that, if we just focus on the largest, tallest, longest, and biggest, we can miss out on some true delights.

The continent of Europe stretches from Iceland in the north, down to the Mediterranean Sea in the south, and extends west as far as the Ural Mountains. After Australia, it is the second smallest continent, however, it holds fifty countries, including Portugal, Andorra, Monaco, and Montenegro. Major rivers like the Danube, Thames, Rhine, and Volga have helped to shape both the physical and social aspects of the geography of this continent, just as the surrounding seas and oceans define it. Technically, given its shape, Europe is a peninsula because it is surrounded by water on three sides: the Arctic Ocean in the north; the Mediterranean, Black, and Caspian Seas to the south; and the Atlantic Ocean to the west. Some geographers even refer to Europe as the peninsula of peninsulas. This is because the Balkan, Italian, and Iberian peninsulas are found in southern Europe, while Jutland and the Scandinavian peninsulas are located in northern Europe. That's a lot of peninsulas! Within this continent punctuated by peninsulas there is a range of climatic zones, rivers, and mountains. Housing a population of over 740 million, many people call Europe home.

Compared to the smallest nation in the world, Russia is the largest country in the world and, even when taking only the western portion of the country into account, it is still the largest country in Europe. Russia also holds the title for the most populous nation on this continent and the highest mountain in Europe: Mount Elbrus. An ancient volcano in the Caucasus Mountains, Mount Elbrus is in southern Russia, just north of the border between Russia and Georgia. Home to over twenty glaciers, this peak is cloaked in snow all year round. The national capital of Russia is Moscow. Situated on the Moskva River, it is the home of St Basil's Cathedral with its distinctive coloured domes, the Kremlin, Red Square, and, for ballet and opera fans, the spectacular Bolshoi Theatre.

Germany, the United Kingdom, Italy, and France are among the major countries in Europe. The capital cities of these countries are Berlin, London, Rome, and Paris respectively. These global cities are popular destinations for tourists who want to soak up the atmosphere of Europe and enjoy its rich history. It is in Paris that the most visited attraction in Europe is found: the Musée du Louvre. Looking for the famous Pyramid entrance, millions of guests visit each year, eager to see famous artworks like the *Mona Lisa* and making for long queues of people. The Musée du Louvre is one of the most visited museums in the world and one of the largest, with more than 70 rooms and around 35,000 works of art. Paris is also home to the Eiffel Tower and the Seine River. Nearly forty bridges span the river across the city of Paris as the river flows through the capital. Paris is just one of the many cities in Europe that are important historically and serve as significant political and economic hubs. When geographers list global cities they feature New York, Tokyo, Shanghai, and Beijing, as well as London and Paris. These two European cities have a global influence. Paris is just as much about politics and economics as it is art and culture, while London has been a global financial capital for centuries.

In the heart of Europe lies Germany. Sharing borders with nine other nations, Denmark and the North Sea lie at its northern borders. The Danube and Rhine Rivers cut through Germany and much of the central and southern regions of this country feature forested hills and mountains. The Black Forest, made famous by the chocolate, cherry, and cream cake by the same name, is perhaps the most well-known wooded area of Germany. It is the largest nature reserve in the country and the source of the Danube River. This is a place where green conifers stand tall, providing a home to boar, ibex, wildcats, and other mammals.

Italy is a boot-shaped peninsula in southern Europe. The waters of the Adriatic, Tyrrhenian, and Mediterranean Seas wash against the shores of Italy. The Amalfi Coast and Italian Riviera in the south are some of the most famous coastal areas, where the colourful houses of Positano cling to coastlines, offering panoramic views of the Mediterranean Sea. Inland, the Apennine Mountains effectively create the spine of the country of Italy, providing a beautiful landscape of peaks and forested valleys. The cities of Milan, Turin, and Venice lie in northern Italy, along with the Italian Alps, which offer opportunities to ski in the winter months and hike during the summer. Florence and Rome are within central Italy, along with the famous region of Tuscany, known for its rolling hills, sunflowers, fields of olive trees, and vineyards. Rome is the national capital of Italy, made famous by the landmarks left from the ancient Romans, such as the Colosseum and Pantheon.

However, this part of the world isn't just about global cities, as there are also towns, villages, and hamlets found within the continent. From small towns in the Lake District where Charlotte Mason lived in her pocket of England, to quaint villages nestled within the mountainous landscape of Switzerland, there is more to Europe than just the cities shown on a map. There are various houses and homes to gaze at, such as the whitewashed villas on Greek islands, alpine chalets tucked high within the mountains, spacious Spanish haciendas, and châteaus dotted around the French countryside. Châteaus are large country houses, passed down through the generations of noble families, many of which were built during the Middle Ages and Renaissance. Some were originally designed as defence fortifications, while others were intended as luxurious palatial residences for the wealthy and for royal families.

Ornate decorations, gilded embellishments, and extensive landscaped parklands characterise these building. Spreading over 800 hectares in the city of Versailles in northern France, the Palace of Versailles is an excellent example of one such opulent estate.

In France and Germany you can explore castles. It is not known exactly how many castles there are in Germany but some estimate around 25,000. Many were built for noblemen, providing both protection to their inhabitants and a space large enough to enable them to enjoy the lavish lifestyles of the aristocracy. Castles are found in other European countries, including Scotland and Austria and today many are popular tourist attractions. Visitors are keen to see these parts of the European continent that echo fairy tales.

There is great diversity within the places and people of Europe. The scenery and climate of the Scandinavian countries of Sweden, Norway, and Denmark with its fjords and forests, is very different to that experienced in Portugal and Spain. Portugal and Spain are on the Iberian Peninsula in southwest Europe, where the waters wash from both the Atlantic Ocean and the Mediterranean Sea. Many nations lie within the Mediterranean, including Greece, Spain, Cyprus and the island of Sardinia and all feature turquoise seas.

While some like to dip their toes in the Mediterranean from the white sand beaches, others prefer the vivid white ski fields of the Alps during the winter. Heading to Austria, France, Italy, Switzerland, or Liechtenstein, they wish to enjoy the snow. Zermatt in Switzerland, at the foot of the Matterhorn, offers the highest ski fields in Europe. Zermatt is famous for mountaineering and skiing and is popular throughout the year, but is particularly busy during the winter months. The vehicles you will see in this village are electric vans for the local hotels, with travellers reaching Zermatt by train, and there are mountains as far as the eye can see.

While the Alps are known for their high, snow topped mountains, this is very different to the flat of the Baltic States within northeast Europe. Bordering the Baltic Sea, Estonia, Latvia, and Lithuania form the Baltic States. In this part of Europe, the contours of the land are gentle and level. Here, the tallest peak is just 318 metres (1,040 feet) tall. Located in Estonia, Suur Munamägi ("Great Egg Mountain") is more like a delicate hill within this flatter part of Europe. Thousands of islands of Estonia lie within the Baltic Sea, while forest blankets large areas of this part of the continent.

Tall alps and small hills, large and tiny nations, small cottages and sprawling castles, they are all a part of Europe. From its vibrant global cities to small hamlets there are many historical landmarks that tell the stories of the rich history of this part of the Northern Hemisphere. From polar climates in the north to the Mediterranean in the south, there are a range of places to experience in this part of the world.

Questions on Chapter 20

For answers see page 206

1. What is the smallest nation in Europe and the world?
2. Moscow is the capital city of which nation?
3. Name the highest peak in Europe.
4. Which river flows through Paris?
5. Name the three Baltic States.
6. Portugal and Spain are located on which peninsula?
7. Name three Scandinavian countries.

Map Questions on Chapter 20

For answers see page 206

1. Vatican City is the world's smallest independent state. It is entirely landlocked by one nation. Name that country.
2. The water bodies surrounding the European peninsula include two oceans and three seas. Please find the Arctic Ocean to the north of Europe and the Atlantic Ocean in the west. Then find the Mediterranean, Black, and Caspian Seas, which are located to the south.
3. Find the capital city of England and note whether it is located in the east or west of the country.
4. The national capital of France, Paris, is situated on the Seine River. The river runs in a northwesterly direction and at the port city of Le Havre it flows into which major water body?
5. Germany shares its borders with nine countries. Name these countries.

CHAPTER 21

Our Oceans and Seas — Part 1

Sailing "the seven seas" has been a phrase since ancient days, but it is more of a poetic one. With around fifty bodies of water that could be called a sea, there are far more than seven! There are just five oceans, each bordered by continents. Oceans are the largest expanses of salt water and cover just over 70% of the Earth's surface. The waters of the oceans are what create our "blue planet" as seen from space. Earth is the only known planet to have liquid water on its surface and 98% of our planet's water is held within the oceans and the many seas, gulfs, and straits.

Earth's five oceans are the Pacific, Atlantic, Indian, Arctic, and Southern Oceans. The Southern Ocean is the most recently recognised ocean, only being officially named in 2000, so you won't find it labelled on older maps and globes. The Southern Ocean is the body of water surrounding Antarctica and meets the Pacific, Atlantic, and Indian Oceans at a latitude of precisely 60° south.

While the Arctic Ocean is the smallest ocean, the Pacific is the largest. Even if all the continents and islands of the world were combined together into one mass, the Pacific Ocean would still be larger than that land area. A vast ocean, it covers more than one-third of the Earth's surface. It is also the deepest ocean, with the Mariana Trench extending down 10,994 metres (36,070 feet).

Just as we can see hills, mountains, valleys and plains on land, the ocean floor has various geological features too. It is not just flat. There are extraordinarily deep trenches like the Mariana Trench, as well as rift valleys, underwater volcanoes, and hydrothermal vents. The study and measurement of the depths of the ocean and sea floors is called bathymetry. Bathymetric scientists map the sea floor. They chart the ocean trenches, submarine canyons, seamounts, and abyssal plains, mapping the forms and features of the ocean floor. These maps are valuable for navigation and scientific research as they help us to understand the marine environment. They are also economically valuable to deep-sea mining companies who want to plan resource exploration and extraction projects. Scientists use a range of tools and technologies to collect the data, including satellite-based remote sensing and sonar. Accurately measuring the depth of the oceans, scientists then analyse the data to create these important maps, oceanographers and marine geologists working to better understand the geography and geology of the depths of the sea.

Extensive and deep, oceanic waters are always in motion. Ocean currents move these waters all around the Earth in distinct patterns. Some ocean currents are warm, but others are cold. Maps show the ways these paths of water move around the Earth like giant conveyor belts, transporting seawater around the planet. The Humboldt Current, sometimes called the Peruvian Current, is a cold Pacific Ocean current that moves around the coast of South America. Also within the Pacific Ocean is the East Australian Current. Unlike the cold Humboldt Current, this is a warm flow of water. It moves south along the eastern coast of Australia. While different temperatures and locations, both ocean currents follow a set path, moving around in a circular motion due to the heat of the sun and the movement of wind.

Another famous ocean current is a warm and swift one. Called the Gulf Stream, this ocean current moves water within the Atlantic Ocean. It brings warmer waters and climate to the east coast of the United States of America and to parts of the United Kingdom too. Famously, Benjamin Franklin produced a map of the Gulf Stream in the late 1700's. Franklin had observed this maritime movement, charting it to show how the warm current of water swept through the Atlantic Ocean. Since then, further maps have been created and shipping companies have learned the benefits of these ocean currents. Harnessing the power and predictability of ocean currents, travel time and fuel consumption can be reduced when vessels travel with the current.

Some ocean currents can be very deep, flowing within the depths of the sea floor, circling large parts of the globe. These waters continually move in their own cyclical patterns, with hot water from the equator moving towards the north and south poles, colliding with cold water from these regions. Ocean water spins in a circular pattern with the Earth's rotation. This means that oceans in the northern hemisphere tend to move clockwise, but within the southern hemisphere they move in an anti-clockwise direction.

Other ocean currents sit just under the surface. These are affected by wind. Air dragging along the surface of the water pulls the water to flow in the same direction as the wind blows. In some regions of the world there are steady, persistent winds that blow in certain directions and these affect ocean currents. For example, the Trade Winds blow just above the equator, in the Northern Hemisphere, moving from east to west. These winds create surface currents as they pull ocean water in their direction.

Air movement, the topography of the seafloor, the shape of the coastline, the rotation of the Earth, and the circulation of the atmosphere all influence the way currents of water move through our oceans. The rotation of the Earth drives warm equatorial currents and also determines the direction of cyclones. Named the Coriolis Effect, this means that cyclones will rotate clockwise in the Southern Hemisphere and in an anti-clockwise direction in the Northern. French scientist and mathematician Gaspard-Gustave de Coriolis first described this force in the 1800's. The phenomenon of the Coriolis Effect is foundational to oceanography and the study of the atmosphere in relation to weather and climate, known as meteorology. Oceanographers examine data from satellites that track and observe ocean currents from space, using advanced technology to get a picture of our surface and deep ocean currents.

The movement of winds and tides affects ocean currents and creates waves. Gentle breezes result in soft ripples across the seas, while powerful winds and stormy weather will generate strong waves and large swells, revealing the immense force of our oceans. Waves are formed as the water surface rises with the wind but is then pulled back again due to the force of gravity, creating a circular movement of water. Out in the ocean the water is deeper so there is more energy in the waters. However, as it comes closer to the coast, the waters become shallower. The bottom of the wave is slowed down by the seafloor, but there is nothing to stop the top, so the crest of the wave continues moving until it crashes onto the shore. This gives us the beautiful view of waves rolling onto the beach.

Harsh and tall, or soft and gentle, waves are different to tides. Unlike waves, tides are not formed through air movement. Rather, tides are created through the force of gravity between the Earth, moon, and the sun. Tidal movement is the rise and fall of ocean levels that occur each and every day as these parts of our solar system interact. Perhaps you have seen a beach on full tide and noticed just how far the water comes onto the land. If you walked along that same beach at low tide, you not only see far more sand and waves out to the horizon, but maybe also rock pools, shells, and seaweed scattered along the shore.

The study of the tides, waves, currents, seafloor geology, and marine ecosystems is oceanography. Oceanographers understand the crucial role the world's oceans play in sustaining life on Earth. Oceans store heat from the sun, which helps to stabilise the climate, and they provide a vital food source for people worldwide. The oceans are also home to algae and phytoplankton, which produce much of the world's oxygen. Oceanographers understand that oceans are vital, supporting communities and economies, and help maintain the overall health of our planet.

A typhoon from space

CHAPTER 22

Our Oceans and Seas — Part 2

The blue of saltwater is perhaps the most prominent feature of the photos of Earth taken from space. Along with the five oceans there are around fifty seas, as well as straits, gulfs, bays, and lagoons, all covering nearly three-quarters of our planet. Despite their name, oceanographers do study more than just oceans; they study the seas too. The terms "ocean" and "sea" are used interchangeably, but what is the difference between the two?

The key difference between seas and oceans is their size. Seas are smaller than oceans but vary in size. The Sea of Marmara in Türkiye is the smallest sea in the world, while the South China Sea and Caribbean Sea are two of the largest. The South China Sea is part of the Pacific Ocean and is surrounded by several countries, including China as its name suggests. The Caribbean Sea is found within the Atlantic Ocean, close to the Caribbean Islands. Other seas bring cold ocean currents, like the Bering Sea. This sea is cold and icy, lying along the coasts of Russia and Japan. This division of the Pacific Ocean is very different to the warmer waters enjoyed along the eastern seaboard of Australia and throughout Southeast Asia.

Oceanic seas are distinct because of their location or proximity to surrounding landmasses. Examine a map of an ocean and you will find a range of seas held within the boundaries of that ocean. For example, the Caribbean Sea, the North Sea, and the Sargasso Sea all lie within the Atlantic Ocean. The North Sea is bordered by Great Britain, Denmark, Norway, Germany, the Netherlands, Belgium, and France. Located in the northern part of the Atlantic Ocean, it is easy to tell where the name for this sea came from. Other seas also have unique characteristics, like the Sargasso Sea. This sea is named after brown algae found in these waters, a type of seaweed called Sargassum. Similarly, the Coral Sea is named for its proximity to the corals of the Great Barrier Reef, while the East China Sea is named after the country it borders. Each sea is within broader oceanic waters, but distinguished by their specific locations or characteristics.

Along with oceanic seas there are also inland seas. These are bordered by land to such an extent that they are often only connected by a narrow strait. For example, the Mediterranean Sea is an inland sea, the world's largest. It is only connected to the Atlantic Ocean by a narrow strait, the Strait of Gibraltar. This historically significant sea has been the geographic backdrop for ancient civilisations in Egypt and Greece, as well as the Romans, Arabs, and Phoenicians. Being an inland sea, it is relatively more protected, allowing for active trade and so some of the most important ports in history grew within the Mediterranean Sea.

Another inland sea close to the Atlantic Ocean is the Baltic Sea. This body of water is bordered by Scandinavian countries and nations of north-central Europe. It lends its name to the Baltic states of Lithuania, Estonia, and Latvia. Only connected to the North Sea by the narrow Danish Straits, the Baltic Sea is the world's second largest inland sea. Almost landlocked, it is also very shallow and not all that salty. This means that the Baltic Sea sometimes freezes over during the winter months.

Along with oceans and seas, there are also bays, gulfs, and straits. A strait is a narrow channel of water that lies between two land areas. It connects two bodies of water, such as two seas, and its defining feature is that it is a very narrow part of the sea. For example, Bass Strait lies between mainland Australia and the southern-most island state of Tasmania. This strait connects the Tasman Sea and the Great Australian Bight. Like other straits around the world, it is relatively narrow, but economically and strategically important. Straits are key gateways to maritime trade. One notable global strait is the Straits of Malacca in Asia. This is one of the world's most important trade routes, connecting the Pacific Ocean with the South China Sea and Indian Ocean. This makes it a crucial route for international shipping, linking major economies like China, India, Japan, and Singapore. Navigation can be difficult due to how narrow the strait is, but also how congested it becomes with so many ships passing through.

Along with oceans, seas, and straits, there are also bays and gulfs to be explored. While these two are similar, they are distinguished by their shape and depth. A bay is a large coastal body where the land recesses, often in a curved shape. That means that the waters lapping this shore are enclosed on three sides by coastline. Bays are wide mouthed, making them easy to access as they curve inwards towards the land. There are huge sweeping bays, but also small and sheltered ones, often called coves.

In comparison, gulfs are larger and deeper than bays. The mouth of a bay or gulf is where the water flows in and out, and while bays are defined by a wide mouth, the mouth of a gulf is relatively narrow. The movement of the water flowing in and out makes the mouth of the gulf narrow and deep. South of the Mississippi Delta lies the largest gulf on Earth. This is a place of sandy beaches, historical forts, stunning plants and wildlife, and shipwrecks, after many sea captains have struggled in the waters. Another famous gulf is the Persian Gulf. This borders Iran, Iraq, Kuwait, Saudi Arabia, Bahrain, Qatar, United Arab Emirates, and Oman.

Bays and gulfs are part of a sea or ocean and both of these inlets have specific characteristics. However, the names of these geographic landforms can be deceiving because sometimes explorers themselves weren't quite sure what they were. While by definition, a gulf should be larger than a bay, the Persian Gulf is actually smaller than Hudson Bay in Canada. A key location for trade in Canada, the Hudson's Bay Company established posts along the shores of this bay back in the 1600s. Trading in furs, this was the very beginnings of the modern department stores found within North America. Hudson Bay is a large and relatively shallow water body and is one of the largest inland seas in the world, however, it is called a bay because explorer Henry Hudson thought it was one and named it so.

There are many different names that are used to describe bodies of water, including bights, lagoons, and sounds. McMurdo Sound is a large bay in Antarctica. Early explorers thought it was much bigger than a bay and less protected, so they called it a sound. Another misnamed sound is found on the south island of New Zealand | Aotearoa. Milford Sound | Piopiotahi boasts a stunning bay, surrounded by cliffs and some of the world's tallest waterfalls. Much like Hudson and his mistaken bay, European explorers named it Milford Sound, thinking the long, narrow inlet was a type of bay connected to the Tasman Sea. However, it is a fjord, a landscape shaped by eroding and retreating glaciers, not the nearby sea.

While some terms have been proven to be inaccurate, other times they are just used more poetically. It isn't always about following strict definitions. Consider the first verse of *America the Beautiful* by Katharine Lee Bates:

> O beautiful for spacious skies,
> For amber waves of grain,
> For purple mountain majesties,
> Above the fruited plain!
> America! America!
> God shed His grace on thee
> And crown thy good with brotherhood
> From sea to shining sea!

Contrary to the poetics of the song, the United States of America is actually bordered by oceans, not seas. However, if you are ever concerned about not being able to hold strictly to these geographical terms, take heart in what we are said to be if we feel lost, because then we are said to be "all at sea"!

Millford Sound in New Zealand

Questions on Chapters 21 and 22

For answers see page 207

1. Which continent does the Southern Ocean encircle?
2. What is the smallest ocean on Earth?
3. Challenger Deep, the deepest sea-trench on Earth in the Mariana Trench, is located in which ocean?
4. What work are bathymetric scientists involved in?
5. What branch of science studies the features of oceans?
6. Which ocean is the Caribbean Sea a division of?
7. Which warm ocean current of the Atlantic Ocean originates from the Gulf of Mexico?
8. How is a bay different to a gulf?

Map Questions on Chapters 21 and 22

For answers see page 207

1. Find all five oceans on the map and name them.
2. The Black Sea is an inland sea in Europe. Which ocean is it a division of and how are they connected?
3. There are over twenty islands located within the Caribbean Sea, but Cuba and Jamaica are two main islands. On a map, find the capital cities of both Cuba and Jamaica.
4. The island city of Singapore dominates the Strait of Malacca. The Strait of Malacca connects the Indian Ocean to what sea and ocean?
5. McMurdo Sound borders the Antarctic continent. It is a large bay within the Southern Ocean and this icy body of water is the location for a large research station. Which sea is to the north of McMurdo Sound?

CHAPTER 23

Freshwater and the Water Cycle

Water, *water everywhere, but not a drop to drink* is a modern paraphrasing of a line from English poet Samuel Taylor Coleridge's famous lyrical ballad, *The Rime of the Ancient Mariner*. At this point in the poem the crew have been blown from the icy winds of the Southern Ocean, north to the Trade Winds of the equator, where it is hot and they are thirsting for freshwater:

> Day after day, day after day,
> We stuck, nor breath nor motion;
> As idle as a painted ship
> Upon a painted ocean.
>
> Water, water, everywhere,
> And all the boards did shrink;
> Water, water, everywhere,
> Nor any drop to drink.

The crew might have been surrounded by water, but oceans, seas, bays, gulfs, lagoons, sounds, and bights are all defined by saltwater, not the freshwater they longed to drink and so desperately needed. 97% of the Earth's water is saltwater, leaving just 3% of our water resources as the freshwater we thirst for and need.

Yet, most freshwater is inaccessible because it is ice or deep in the ground. Over two-thirds of the freshwater on Earth is within glaciers and icecaps, and just under one-third is groundwater. As its name suggests, groundwater is held in the ground, within rocks, soil, sand, and the earth. This leaves very little freshwater available as surface water. Only around 0.3% of all freshwater is found within rivers, lakes, ponds, wetlands, and swamps. That means more than 99% of all the water on Earth is difficult for humans and living things to access. As freshwater that supports life is surprisingly scarce, it needs to be used wisely.

All water circulates around the Earth through a process called the water cycle. This hydrological cycle is an important global system of our planet. Sunlight and heat causes surface water from our seas and oceans, lakes and rivers to evaporate in warm air, changing from liquid to a gas. Only freshwater vapour rises. Salts and minerals are left behind. Rising higher in the atmosphere, the air cools. As it cools, the water vapour condenses into clouds. Its state changes to become liquid again. As more and more water molecules condense, this moisture is added to the atmosphere. This condensation is what causes clouds and fog to form, along with the dew you see on flowers and blades of grass in the early morning. Moisture building up in the clouds can also result in rainfall because when there is sufficient weight in the clouds, precipitation occurs. This can be in the form of rain, but it might also be hail, snow, or ice when the cold air in the atmosphere converts water droplets to a solid form, whether it is soft snowflakes silently falling or hard icy hail

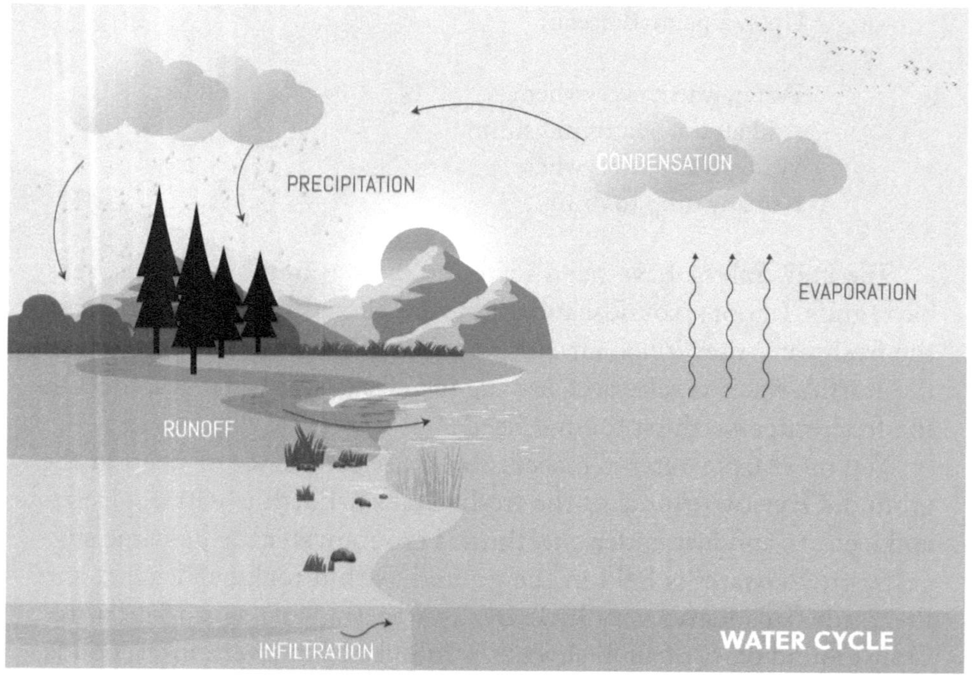

pelting from the sky. This movement of water changing through three states, evaporating, condensing, and then falling as precipitation is the essence of the water cycle. Water is always cycling around the Earth in these different forms.

In geographical landforms and processes we mainly see freshwater in liquid and solid states. We can however, see water in vapour form within the spectacular Cloud Forests. These are found in the Amazon and parts of Africa and Southeast Asia, where clouds of vapour cling to rainforested areas. Water in its solid form can make a stunning sight, with ice landscapes forming within mountain glaciers, pack ice, polar ice caps, and icebergs. This frozen storage of water as ice is an important resource for our Earth. It plays a crucial role in the global climate system too, with these icy white surfaces reflecting solar energy back to space. This is called the albedo effect.

When we think about water in our landscapes we tend to think of it as a liquid, flowing through the land. Lakes and ponds, rivers and streams, hot springs and geysers, wetlands and swamps, as well as magnificent waterfalls, are all defined by moving water. A lake is a relatively large body of inland water. Surrounded by land on all sides, the water is generally slow-moving or still. The largest lake in the world is the Caspian Sea. Despite its name, it is a lake. The Caspian Sea is about the size of the countries of Japan or Germany, and is bordered by five nations: Azerbaijan, Iran, Turkmenistan, Kazakhstan, and Russia. The country of Iran is known for exporting the famous Beluga caviar all around the world. Fish roe is harvested from the Beluga sturgeon, a fish found in the Caspian Sea, and is then salt-cured. Beluga Caviar is perhaps the most prestigious caviar in the world, considered to be a luxurious delicacy.

Nearby to the Caspian Sea is the Aral Sea. Again, despite its name, it too is a lake. However, there is one characteristic of both lakes which can help to explain why they are referred to as "seas". It is the water. Both the Aral and Caspian Seas are known for having more saline water. This means that, compared with true freshwater lakes, their waters are more salty. Though not as salty as seawater, this is why both were named as seas, not lakes.

While the Caspian and Aral Seas are large, others lakes are much smaller. Some are so small they are simply called ponds. However, no matter what size they are, lakes provide important habitat for a range of wildlife. They also offer people beautiful recreational areas to enjoy and these reservoirs serve as a key element of the water cycle. Around the world there are many lakes, all different shapes and sizes. This includes the Great Lakes of the United States of America and Canada; Lakes Victoria, Tanganyika, and Malawi in Africa; and Lake Titicaca on the border of Peru and Bolivia in the Andes Mountains of the South American continent. These are all significant freshwater features that communities rely on in many ways.

Most lakes have water all year round, however, some are only inundated with water seasonally. For example, in Central Australia lies Lake Eyre | Kati Thanda. It is an endorheic lake, meaning it is a water system that is separate from others. It doesn't drain towards the ocean. Water can only flow into it. It doesn't flow out again, only evaporates. During dry seasons, Lake Eyre is a glistening salt pan, with its distinctive pink hues, but when there are downpours upstream, this lake transforms. Floodplains, streams, and channels converge, and the desert landscape is altered to a glorious lake with an abundance of wildlife.

While lakes are valued for their relatively still waters, rivers are prized for the way they move and flow through the landscape. Often referred to as lifelines, rivers are essential sources of water, making them crucial for sustaining life. Rivers are known by many different names across the world, including stream, brooklet, rivulet, estuary, creek, beck, water way, and burn. These terms signify the great diversity of our river systems across different regions of the world. Even though some rivers may be very broad and move rapidly, all rivers start from a small source of water. Many begin as a tiny stream high in the mountains, from melting ice. Moving from the high point on the mountain or hill, the water flows through the landscape, down the slope to lower ground. Smaller rivers may trickle into larger ones, with these smaller rivers being called tributaries. Some rivers babble into lakes or dams, while others flow out to the sea. Rivers and lakes are key parts of our environment, providing essential freshwater, important for animal habitats and for human uses. A wide variety of plant and animal species are supported by rivers. For thousands of years rivers and lakes have captivated many people, including explorers, scientists, and nature lovers, and have served important roles for trade, geo-political, and spiritual purposes.

CHAPTER 24

Rivers of the World

Alfred Lord Tennyson's poem *The Brook* shares the journey of a little brook travelling through the landscape to join a bigger river. This waterway passes down ridges, through valleys and towns, under bridges, continuously moving forward to the river. Tennyson captures the movement and sound of the water:

> I chatter, chatter, as I flow
> To join the brimming river,
> For men may come and men may go,
> But I go on forever.

Tennyson also reflects on the continuous nature of the hydrological cycle. The water in rivers does go on forever, circling through the water cycle, but freshwater is a limited resource. As described in the poem, rivers traverse the land from their high point at the source, through to the lake, dam, or sea they may flow into. Smaller tributaries gather into larger rivers and continue to carve through the landscape.

During this flowing course, rivers may meander gently, quietly and calmly moving through the landscape, but others move with a strong force. For instance, the Futaleufú River in the Patagonia region of Chile has some of the biggest and fastest moving rapids. Fed by glacial waters from the Andes, this is an impressive whitewater river, the churning of the water making it foam and look white in colour. Rapids are often found in whitewater rivers. These are shallower areas of a fast-moving river, where water rushes over the riverbed or rocks. The depth of the river, the sharp incline, and the rocks create more turbulence, so the river waters are pushed through these obstacles. This increased movement traps air in the water, causing bubbles to form as the water is agitated, transforming it into whitewater, and creating exciting parts of the river to navigate.

A range of geographic terms are used to describe different parts of a river, such as mouth, riverbed, and watershed. The watershed is the land area that drains into a particular river and is also sometimes called a river basin. The mouth of a river is the place where the river flows into a larger waterbody, whether it is a lake, sea, or an ocean. The channel refers to the path a river follows, while a meander is the name given to the curves and bends.

In Kenneth Graham's classic book, *Wind in the Willows*, the riverbank is the place where Mole first meets Ratty, the Water Rat who becomes a firm friend and fellow adventurer. The sides of land along the river are called the riverbank. Some riverbanks are gradual and grassy, ideal for picnics, games, or fishing. This the place where Ratty and Mole enjoy their cold chicken, cress sandwiches, ham, lemonade, and ginger beer. These are generally beside calmer and slower flowing rivers. Other riverbanks can be stony and steep. A steeper slope of a riverbank shows that the movement of the river is causing more erosion. As the flowing water carries sand, rocks, and other debris, carrying it along with the river, the movement of this sediment can erode the riverbank further. More broadly, the space where land and rivers meet is called the riparian zone. This is another example of where a Latin term has been folded into English because "ripa" in Latin refers to a bank.

As water moves through the landscape, some rivers create spectacular waterfalls because the waters drop from a great height. Victoria Falls are located on the border between Zambia and Zimbabwe in Africa. Here, the Zambezi River thunders and sprays over the cliff, into the gorge below. Named after the then Queen of England, Victoria Falls are nearly two kilometres (5,604 feet) wide and drop over 100 metres (354 feet) in height. The flow of the river through this African landscape creates the stunning waterfalls. In North America, it is the drop of the Niagara River over a cliff that creates Niagara Falls. While it sounds like just one waterfall, there are actually three: the American Falls, Bridal Veil Falls, and Horseshoe Falls. These are located within the American and Canadian border. They are the largest falls on the North American continent and large volumes of water pour over the rocks each second, all sourced from the world's largest freshwater system.

However, waterfalls aren't always associated with sheer cliffs. There are cascades, which are areas where the water flows over smaller rock steps. There are beautiful cascades within the Blue Mountains in Australia. Visitors can walk the path beside the falls and watch the movement of the water as it passes through the series of steps. Some waterfalls are called "Bridal Veil Falls" owing to the fact that they look like a veil a bride would wear, while others are multi-stepped. The Baishui River in China creates the Huangguoshu Falls which are tiered waterfalls. The water moves through different steps and tiers. In some places waterfalls are glacial waters. For example, the Jökulsá á Fjöllum River flows from the Vatnajökull glacier, moving over the landscape of Iceland. This creates the powerful Dettifloss waterfall as the river continues to flow out into the Greenland Sea. Given the movement, the water is white from foam and creates a lot of spray. This is a huge and dramatic water landscape due to the sheer power and mass of moving water.

The end of a river and the way it deposits the sediment it carries can also create some stunning landscape features, such as deltas and alluvial fans. The place where a river meets the coast and fans out to

Victoria Falls

deposit this sediment is called a delta. For thousands of years the Nile River has provided freshwater and fertile land to those living along its banks as sediment and silt is carried by the river. This sediment load has created the Nile Delta which currently covers an area of 70,000 square kilometres (27,027 square miles).

Similar to a delta but created inland rather than on the coast, a river may create an alluvial fan. Like a delta, this is formed when the river fans out along the ground, foothills, hillsides, mountains, or plains. An alluvial fan is a triangular-shaped area where gravel, sand, and silt has been deposited by the flowing water. The particles deposited are called alluvium. While flowing, the river carries the alluvium, but as the river waters fan out, the alluvium spreads into the space, creating this distinctive fan shaped feature. Death Valley in California is the site of an ancient alluvial fan. Others are found along the Koshi River in Nepal and in the Zagreb Mountains in Iran. Like deltas, these can be fertile, productive areas given the alluvium contains rich minerals and organic matter.

Of all the rivers in the world, the Nile River in Africa is the longest. Stretching over 6,600 kilometres (4,100 miles), the river flows north to empty into the Mediterranean Sea and create the Nile Delta. Like the Tigris and Euphrates Rivers, which were once central to ancient Mesopotamian societies, the Nile was vital to the success of early Egyptian civilisations. It remains an essential lifeline for northeast Africa today. The second longest river in the world is found on the South American continent, the Amazon River, while the third is the Yangtze River. This starts on the Tibetan plateau and flows to the East China Sea.

There is one river in Europe which you probably know from music, not just geography. This is the Danube, famously celebrated with the Blue Danube Waltz by Johann Strauss. It is a river that dances through ten countries: Germany, Austria, Slovakia, Hungary, Croatia, Serbia, Romania, Bulgaria, Moldova, and Ukraine. Large sections of the river serve as borders between these nations, and it has long been vital for trade and transportation. Along with the Danube, other rivers flowing within Europe include the Elbe, Po, Rhine, and Volga, winding within mountains, plains, towns, and cities.

Within Asia the major rivers are the Yangtze, Ganges, Mekong, Yellow (Huang He), and Lena Rivers. The Yangtze flows from west to east for 6,300 kilometres (3,915 miles), originating in the Tibetan Plateau and ending in Shanghai, China where it drains into the East China Sea. The longest river in Asia, it is also one of the busiest in the world. Nearly 500 million people live along the Yangtze and a mass of cargo and passengers move along its waters. The Yangtze Delta is perhaps the most hectic shipping junction on Earth. It is also the largest economic centre of China. This is where heavy loaded barges that have travelled down the river meet ocean freighters, oil tankers, container ships, along with small fishing vessels. It is an important gateway to the Asia-Pacific region and supports an array of global manufacturing operations.

Several noteworthy rivers dominate the two American continents. In North America, the St Lawrence River is part of the Great Lakes catchment. Many readers discover this river through Holling C Holling's book *Paddle-to-the-Sea*, following its journey through Canada and out to the Atlantic Ocean. Other rivers include the Colorado River, and the famous Mississippi which passes through ten American states, including Wisconsin, Kentucky, and Tennessee. Within South America, the Amazon River is perhaps the best-known river, but by no means the only one. There is the Paraná River which supplies energy to parts of Brazil, Paraguay, and Argentina, and also the Orinoco River, a river famous for its secrets. The source of the Orinoco is within one of the most remote regions of South America, where the impressive rapids were described by explorer Alexander von Humboldt as being "the eighth wonder of the world". Of all the rivers in the world, this one is considered to be the least understood and most mysterious.

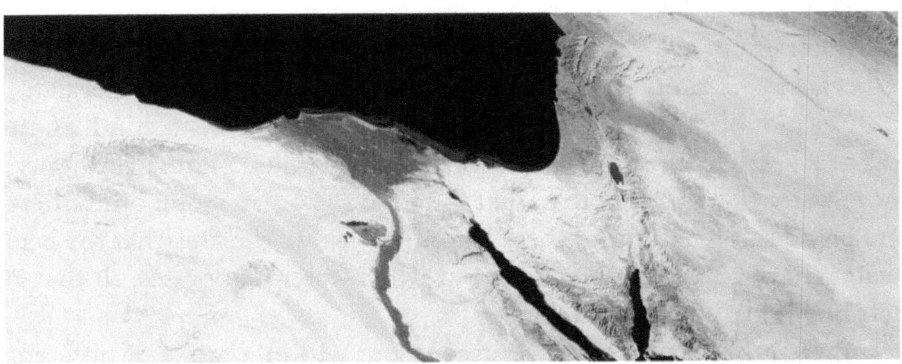

The lush Nile delta

CHAPTER 25

Lakes, Dams and Wetlands

Compared to a river, which can flow quickly through a landscape, lake waters are generally slow-moving. A lake is a stable body of water that is surrounded by land, so all lakes are located inland. There are numerous lakes across Earth, ranging from small ponds to great lakes that cover a huge area and hold a large amount of freshwater. As covered in Chapter 22, some lakes are so big that they are referred to as seas, such as the Caspian Sea, which is actually the world's largest lake. While some lakes are relatively shallow, others are very deep. For instance, the bed of Lake Baikal in Russia extends to nearly 2 kilometres (1.4 miles) at its deepest point. This great depth means that it holds about one-fifth of all the surface freshwater on the planet.

The water source for lakes and ponds can be precipitation (rain or snow), ice melt, streams flowing into the lake, or groundwater seeping up from an aquifer. Regardless of their source, geographers often classify lakes in the way water flows out. Some lakes sit within closed basins, meaning that there may be some water loss through seepage or evaporation, but water does not flow out of the lake again. These are called closed lakes. Other lakes are open lakes as the water continues to flow out through a river or stream.

While most lakes are freshwater, some can be salty, similar to the saltwater of our oceans and seas. Salty lakes tend to be closed lakes. This is because over time, closed lakes become more saline as the water naturally evaporates from the lake, leaving salts and minerals behind. Some saline lakes, like Great Salt Lake in Utah, the United States of America, have water that is saltier than that found in the ocean. Sometimes there are broad salt flats around these lakes. This shows the area that the lake waters have covered at one time, but when water evaporates, all that is left behind are the salt minerals.

There are lakes on every continent and within a range of different environments. Lakes are even found in Antarctica, where they are called subglacial lakes, and within deserts, such as the Lakes of Ounianga in the Sahara Desert. They are also found at different elevations. For example, Lake Titicaca is located high within the Andes Mountains, between the nations of Peru and Bolivia. It is one of the world's highest lakes. In comparison, the Dead Sea, which lies between Israel and Jordan, is the lowest, lying below sea level. No matter where it is located, a lake is simply where water has accumulated in a spot that is lower than the surrounding countryside, regardless of longitude, latitude, or altitude.

Forming a natural basin in the landscape, some lakes are found in the craters of inactive volcanoes, sit within the plain off the meander of a river, or within a natural depression carved out by glaciers. Most have formed naturally, but not all. Sometimes artificial lakes are created to provide a water-setting for a city or town, or as part of a project to provide hydroelectric power. Lake Burley Griffin in Canberra, Australia was created for the nation's capital. Part of the Molonglo River was dammed when the capital city was built. The Central Basin of the lake adds to the Parliamentary Area which includes Parliament House, the National Library, and the High Court of Australia.

Only a couple of hours drive from the city of Canberra, in the Australian Alps region, lies the Snowy Mountains Hydro-Electric Scheme. A marvel of civil engineering, the Scheme, known locally as "The Snowy", includes major dams, power stations, and many kilometres of aqueducts and tunnels. Through this extensive scheme, water from the Snowy River is diverted and used to generate hydroelectricity for Australians. Lakes and dams were created as a part of this massive scheme, dramatically changing the natural landscape of the Australian Alps.

While lakes can be natural or artificial, dams are constructed bodies of water in the landscape. The creation of the dams within the Snowy Scheme in Australia allowed engineers to harness the power of water to generate electricity. A series of structures were built to hold back the natural flow of water and control it to power through a series of interconnecting underground tunnels. Similarly, the Colorado River, which moves through seven American states, including desert regions in Arizona, Nevada, and California, is also harnessed for hydroelectric power. Two of America's largest dams are situated on the Colorado River: the Hoover

Dam at Lake Mead and the Glen Canyon Dam at Lake Powell. Such dams restrict the natural flow of a river, lake, or stream with engineers using earth, rock, stone, and cement to hold water in the dam. They alter the natural landscape and use water resources for human needs.

Similar to dams, weirs are another constructed water landform. Weirs are like small-scale dams, but the flow of water isn't fully obstructed. A barrier structure is put into place over a river or stream, allowing the water level on the upstream side to be raised slightly. Weirs are often put in place to prevent flooding in certain areas, as they allow for the rising and lowering of the water level. The Pretzien Weir in Germany is located on the banks of the river Elbe, close to the city of Magdeburg. Given the flooding experienced in this area, the construction of the weir was completed in 1875 and was part of an initiative to protect residences and farms. It also enabled better shipping in the area. The iron sluice gates could be raised or lowered, acting like a floodgate to block or move more water through. Along with flooding protection and supporting shipping, weirs are also used in some agricultural areas to support irrigation and to provide water-based recreational opportunities.

Lakes can be all different shapes, sizes, and depths, but smaller lakes are often referred to as ponds. Ponds may be very stable water environments (such as bog ponds), but they may also be rather shallow and not able to hold water all year round. Ponds are often found within moors, grasslands, floodplains, and agricultural areas. Some occur naturally and others are created by people. There are many ponds in Britain and they provide an important freshwater habitat for various plants and animals.

Glen Canyon Dam

The Royal Botanic Gardens in Kew, London, has the famous Waterlily Pond with giant waterlilies and their striking blooms. Across the English Channel, over in France, Claude Monet's Garden in Giverny features a gorgeous pond, also with waterlilies. This one was inspired by Japanese gardens, where water is prized for tranquillity.

Lakes and ponds are quite different to wetlands and swamps, which serve as transition areas. Transition areas are places in the landscape that are neither totally dry, like land, nor totally underwater, like a lake. Often inundated with water seasonally, wetlands and swamps are characterised by their vegetation. There are often a lot of trees and a variety of plants, making rich, ecologically diverse areas. Wetlands and swamps are found on every continent except Antarctica and can be known by a range of names, such as peatlands, sloughs, bogs, fens, mires, and potholes. While varying immensely across locations, these transition zones are an important part of the freshwater landscape on Earth.

One important transition area is the Okavango Delta in Botswana, Africa. Despite its name, this delta doesn't drain out to the ocean. Instead, the water drains into the Kalahari Desert. It is a vast grassland plain which is seasonally inundated to create a spectacular wetland environment. Experiencing both wet and dry seasons, the Okavango Delta is annually flooded by the River Okavango, which transforms an arid landscape into a vibrant wetland. This attracts large herds of African elephants, zebra, and buffalo, which seasonally migrate to this lush area. Rhinoceros, cheetahs, lions, wild dogs, and many species of birds and reptiles also live within the rivers, lagoons, swamps, and flooded grasslands.

<u>An old silent pond.</u>

An old silent pond…
A frog jumps into the pond,
splash! Silence again.

by Matsuo Basho

Questions on Chapters 23, 24 and 25

For answers see page 208

1. Please name the three processes of the water cycle and briefly describe each.
2. Name two rivers found on the South and North American continents.
3. Are alluvial fans found on land or at sea?
4. The Yangtze Delta is formed where the Yangtze River meets which sea?
5. Name the world's largest lake.
6. What is the capital city of Australia and the name of the lake that was created for the capital?
7. How is a dam different to a lake?
8. In which country and continent do you find the Okavango Delta?

Map Questions on Chapters 23, 24 and 25

For answers see page 209

1. Which five countries border the Caspian Sea?
2. Lake Eyre | Kati Thanda is a lake located within Central Australia. The country of Australia is made up of six states and two territories. Using a map, list the names of the states and territories of Australia.
3. Follow the path of the Danube River in Europe and note which countries it passes through.
4. The Amazon River ends at the Atlantic Ocean, where the Amazon Delta is located. Name the bay that the Amazon flows into.
5. The powerful Dettifloss waterfalls are found on Iceland as the Jökulsá á Fjöllum River flows from the Vatnajökull glacier to the Greenland Sea. Name the national capital of Iceland.
6. The world-famous Kew Gardens are an important part of the Royal Botanic Gardens in England and feature some beautiful ponds. The Kew Garden are in southwest London. Name the river that passes through London.
7. Find Botswana on a map of Africa and list which countries border it.

CHAPTER 26

Icesheets, Glaciers and Fjords

Of all the water found on Earth, 97% is held within our oceans and seas. Given this is all saltwater it only leaves 3% as freshwater. Very little of Earth's freshwater flows through rivers and lakes. Instead of rushing through river channels, gliding around meanders, or cascading over waterfalls, three-quarters is stored within glaciers and ice caps, making glacial ice the largest reservoir of freshwater on Earth. Antarctica and Greenland hold most of this frozen store of water, with over 99% of ice locked within the continent of Antarctica and the Greenland Ice Sheet. These frozen landscapes play a crucial role in regulating our climate as their bright white surfaces reflect sunlight back into the atmosphere, rather than absorbing it as darker surfaces do. This reflection helps moderate global temperatures, influencing climate and weather patterns worldwide.

Currently, about 10% of the world's landmass is covered by ice. Geographers use specific terms to describe these areas, differentiating between the size and appearance of the ice covering the land. Ice sheets are the largest. These cover more than 50,000 square kilometres (19,000 square miles) and lie relatively flat on the landscape. Today ice sheets are only found in Antarctica and Greenland.

Areas smaller than 50,000 square kilometres (19,000 square miles) are ice caps and icefields. Ice caps are a type of glacier, with a distinctive dome-like shape, formed by slow-moving ice. They are found in high-latitude polar regions as well as mountainous areas of subpolar regions.

Icefields are similar to ice caps, but they don't have the dome-like shape that is the tell-tale sign of an ice cap. Instead, icefields can have mountains and ridges jutting above the ice, places where the bedrock has pierced through. These parts are known as nunataks, meaning "lonely peaks", with the summit of the mountain or a rocky ridge protruding through the ice. These rocky outcrops can serve as important landmarks and points of reference for navigation and scientific study in glacial regions. The Harding Icefield in Kenai Fjords National Park, Alaska extends over 1,126 kilometres (700 square miles). More than thirty glaciers of different sizes and types are found within the icefield but not all the underlying mountains are completely buried. Outside the polar regions, the state of Alaska is one of the world's most heavily glaciated regions and the Harding Icefield is a spectacular sight.

Glaciers are conglomerations of ice, snow, sediment, rock, and sometimes liquid water. They form on land and, flowing slowly like a frozen river, can carve through the landscape, eroding it. Glaciers can be found on every continent except Australia. Given the cold temperatures required and the fact that many are formed where there is significant snow accumulating, in the course of a year it isn't cold enough for glaciers to form. While most of the world's glaciers are found in Antarctica, others are located on the world's largest island, Greenland, and within the state of Alaska in the United States of America. However, glaciers aren't just found in the polar regions. There are glaciers in New Zealand and even rare tropical glaciers in Indonesia.

It takes many years for a glacier to form. As snow falls, some melts a little. Melting, the snow becomes harder and more dense compared to fluffy powder snow. The slight melt makes it more like a pellet of ice. When more snow falls this pellet is compressed by the new layer of snow. These layers of hard snow are called firn. Sediment, like rocks, may be trapped within this frozen mass and over time, layers of firn form and meld together. This structure can become very thick. With the layers of thick ice and sediment, glaciers can be very heavy! Due to this weight, and the forces of gravity, some glaciers may start to budge slowly through the landscape, moving slowly like a frozen river, with those layers of ice eroding the land as it moves. The world's fastest glacier is the Jakobshavn Glacier, in Greenland, but other glaciers are frozen solid and do not move at all.

Given they are made of snow and ice, it is tempting to imagine glaciers as vivid white in colour. However, they have a slight blue tint. This is because glacier ice is a mono-mineralic rock, a crystalline form of water, sometimes called Hexagonal Water because of the shape of its crystals. Through the geological process of creating a glacier, thousands of individual snowflakes are compressed, transforming them into dense crystals of glacier ice. This compression not only increases their size and density compared to the fluffy white snowflakes that swirl and fall from the sky, but it also gives the ice its blue hue. This colour is significant because it influences how the frozen surfaces reflect sunlight, which in turn, affects our climate.

Vatnajökull glacier in Iceland is the largest ice cap in Europe. Spreading over 8,100 square kilometres (3,127 square miles), it is big and thick, being 1,000 kilometres (3,000 feet) deep in parts. Vatnajökull serves as a key store of freshwater and as a popular tourist attraction. People love to hike within Vatnajökull National Park, admiring the glacier, exploring the ice caves, viewing the glacier lagoons, and witnessing the most powerful waterfall in Europe, the Dettifoss. This is a striking landscape perfect for keen photographers, with the vivid blue of the glacial ice set against the grey of the surrounding terrain of volcanic ash.

Just as geographers and travellers delight in the sights of Iceland, many are lured to the beauty of New Zealand, also shaped by frozen forces. Glaciers have created some impressive landforms, including fjords in Milford Sound | Piopiotahi on the South Island. Fjords are a bodies of water nestled within cold mountain regions. Generally long, narrow, and deep, they are tucked into valleys with steep and rocky sides that show where the glacier moved through the landscape to create the fjord. Milford Sound is a long, narrow inlet within Fiordland National Park in New Zealand's South Island | Te Waipounamu. Despite being called a sound, it is actually a fjord.

Some of the biggest fjords on Earth meet the sea. This connection to the ocean means sea water floods the valley created by the glacier, filling the fjord. The mix of saltwater from the ocean with freshwater from the glacier, and snow and rain, means that the water within a fjord is brackish. Brackish water is a mix of both saltwater and freshwater. However, some inland fjord lakes do not open to the ocean. Instead, freshwater fills inland fjord lakes. This is because of a connection to a lake, rivers, or streams. Many fjords are a spectacular blue or sea-green colour due to the silt and sediment carried by the glacier into the lake.

The sunlight reflecting on the sediment in the water creates their unique and stunning colour. It also makes them look very enticing for a swim, but they are icy cold.

While used internationally to describe this geographical landform, the word fjord is a Norwegian term. The Norwegian coastland is dominated by fjords, with an estimated 1,200 fjords defining this Scandinavian country. There are many majestic fjords in Norway, but they can be found in other countries too, including Chile, New Zealand, Canada, Greenland, and the American state of Alaska. The world's longest fjord is in Greenland. Called Scoresbysund Et in Danish, or Scoresby Sound, it lies on the eastern coast of Greenland. What may be an unexpected feature of some deep fjords is what lies at the bottom. This is because coral reefs have formed within some fjords. Normally coral reefs are associated with tropical islands, however, Norway has some of the most extensive deep sea coral reefs on the planet. Similar reefs are also found in New Zealand due to the depths of the ocean water in the glacial environment.

Along with adopting the word fjord into our geographical vocabulary, there is another Old Norse term used: "skerry". Skerries are small rocky islands found near fjords. Like fjords, skerries are created by glaciers,

Kenai Fjords

with little islands and rocky reefs forming along the coastline where the glacial valley meets the ocean. Just as glaciers cut into the valley to create a fjord, skerries are created where land is carved out by a glacier, resulting in thousands of rocky islands, reefs, and jagged points in the water, all of which are referred to as skerries. Most of the Scandinavian coastline is defined by skerries and they can also be found along the coastline of the American states of Washington and Alaska.

While most glaciers and fjords are located in polar colder regions, there are rare occurrences of glaciers in the tropical zone. High up in the Jayawijaya mountains in the region of Papua in Indonesia are tropical glaciers. Within the Lorentz National Park, they are called the Eternity Glaciers. These glaciers exist because of the high altitude of Puncak Jaya, the highest peak in Indonesia, and local tribes live close to the glaciers, regarding them as sacred sites. There are only a few tropical glaciers in the world, with others located within the Andes Mountains in Peru and the high mountains of Africa. Yet, scientists record that these are showing signs of retreat, and there is real concern that these natural treasures may be lost forever.

Many scientists are concerned about the decreasing area glaciers occupy on Earth due to climate change. Using techniques like repeating aerial and satellite photography, scientists can examine the loss of glaciers and ice. They assess how their shape and area changes and the amount of glacial ice on the planet. This is a key issue as data monitors rising global temperatures which can cause ice to melt, leading to more freshwater flowing through the water cycle. This is why understanding the role our frozen landscapes play is critical.

CHAPTER 27

Groundwater Resources

When we stand by a river or a waterfall we see water moving through the landscape. We may feel the spray on our faces and hear the sound of rushing water. These can be gentle, tranquil places, but also sites where great power and force are exerted. In addition to moving freshwater, we understand that frozen ice is also a force within the landscape, with ice sheets, ice caps, and glaciers being important and beautiful features of our geography. The hydrological cycle explains how water continually loops through the landscape, evaporating into the atmosphere, condensing into cloud, and then falling as precipitation. It is a key cycle of our planet.

In addition to these water features, there are water resources beneath the surface of the Earth. This is water that we cannot see. It is called groundwater. As its name suggests, groundwater is water found within the ground. It lies within empty spaces under the ground known as aquifers. An aquifer is an underground layer of rock that can store and move water. These rocks hold some of the world's most precious water resources. Aquifers are porous, meaning water can pass through. They can be all shapes and sizes and are found at varying depths in the ground. The Great Artesian Basin in Australia is a huge groundwater resource. It covers 22% of the Australian continent and is a system of aquifers, holding a massive water source underground.

In the same way that raindrops can seep through into the soil, groundwater can move through these underground geological landforms. Water percolates downward into aquifers through a process known as infiltration. Surface water seeps into the earth, moving through soil, sand, and rock to create underground water supplies within aquifers.

Groundwater is a significant water source for irrigation, drinking and household use, and is used by various industries. Hidden underground, it is a vital part of the water cycle because it helps to replenish and maintain the levels of surface water in rivers and lakes. Just as water can pass down into the ground, it can also bubble up to the surface. This means that groundwater can replenish surface water sources or be discharged into rivers and lakes.

While it may not be seen, groundwater is an essential natural resource. In some places around the world people are critically reliant on groundwater resources. This includes millions of people within the Rio Grande and Rio Bravo basin between Texas and Mexico. Straddling the border between the United States of America and Mexico, this groundwater basin provides part of the public water supply and water for irrigated agriculture. It also supports key wetlands and springs for wildlife, including migratory birds, because groundwater plays an important role in natural ecosystems.

Groundwater held in aquifers naturally discharges at springs and within wetlands. These vast water reserves can also be accessed with the installation of a well and bores. While there are different types of wells, essentially a well is a hole that is dug into the ground, using pipes and a pump to draw the water from the aquifer to the surface. In places where surface water is scarce, wells can transform a local community, providing a reliable and ample supply of water. However, given this water resource is not seen by the naked eye, it can be difficult to determine the amount of water available underground, so there can be concerns that this precious resource might not always be managed well. While groundwater supplies are recharged through rain and snow melt, as the water droplets seep through the cracks and crevices to move beneath the land's surface, in some regions the groundwater is being used much faster than it can be replenished. This means that the resource is being depleted. In other areas, groundwater can be polluted.

Being stored under the ground, groundwater may naturally contain dissolved minerals and gases. This means it often tastes a little different to surface water, with almost a tangy taste. It can look different too. It often looks a little cloudy in a glass. Another intriguing feature of groundwater is its temperature. Water in lakes, rivers, and our oceans is generally cool, sometimes even icy or completely frozen. However, while groundwater can be cool in some places, in others it can be warm or very hot, sometimes even to boiling point. This is because there is an incredible amount of heat and pressure under the ground which can affect the temperature of groundwater as the warmth and energy heats the water up.

This heat within the earth creates hot springs. Hot springs are pools of water heated by the hot or molten rock within the ground, making the water warmer than the surrounding ground and air. This is why they are often known as thermal or geothermal springs. Due to the thermal heat of the Earth, these water features can range from lukewarm to extremely hot. Hot springs are found in many countries around the world. This includes Australia, Chile, Greece, Iceland, Japan, and Türkiye, where the famous Pamukkale World Heritage site is located. Pamukkale is one of Türkiye's most popular tourist attractions and is a series of petrified waterfalls and mineral salt forests. Flourishing in ancient Greece and Rome, the waters here were considered therapeutic, with hot springs, basins, and pools for bathing and swimming. Today, Greco-Roman ruins still stand in the area, all centred around the complex groundwater system so many favoured for their healing qualities. Literally called "Cotton Castle" in Turkish, the landscape at Pamukkale is dazzling white, like cotton bursting open from their pods. This landscape is white due to minerals left by underground thermal spring water, creating a unique water-based scenery that many flock to see each year.

Hot springs are also popular in Asia, particularly in Japan where they are known as onsens (温泉). Just as many did in the ancient days of Pamukkale, visitors to onsens like to bathe in these natural thermal springs, staying in traditional inns and benefiting from the health properties of plunging into the mineral-rich waters. More than 1,300 years old, Nishiyama Onsen Keiunkan in Japan is considered the oldest inn in the world. It is located near volcanic hot springs in the mountains surrounding Mount Fuji, Japan's most sacred mountain. The energy of the earth heats the water, making the inn is a popular destination for bathing and relaxation. However, it is not just humans who appreciate the hot springs. Japanese macaques are known for sitting and bathing in the snow and the steaming hot springs, which is why they are often called "snow monkeys".

Across the Atlantic Ocean from Japan, in the United States of

America, there is a rare type of hot spring. This is called a geyser. It is a hot spring which is pushed through a vent in the ground, forcing a jet of steam through the earth to burst forth to the surface. The power by which this explodes, and the amount of steam released, makes for a spectacular sight. This is why millions of visitors venture to Yellowstone National Park in Wyoming every year to see this amazing water force. Old Faithful, the famous geyser in Yellowstone, erupts every 90 minutes, spilling jets of boiling water and steam from deep under the ground. After the geyser erupts, the water seeps back into the groundwater. Underground, the water will become heated and, placed under geological pressure, it will then erupt again. The eruptions of Old Faithful can be reliably tracked and predicted, information which is shared online and through an app.

While almost half of the world's active geysers are found in Yellowstone National Park, representing the largest concentration of geysers on the planet, geysers can be found in other places around the world too. New Zealand, parts of Russia, Chile and Iceland all feature geysers, and just like Old Faithful, these are dynamic movements in the landscape and evidence of the geothermal processes underground.

Whether it is a geyser erupting, the white landscape of Pamukkale, the onsens of Japan, or spectacular caves, water moving through the ground can create some remarkable natural structures. Caves are formed by the slow and sustained movement of water. Known as karst landscapes, these are places where water and carbon dioxide dissolve stone to create underground cavities. When combined, the water and carbon dioxide from the air form a weak acid. As this percolates through the ground, it wears the stone away. Over time, the rock is broken down and fractures, with hollows appearing within the earth. It takes a long time, but this movement of water creates some impressive and deep caves in the earth.

Due to the constant dripping of water moving through the rock, caves are naturally moist environments. This is why, when you visit a cave, you may hear the slow, steady sound of water passing through the underground landscape. The dripping water within a cave can create stalagmites and stalactites. These are rock formations, but they can look a bit like icicles. Stalagmites grow upwards from the floor, created by the minerals from the weeping water as it drips from the cave ceiling onto the floor. Stalactites hang from the roof of the cave, water dripping from its pointed tip. A good way to remember the difference between the two is this: Stalactites hang tight to the ceiling, but stalagmites push up with all their might. Over time the stalagmites and stalactites can actually connect, forming a column inside the cave.

Caves, along with subterranean rivers and sinkholes, are common features of karst landscapes, although not all caves are found on land. There are sea caves too. Some of these are partially submerged, while others are entirely underwater. Just like land-based caves, sea caves can be dramatic landscapes with narrow passages and wide-open chambers. Some famous sea caves are the Blue Grotto in Capri, Italy and Fingal's Cave in Scotland, both providing a glimpse into the powerful forces of water that sculpt our world.

Fingal's Cave

Questions on Chapter 26 and 27

For answers see page 209

1. On which continents can glaciers be found?

2. What is the difference between an ice sheet and an ice cap?

3. In which national park is Old Faithful located?

4. Name two countries where hot springs can be found.

5. Do stalagmites grow upwards from the floor of a cave or down from the ceiling?

Map Questions on Chapters 26 and 27

For answers see page 210

1. Fjords are found mainly in Norway, Chile, New Zealand, Canada, Greenland, and the American state of Alaska. Find these five countries and the state of Alaska on a map.

2. Many glaciers and fjords are found in Scandinavia. Which countries form Scandinavia and what are the major water bodies in this region?

3. Locate Milford Sound | Piopiotahi on a map of New Zealand.

4. Find the Outer Hebrides of the west coast of Scotland. This is an archipelago, made up of islands and skerries. Name the ocean it lies within.

5. Hot springs with bathing facilities and traditional inns, known as onsens (温泉), are popular in Japan. Find Japan on a map and name the four main large islands.

6. Name the ocean and four seas that surround Japan.

CHAPTER 28

The Coast

Along the coastlines of the world, you can witness some of the most incredible transition zones between land and sea. The land that runs along the sea is the coast, while the coastline marks the boundary where land meets seawater. In some places this meeting is calm and gentle, with salty seawater softly lapping against white sandy beaches. In other areas the coast is rugged and dramatic. Some coastlines of the world are made up of steep cliffs and powerful, towering waves that crash forcefully. These create a wild, and sometimes treacherous, coastal landscape.

Wave action, water currents, and tides shape the varied coastlines of our world. Whether they lap delicately or powerfully crash in, waves hit the shore and shape the land. This wave action erodes and carves out the coastline, and also deposits particles from the sea, adding sand, shells, seaweed, and marine creatures to build and form new coastal features. Both of these actions – erosion and deposition – change the coastal landscape over time.

Strong wave action can cause coastal retreat in some regions of the world. Parts of Australia's beautiful beaches are retreating due to a range of factors, including erosion and storm surges, and the famous White Cliffs of Dover in England are monitored for increased rates of erosion. These majestic walls look over the English Channel on the coastline of southeast England. They are white in colour due to the chalk in the landscape. Once described by William Shakespeare as "This fortress built by Nature for herself," parts of the coastline are slowly crumbling into the sea. Experts regularly check the stability of these cliffs where many people like to ramble. In contrast, some coastlines are far more resistant to wave action. Sugarloaf Mountain in Rio de Janeiro, Brazil, is made of tough, dense rock. While powerful waves mightily crash and hammer, the landform remains largely unchanged.

Around the world people love time at the beach. While keen surfers favour a high energy beach, with tall, breaking waves, others prefer those with lazy pleasant waves where they can swim and splash. These are languid beaches and are often places where waves will deposit particles from the seas rather than those where the landscape is fiercely worn away. Beaches, sand dunes, sand bars, spits, and tombolos are all coastal landforms that are created by depositional processes. They are shaped by the sand that forms them.

Coastal geography examines the processes that create landforms such as sandbars, spits, and tombolos and the coastal zone between land and sea, monitoring the constant shaping of the coast from wave action. This movement creates new landforms, but can also clog harbours and river mouths as sand moves away from beaches and into these areas. As you may guess from its name, a sand bar is literally a bar of sand. It is a strip of land along the coast, formed by sediment being deposited in this area. Long sand bars point out into the ocean as the water currents and waves strike the coast at an angle. The swash of a wave picks up sand and carries it from the beach. The next wave to follow will also move sand, and then the next, and so on. This continual wave action carries grains of sand from the beach to create a sandbar. A long sandbar is called a spit and so much sediment can build up that lagoons form, creating an area of calmer waters sheltered by the spit. Another type of spit is a tombolo. A tombolo connects an island to the shore, acting as a type of sandy land bridge between the mainland and island, reshaping the coastline.

In 333 BC Alexander the Great made clever use of a sandbar that had begun to form in the Mediterranean Sea. Back then the city of Tyre was on an island not too far from the coast and Alexander wanted to take control of it. Cutting down trees on the island for agriculture had resulted in gradual erosion. As sediment ran off the land into the sea, a long, thin sandbar had formed, stretching all the way to the mainland. It was a few meters underwater, but nevertheless the beginnings of a tombolo. Unwilling to wait for natural processes, Alexander's engineers piled up stone, timber, and rubble on the sandbar, creating a causeway and setting the scene for their siege of Tyre. This construction had a long-lasting effect. It interrupted the currents, and the area slowly silted up, so much so that today the city of Tyre, in southern Lebanon, is a peninsula. Alexander's construction of the causeway altered the coastal geography of this area.

While some coastal landforms are shaped by deposition, others are created through erosion. Cliffs, sea arches, caves, and stacks are all landscape features that change over time due to constant wave action. Cliffs are generally associated with a headland. This is the part of land that juts out into the sea, offering a commanding view. Generally made of materials that are more resistant to erosion, a headland is often characterised by a flatter top. Land's End in Cornwall, England is a famous headland. It is the southwestern most tip of England. Here, the headland extends over into the Atlantic Ocean, making Land's End a popular tourist destination. The cliffs and coastline here are notoriously wild as the waves, winds, and sea-spray have eroded the landscape, making rocky, rugged cliffs.

Along some parts of the coast you may spot sea caves, arches, and stacks. All are the result of wave action eroding sea cliffs. As waves crash along the cliffs, rock is worn away. The sand, salt, and shell particles within the sea waters are abrasive and cut into the rock. Over time, cracks form. With repeated wave action, these coastal rock formations gradually open up. Although they may look like strong and mighty fortresses, the force of water shapes these parts of the coast. These cracks may gradually open up, forming a sea cave. As the waves pound into the sea caves, the sea water hits the back wall of the cave and the force of this will form a sea arch as the sea cave continues to erode. While sea caves and arches are beautiful, the forces of erosion don't stop there. In time, the remaining bridge will collapse, leaving just a sea stack standing in the ocean waters.

The Twelve Apostles along the Great Ocean Road in Victoria, Australia are a great example of coastal erosion at work. Within this part of southeastern Australia there are sheer cliff walls, sea caves, arches, and stacks, along with blowholes, where the water whooshes up through a hole in the rock. There were once twelve sea stacks standing within Port Campbell National Park in the Pacific Ocean. These were named after Jesus' twelve disciples. However, because these coastal processes just don't stop, there are currently only eight still standing. This is an amazing stretch of Australia's coastline. You can stand on the coast and feel the sea spray as the cold ocean waters roll in, watching the dynamic forces constantly at work.

There are many stunning coastlines to explore around the world. Ha Long Bay in the Gulf of Tonkin, Vietnam, features over 1,600 islands and islets. These are tropical jungle islands and mostly not inhabited. This is a seascape of towering limestone pillars, a Karst landscape in the sea. You can see sea stacks, arches, pillars, and sea caves. The steady erosion of the limestone from rainwater and the sea has carved out these beautiful geographical features, making it a breathtaking coastal area. For generations, the Kinh people have lived within Ha Long Bay on floating fishing villages. A popular tourist destination, many sell handmade crafts or local delicacies to visitors, many featuring locally caught fish and seafood.

Other coastlines are desolate places where few people live or visit. In the south-west of Africa, in Namibia, the Skeleton Coast borders the Atlantic Ocean. Once littered with the skeletons of whales from that prosperous industry, it is still punctuated by the many shipwrecks that dot the coast. Quite the opposite of a popular coastal city, the Skeleton Coast is one of the last great wildernesses of the world. Despite being in the tropical zone, the Skeleton Coast is chilly. The cold Benguela sea current brings a dense fog that shrouds the coast for most months of the year and brings icy cold surf. Treacherous conditions, rough waves, changeable weather, and shifting shores make it a difficult part of the coastline to navigate. It is so difficult that some refer to the Skeleton Coast National Park as the world's largest ship cemetery. Here, tall sand dunes meet the cold waters of the Atlantic Ocean, offering an important refuge for many animals, including Cape fur seals, elephants, zebras, giraffes, chacma baboons, hyenas, antelope, and various species of birds.

Around the world, coastlines have long been among the most populated areas. Many people like the coast and today over half of Earth's population lives on, or near, a coast. Beaches are a beloved recreation area and important for tourism and industry too. Coastal regions support important sea-based industries, including marine fishing, national defence installations, and strategic ports vital to trade. In the United States, there are coastal cities like Honolulu in Hawai'i, rich in Hawaiian and Polynesian heritage, and Los Angeles in California, famed for its beautiful ocean views. In Asia, the audacious architecture of Dubai in the United Arab Emirates looks out from the desert to face the Persian Gulf, while in Hong Kong, skyscrapers offer views of the South China Sea. Coastal cities around the world are home to millions of people and serve as popular tourist destinations for many more.

Questions on Chapter 28

For answers see page 211

1. Which body of water does the White Cliffs of Dover look out upon?
2. Coastal landforms are created through both erosion and depositional processes. Name two depositional landforms found in coastal zones.
3. Name at least one feature of a coastal zone that is created by erosional processes.
4. A tombolo is a type of spit. Please describe it.
5. In which country do you find Ha Long Bay and the Gulf of Tonkin?

Map Questions on Chapter 28

For answers see page 211

1. Sugarloaf Mountain is in Rio di Janeiro in Brazil. On a map, find the capital city of Brazil and name the ocean that runs along the east coast of this country.
2. Find the Gulf of Tonkin and identify which countries and sea border Vietnam.
3. The more densely populated parts of Hong Kong are Hong Kong Island and Kowloon Peninsula. Victoria Harbour lies between the two. In which direction from Hong Kong Island does Lamma Island lie?
4. The Skeleton Coast is in Namibia, Africa. Which ocean adjoins this coastline?

CHAPTER 29

Mountain Ranges

Stories in history include accounts of explorers and climbers making their ascents to mountain tops; some successful, others to their peril. These quests to conquer the topmost parts of the landscape make for some legendary tales, such as mountaineer Sir Edmund Hillary and Tenzing Norgay being the first to summit Mount Everest in 1953. Atop the highest peak on Earth, these two men stood higher than any other point in all the surrounding mountains. They looked out upon the Himalayan Mountain ranges and through to the Tibetan plateau, located to the north of Mount Everest.

What makes a mountain a mountain? How is a mountain different to a hill? These are questions that students often have when thinking about the towering locales of our world. They are great questions, but most geographers don't have an exact definition to answer them. Years ago, mountains were primarily defined by their height. While there is no one universally accepted definition distinguishing a mountain from a hill, there are ways that help tell them apart.

Both hills and mountains are elevated landforms, meaning that they rise higher than the land around them. Hills are smaller than mountains and they are naturally round, almost like bumps in the landscape. They are relatively easy to climb since they rise gradually from the surrounding land. In comparison, mountains rise more dramatically in the landscape and have a well-defined summit. They tend to be steeper than hills and are often the result of a geological process called faulting. Also, most mountains have been given names. Many include the term "mount" in their name (or "mont" in French), such as Mount Rainer, Mount Kilimanjaro, Mount Cook, and Mont Blanc. In comparison, most hills don't have names given to them, though a few special hills do. For example, the Hill of Tara near Dunsany in Ireland has been a significant heritage site since the Iron Age, serving as the inauguration site and high seat of the kings of Ireland. Ruling monarchs would use the hill because it gives a commanding view of a large swathe of country. You can visit this hill and explore the ancient ceremonial and burial site which isn't too far from Dublin, the national capital of the Republic of Ireland.

A sequence of hills is often referred to as a hill chain, and mountains grouped together are called a mountain range. The mountains in ranges are geologically related, with most mountains in the range being formed by the same geological processes. These ranges often form political boundaries between countries, such as the Zagros Mountains bordering Iran and Iraq, the Andes Mountains between Chile and Argentina, and the Pyrenees Mountains between France and Spain. Their height and size offers a natural protective barrier to the land that lies beyond.

Some mountain ranges extend for hundreds or even thousands of miles. The Great Dividing Range in Australia is one of the world's longest mountain ranges. It runs along the length of the eastern coast of Australia, from the northern tip of the state of Queensland to the southern state of Victoria. Australia's tallest peak is found within this mountain range: Mount Kosciuszko. In 1840 Polish explorer Pawel Strzelecki became the first European to climb Mount Kosciuszko and he named it. He noticed that the domed peak of Australia's highest mountain was similar in shape to the tomb of Tadeusz Kościuszko back in Krakow, Poland and so he named the mountain after this.

Further east from Australia, across the Tasman Sea, lies New Zealand | Aotearoa. Like the Great Dividing Range that runs the length of Australia, the Southern Alps is the mountain range that runs the length of New Zealand's South Island | Te Waipounamu. Known as Aoraki in Māori, Mount Cook is the highest mountain in this range and the tallest peak in the country. While climber and New Zealander Sir Edmund Hillary is most commonly associated with Mount Everest, climbing and summiting Mount Cook was his mountaineering challenge and training ground before he tackled the Himalayas. Climbers continue to pursue this challenge today. The most sacred of peaks to the Māori, Mount Cook is loved by adventurers too, with many hikers keen to witness the breathtaking view of New Zealand's largest glacier, Tasman Glacier.

The terms summit and peak are used in relation to mountains and while there is always one summit of a mountain, it may have many peaks. Do you know the difference? The summit is the highest point of a mountain. The word is taken from Latin, with "summus" meaning uppermost, highest, topmost. The summit is what climbers and explorers want to stand on to know they have reached the very heights of a mountain. In comparison, peaks are pointed tops of a mountain, only one of which can be the summit. Often snow blankets the summits of tall mountains, but it can be found on the peaks too.

Each year many climbers attempt to reach the summit of Mount Everest, tackling the extreme conditions to stand on the highest point on Earth. These rocky peaks are covered with snow and ice, making them treacherous to traverse. The mountain climb is gruelling, as are the physical effects of being at such high altitudes. These landforms are so high that there are lower levels of oxygen, making it difficult to breathe.

Other adventurers want to complete the trek to Mount Everest Base Camp. This walk offers views of some of the highest peaks in the world, with four of the six highest mountains in the world found in the Himalayas. Preferring to enjoy the views of the mountains from lower ground, this is still a difficult hike. Some may capture the experience and scenery through photographs, or perhaps paintings or poems. Poet Percy Shelley was captivated by the panorama of the Alps while holidaying near Geneva, Switzerland in Europe. Shelley describes Mont Blanc, the highest mountain in the Alps, in this excerpt of his poem *Mont Blanc: Lines Written in the Vale of Chamouni*:

> Far, far above, piercing the infinite sky,
> Mont Blanc appears—still, snowy, and serene;
> Its subject mountains their unearthly forms
> Pile around it, ice and rock; broad vales between
> Of frozen floods, unfathomable deeps,
> Blue as the overhanging heaven, that spread
> And wind among the accumulated steeps…

The Alps stretch across the European countries of France, Italy, Switzerland, Germany, Austria, Lichtenstein, and Slovenia. The tallest peak in the Alps, Mont Blanc is 4,809 metres (nearly 16,000 feet) high. Its name literally means "the white mountain", with "blanc" being the French word for "white". While called a mountain, Mont Blanc is actually a massif, which is a unique geological feature. Many massifs, like Mont Blanc, have very steep sides, prominent peaks, and rugged rocky terrain. They are like a compact mountain range, with various peaks and one summit.

Some cultures have particular words to describe the high points of a landscape. In the Lake District of England the word *fell* is used to describe mountains and hills, taken from the Old Norse word of *fjäll* which described mountains higher than the tree line. Likewise, in Wales, rocky outcrops on a summit or a peak are sometimes called *tors* or *twrs*. This comes from an old Celtic word for hill. Throughout the United Kingdom many mountains are referred to as *"ben"*, such as Ben Nevis, the highest mountain in Britain. This comes from the Scottish Gaelic word, *beinn*, which means mountain. Other terms used to describe the landscape include *pen* and *crag*.

Plateaus, mesas, and buttes are other features of mountainous landscapes to explore. A plateau is a relatively flat elevated landform, and a defining feature of a plateau is that they rise very steeply on at least one side. The Tibetan Plateau is the largest plateau in the world. It covers an area of 2.5 million square kilometres (1.5 million square miles). Found within the countries of Nepal, Tibet, China, India, and Bhutan, it is the Tibetan Plateau that climbers see to the north when standing at the summit of Mount Everest. Sometimes it is referred to as "the roof of the world".

Like a plateau, a mesa has a flat top, but unlike plateaus, which are found in many different parts of the world, mesas are generally located in arid or semi-arid regions. They can be small or cover a huge area, like the Grand Mesa in Colorado. This flat mountain top covers around 1,300 square kilometres (500 square miles) and includes forests and pine areas, ski fields, and hundreds of alpine lakes, offering a natural habitat for moose, deer, elk, and many birds. All of this stands at an elevation of around 3,400 metres (11,000 feet) above sea level. This makes it the world's largest flat-topped mountain, with its distinctive mesa flat top and steep sides. Not all mesas are big like this one though. It is possible to find small mesas. Mesa is the Spanish word for table, similar to "mensa", the Latin word for table. Just like its name, a mesa is shaped like a table because the weaker vertical sides erode away, leaving the stronger rocks on the flat top.

Just as mesas are found in arid and semi-arid regions, so are buttes. Created by erosion and weathering, these are elevated landforms that were once part of a plateau or mesa, but have changed over time due to weathering processes. While mesas and plateaus can be different sizes, the dimensions of a butte are important. They define this landform. A butte is taller than it is wide. While the sides have worn away, a butte retains the original height of the plateau or mesa.

Monument Valley in the state of Utah, in America's west, has one of the most well-known conglomerations of buttes in the world. These figures rise high in the surrounding desert. This place has often been depicted in films, and images of the two buttes called "the Mittens", are recognisable to many. This area is important to the Navajo nation, who call it Tsé Bii' Ndzisgaii, a name which refers to the characteristic white streaks that are found within the rocks. The beauty of these features attracts many tourists and outdoor enthusiasts, wanting to witness these visually dramatic landforms.

The Mittens

Questions on Chapter 29

For answers see page 211

1. What is the highest peak on Earth and within which mountain range is it found?

2. In the United Kingdom many mountains are named "Ben" after the Scottish Gaelic word, Beinn, which means "mountain". What is the name of the tallest mountain in the United Kingdom?

3. Sir Edmund Hillary and Tenzing Norgay were the first to summit Mount Everest in 1953. Which mountain in New Zealand is also associated with Sir Edmund Hillary?

4. Which landform is referred to as "the roof of the world"?

5. What is the highest point of a mountain called?

6. In which biome are mesas and buttes located?

7. In which American state is the Grand Mesa located?

8. How does a butte differ to a mesa?

Map Questions on Chapter 29

For answers see page 212

1. Mount Rainer is found in the North American continent. It is located in the state of Washington, in the United States of America. On a map find Washington state and list the bordering states, country, and ocean.

2. Mount Kilimanjaro and Table Mountain are both found on the African continent. Identify which countries they are located in.

3. On a map of Europe find the countries that the Alps stretch across.

4. On a map please find a mountain range within the continent that you live in.

5. Please find the Himalayan Mountain Range and the Tibetan Plateau on a map. Name two of the countries within this part of Asia.

6. Monument Valley is found in Utah. On a map, find the states that border Utah.

CHAPTER 30

Crevasses and Canyons

When Hillary and Norgay climbed to the summit of Mount Everest there were many precipitous challenges for them to overcome. Climbers today still face these and one is not far from the South Base Camp in Nepal. Base Camp is a campsite at the beginning of the mountain climb; the place where teams of climbers gather in a pop-up city of tents filled with supplies and equipment. Climbers rest, prepare themselves and their gear, and acclimatise to the high altitudes. Given Mount Everest straddles the Nepal-Tibet border, there are actually two Base Camps for Mount Everest: one in Nepal and one in Tibet. A frozen feature of the landscape close to South Base Camp is the Khumbu Icefall. Part of the Khumbu Glacier in the Khumbu Valley, this is a glacier that constantly moves. That movement makes for treacherous conditions for climbers and sherpas.

While they sound rather similar, mountain climbers are unlikely to confuse the terms "crevice" and "crevasse". A crevice is a little crack in a rock, but a crevasse is a deep, narrow crack in a rock or a glacier and presents a real danger to climbers. A crevasse can be so deep that it appears bottomless. Sometimes they can be narrow enough to jump over, though climbers use equipment to help them cross safely. The Khumbu Icefall in Nepal is a frozen crevasse. Its continual movement means that new crevasses and avalanches can appear in the landscape without much warning. Aluminium ladders are placed horizontally flat over the crevasse so climbers aiming for the summit, in their cumbersome boots and carrying equipment, can cross the dangerous gap. Given the Icefall is always moving the ladders need to be regularly readjusted to ensure a safe passage. Even so, official records show nearly fifty lives were lost at Khumbu Icefall between 1953 and 2023.

Another danger for climbers are seracs, which can be created by crevasses. Seracs are tall pillars of ice, forming where crevasses meet. Icefalls like the Khumbu Icefall can have dozens of seracs which tumble suddenly and unexpectedly. They fall because the column of ice can become unstable due to the terrain shifting or because of ice melt. These monoliths of ice are notoriously dangerous. Climbers fear the devastating effects of a serac falling because they can be as big as a building that is several storeys high.

Warmer temperatures due to climate change have led to a growing number of reports of seracs abruptly collapsing. A large number of seracs are found on K2, the world's second highest mountain. Located within the Karakoram Range in Pakistan and China, the Bottleneck is a famous narrow couloir (corridor) within the route most climbers take to summit K2. The Bottleneck is a passage lined with seracs. If they fall, they can block the route or cause an avalanche. Sadly, on just one day in 2008, eleven climbers died and others were injured due to an ice avalanche at the Bottleneck. Ice melting at unprecedented rates is presenting new risks to climbers as the collapse of glacial ice – known as an "ice release" – sees seracs falling, posing new dangers to climbers.

Water is a dynamic force in nature, creating and defining landscapes. From frozen water creating glaciers and seracs, tranquil lakes with pleasant settings, severe ocean waters presenting challenges to sea-going vessels, or tourists travelling to marvel at rivers and massive waterfalls, the movement of water is an important part of the geography of our Earth. Just as glaciers carve fjords, rivers can create canyons. While these landscapes can be visually stunning, they also pose dangers to intrepid travellers. Canyons are formed by flowing rivers, so it is essential that canyoneers take precautions when exploring. Flash flooding is a significant risk as water can rush through canyons at speed and rise to higher levels than sometimes expected.

A canyon is a deep and narrow valley. One particular feature of canyons is their very steep sides. The pressure and constant flow of water creates the magnificent and vast landscape of a canyon. The Grand Canyon in the American state of Arizona, the Blyde River Canyon Nature Reserve in South Africa, and the Yarlung Zangbo Grand Canyon in Tibet are some of the world's deepest canyons. Swift streams of water running through rocks over a long period of time have formed these river canyons.

Similar to a canyon, a gorge is more narrow and steeper and often smaller too. However, somewhat confusingly, the two terms are sometimes used interchangeably. Typically though, canyons are larger than gorges, having broad, flat valley floors. These are noticeably different to a gorge which can be quite dramatic given they are narrow and enclosed. Both gorges and canyons are created by rivers physically weathering and eroding the rock. As the pressure from the flowing water digs into the surface, it moves sediment. The movement of the sediment gouges out the area, with the force of the water and the sediment load it carries resulting in an erosive action. Over time, the rock is worn down as water continues to push through the landscape that same way. The riverbed gets deeper and deeper.

Running for around 500 kilometres (310 miles), the Yarlung Zangbo Grand Canyon is three times deeper than the well-known Grand Canyon in the United States of America. In the southeastern part of Tibet, this is a harsh environment with glaciers, steep cliffs, sharp slopes with impressive gradients, and great waterfalls. It is often hidden within a sea of misty clouds, framed by snowy mountains. The movement of the

Yarlung Zangbo Grand Canyon

debris down the slopes and the high energy of the Yarlung Tsangpo River has carved out this perilous canyon. This is the home of the ethnic tribes of the Menba and Luoba people and a relatively unexplored part of the world. Some even refer to it as "the Everest of rivers" due to the many failed attempts to hike parts of the canyon which are just inaccessible. Hikers visiting this area are keen to see the canyon and the forests and wide variety of flowers that grow in the region. Explorers need to carefully choose the best time to visit due to potential seasonal obstructions because of snow, debris running down canyon walls, and the potential flooding caused by heavy rains.

While still holding potential dangers, different again to canyons and gorges, are ravines. A ravine is a small, narrow valley with steep-sides, carved out by running water. Typically, ravines are in a V-shape. The stream of water moving across the rock erodes the landform, particularly when seasonal flooding causes a greater volume of water to pass over it. In terms of size, a ravine is smaller than a canyon, but larger than a gully.

Gaze down on the world's third largest canyon and you see many shades of green. The Blyde River Canyon Nature Reserve in South Africa sports sheer escarpments and lush subtropical vegetation. It is very different to the view over the Grand Canyon in America, with its arid features. This nature reserve is one of the most visited sites in South Africa. Many travellers journey to see the majestic rock formations of the canyon and the Drakensberg Escarpment. A popular place to visit within the canyon is Bourke's Luck Potholes. Located at the confluence of the Blyde and Treur Rivers, the swirling and circular motion of the water has created spectacular rock formations through erosion. This includes potholes, cylindrical tubes and tunnels, and perfectly circular plunge pools of water within the sandstone, all of varying colours given the minerals in the rock. While water flows through the canyon all year round, during the rainy season even larger volumes of water pass through. This surge of water can carry an increased sediment load. As the sand, pebbles, and larger rocks are transported by the water, they erode the canyon walls, acting as an abrasive as they tumble along in the wash. However, the larger rocks are the reason why Bourke's Luck Potholes is called a "rock-cut basin". They have created deep rock pits where the water pools. This is a naturally sculptured landscape, where you can see intricate hollows, coloured steep rock faces, and mesmerising waterfalls.

In his poem, *The Grand Canyon*, American poet, author, diplomat, and educator Henry Van Dyke described the "wild splendour" of this landform as the "handiwork of the Most High". Here is part of that poem, describing how the canyon formed:

What force has formed this masterpiece of awe?
What hands have wrought these wonders in the waste?
O river, gleaming in the narrow rift
Of gloom that cleaves the valley's nether deep,—
Fierce Colorado, prisoned by thy toil,
And blindly toiling still to reach the sea,—
Thy waters, gathered from the snows and springs
Amid the Utah hills, have carved this road
Of glory to the California Gulf.
But now, O sunken stream, thy splendour lost,
'Twixt iron walls thou rollest turbid waves,
Too far away to make their fury heard!

Bourke's Luck Potholes

CHAPTER 31

Volcanoes

> I have never seen "Volcanoes"—
> But, when Travellers tell
> How those old — phlegmatic mountains
> Usually so still —
> Bear within — appalling Ordnance,
> Fire, and smoke, and gun,
> Taking Villages for breakfast,
> And appalling Men —

This is the beginning of Emily Dickinson's poem, *I Have Never Seen "Volcanoes"*, declaring she has never seen them. But perhaps you have? While you may not have seen a volcano "taking villages for breakfast" you may have seen mountains which are actually volcanoes."

The explosive nature of volcanoes has shaped large parts of our Earth's landscape and the volcanoes themselves can stand as majestic features, such as Mount Fuji in Japan. These landforms are places where molten hot rock bursts forth from deep under the ground, with the volcano acting as an opening and a pressure valve, resulting in lava, smoke, and ash. Volcanic eruptions may last for just a few days, or they can continue over months or even years. Whole islands have been created by these powerful forces, with the islands of Hawai'i forming through a volcanic hot spot.

A volcano is an opening on the Earth's surface where magma, gas, steam, and ash from deep within escapes through. Known as magma within the Earth, when this hot rock spews on the surface it is called lava. There are different types of volcanoes, each with unique characteristics. Some are shaped like a cone, such as Mount Vesuvius near Naples, Italy. These are called stratovolcanoes or composite volcanoes. Others, like Mauna Loa in Hawai'i, are shield volcanoes.

Mauna Loa

Mauna Loa is the largest active shield volcano on Earth. It is also the highest mountain in the world when measured from its base deep in the Pacific Ocean, rather than measuring from sea level (in which case Mount Everest is the tallest). Mauna Loa has broad, rounded slopes that are characteristic of a shield volcano and its name means "long mountain", a fitting description.

There are also Cinder Cones. These are the most common type of volcanic landform around the world. They are named thus because the ejected rocks from the volcano are known as "cinders". Called scoria, these rocks are light and have a small bubble appearance to them. They are light because gas was trapped within the liquid rock at the time it changed to solid form. Even large scoria rocks are lightweight and are characterised by numerous small cavities. When they are pushed out of the vent, most cinders land close to the vent. Over time, this deposit of cinders builds up the height of the cone itself.

One feature of all volcanoes is the structure at the top from which the magma flows. After the magma has passed through the internal chamber of the volcano and erupted out, there is often a hollow depression left at the top. This shows where the volcano partially emptied and how the summit of the volcano may have collapsed in the violent eruption. Shaped like a bowl, or a large crater, this part of the volcano is called a caldera. Many students will look for this feature when examining a volcano. Some calderas even form a lake as water fills the space in years to come. Crater Lake in Oregon is one such feature, forming after the eruption of Mount Mazama.

The caldera of Krakatoa is a famous geological feature of the Asia-Pacific region, and indeed, the world. An island in the Sunda Strait, between Java and Sumatra in Indonesia, Krakatoa is the site of one of the most destructive volcanic events ever recorded in history. In 1883 a catastrophic volcanic explosion on the island of Krakatoa occurred, resulting in the formation of a significant caldera. After a couple of months of expelling smoke and minor eruptions, on the morning of 27 August 1883, Krakatoa violently erupted. This saw the central part of the volcano collapse, which destroyed nearly three-quarters of the island, generated tsunamis, and killed over 36,000 people. Tremendous volumes of black ash, lava, and pumice spewed out of the volcano and skies around the world were darkened for years afterwards because of the eruption. All that was left was a large caldera as the main part of Krakatoa disintegrated into the magma chamber.

As scientists monitor the dangers that such explosions can bring, volcanoes are classified as being extinct, dormant, or active. Active volcanoes are those that have regular activity and are closely monitored for risk of explosion. This regular monitoring is key, particularly given it is estimated that at least 350 million people live within the danger range of the world's active volcanoes. The opposite to active, extinct volcanoes are those that erupted so long ago that they are considered unlikely to erupt ever again. Dormant volcanoes lie between these two categories. Dormant volcanoes are on watch. While they are currently quiet, they still require surveillance.

Mount Vesuvius, near the Bay of Naples in Italy, is an active strato-volcano. It is one of the few active volcanoes in Europe, but with around 800,000 people living on the slopes of this volcano, it is considered one of the most dangerous on Earth. Thus, it remains one of the most studied and monitored. Mount Vesuvius erupted back in 79 AD. The thick clouds of volcanic ash, gas, and hot, flowing rock destroyed the ancient Roman cities of Pompeii and Herculaneum. More recently, an eruption in 1944 lasted for nearly a fortnight and destroyed the village of San Sebastiano. For days the volcano rumbled and roared and the ground shook. Smoke, lava, and rocks erupted from the crater top. This eruption occurred during World War II and soldiers were stationed at an airfield not far from Mount Vesuvius. Sergeant Robert F. McRae, a solider with the US Army, wrote diary entries describing the eruption, providing details of this geological event: "…The noise is like that of bowling balls slapping into the pins on a giant bowling alley. To look above the mountain tonight, one would think that the world was on fire."

The reason why Mount Vesuvius is closely monitored is because it can erupt again and again. This is because the cracks within and beneath Mount Vesuvius connect the vent of the volcano from the outside air to storage areas of molten rock, the magma. Magma is much lighter than solid rock, so it can easily and quickly travel upwards through the vent and land in areas outside, areas close to residential zones. Worldwide there are approximately 1,300 potentially active volcanoes and Mount Vesuvius is just one of these.

About three-quarters of the world's active volcanoes are located in the Ring of Fire in the Pacific Ocean. The Ring of Fire extends from Mount Erebus, the southernmost active volcano, located in Antarctica, along the western coast of South and North America across to Alaska, across the Bering Strait, and through to Japan, the Philippines, and south to New Zealand. It is one of the most geologically active areas

Popocatépetl

on Earth. Close to 90% of all earthquakes occur within this zone. This is due to tectonic plates, the massive sheets of the Earth's crust that are constantly moving. The sliding and colliding of the tectonic plates contributes to this geological activity. Krakatoa, Mount Ruapehu, Mount St. Helens, and Popocatépetl, are all volcanoes found within the Ring of Fire. Mount Ruapehu is in New Zealand and has minor eruptions almost every year, while Mount St. Helens is located on a weak section of crust within the Cascade Mountains in the US state of Washington. Its last recorded major explosive eruption occurred in 1980. Popocatépetl is in Mexico, not far from Mexico City, which potentially puts millions of people at risk if it were to erupt.

Volcanoes don't just form on land. They can form within the ocean. Volcanoes can even sit under ice caps. Eyjafjallajökull in Iceland is a volcano completely covered by an ice cap and located below a glacier. The ice cap covers an area of 100 square kilometres (39 square miles) and the mountain itself is a stratovolcano. There are several magma chambers within the volcano which means an explosion can continue for a sustained period of time and be very powerful. Eyjafjallajökull has erupted a number of times over the years and in 2010 there were a series of eruptions between March and June. The area around the volcano needed to be evacuated and homes, property, and crops were lost. The eruptions caused massive disruptions to flights across Europe as large amounts of volcanic ash blasted into the air. A no-fly zone was established across parts of Europe as the plume of volcanic ash reached up to nine kilometres into the sky. Over 100,000 flights were cancelled, and millions of passengers were left stranded for long periods due to the disruption.

Volcanoes can be a spectacular part of our landscape but are also destructive too. This is why it is imperative that volcanoes are monitored by scientists. Both seismic and Global Positioning System (GPS) stations are positioned to detect and monitor ground movement that could indicate a volcano awakening, showing how applying new technology is helping geologists and geographers to better understand our Earth in the 21st Century.

Questions on Chapters 30 and 31

For answers see page 213

1. On which mountain is the Khumbu Icefall located?
2. How is a crevice different to a crevasse?
3. Why are seracs dangerous?
4. How is a gorge different to a canyon?
5. Which canyon is deeper: the Grand Canyon in the United States of America or the Yarlung Zangbo Grand Canyon?
6. In which country is the Blyde River Canyon Nature Reserve located?
7. Volcanoes are classified into three categories, one of which is active. What are the other two categories?
8. Which is the largest active volcano in the world?
9. There are three main different types of volcanoes. Name the three types.

Map Questions on Chapters 30 and 31

For answers see page 214

1. The Grand Canyon National Park is found in the state of Arizona. Name the country and American states bordering Arizona.
2. The Drakensberg Mountain Range is located within both the countries of South Africa and the Kingdom of Lesotho. Find the capital city of Lesotho.
3. Mount Fuji is a volcano on the Japanese island of Honshu. Find the island of Honshu on a map and also Okinawa, another Japanese island.
4. The Ring of Fire is an area of seismic activity around the Pacific Ocean. Find the Ring of Fire on a map, tracing around its location.
5. Mauna Loa is an active volcano in the American state of Hawai'i. Name the capital of the Hawaiian Islands and find it on a map.
6. In which country is Eyjafjallajökull found?
7. Name the ocean that surrounds Iceland and list the closest countries.

CHAPTER 32

Earthquakes and Tsunamis

Along with many active volcanoes, the Ring of Fire is where around 80% of the world's largest earthquakes occur. Both are due to tectonic plate movement. It is this movement that creates volcanoes, earthquakes, and tsunamis. As the plates slide closer to one another, move further apart, or collide, they cause this geological activity. There is a huge amount of energy stored within the movement of the tectonic plates and this creates dramatic elements of our world. Deep oceanic trenches are formed, lava bursts forth from the depths of the earth, the earth shakes and quakes, and large volumes of ocean water are displaced in the violent changes. While earthquakes can occur in other areas around the world, most happen along the tectonic plate boundaries.

When two tectonic plates collide, the pressure and energy of this accumulates within the edges of the plate. Eventually though, this energy needs to be released. This happens through seismic waves which effectively ripple out as the pressure is released. It is this release of pressure that creates a shock through the landscape, which is called an earthquake. Some shocks may be slight, people noticing only a slight shake or tremor, but other earthquakes can be severe and cause widespread devastation to people and the landscape. These are huge forces of planet Earth, literally making the earth shudder and rupture.

Earthquakes are measured by magnitude, in a scale called the Moment Magnitude scale. This indicates the power of the earthquake and helps seismologists seeking to understand earthquakes. The higher the number, the more energy that is released from the depths of the Earth. Previously, the Richter scale was used. Developed by Charles Francis Richter in the 1930's, this scale focused specifically on earthquakes in California and required the seismic waves to be within a certain proximity of the seismometers. As a result, it wasn't always accurate when measuring earthquakes in other parts of the world or smaller tremors. In comparison, the Moment Magnitude scale measures the energy at the moment of release and involves recordings from multiple stations in the seismographic network, giving greater accuracy. It also helps to record data about earthquakes that are so small people do not even notice the ground motion.

Damage to property and infrastructure, landslides, avalanches, and tsunamis are just some consequences of more powerful earthquakes. The amount of damage varies widely, depending on the magnitude and depth of the quake. In some instances, people may barely notice the ground shaking, but at other times they can be catastrophic. The largest magnitude earthquake in recorded history occurred in May 1960 near Valdivia in Chile. Measuring a magnitude of 9.5, the rupture zone of this massive earthquake was estimated to be between 500 – 1000 kilometres (311 to 621 miles) long. Parts of the ground along the rupture sank, and being low-lying, there was wide-spread flooding. The natural disaster resulted in many deaths, with the loss of between 500 to 5,000 lives. In addition, more than 2 million people were left homeless as it destroyed homes, buildings, and infrastructure, and caused landslides.

A tsunami

The earthquake, sometimes called the Great Chilean Earthquake, also triggered a tsunami across the Pacific Ocean.

A tsunami is a series of ocean waves triggered by a powerful disturbance. This can be a volcanic eruption, or, as in the case of the Great Chilean Earthquake, an underwater earthquake. The tsunami in Chile devastated parts of Hawaii, Japan, and the Philippines. Increased tides due to the tsunami were even felt in New Zealand, Samoa, and Australia. Wave action reached Australian shores around eleven hours after the earthquake. Then, days after the earthquake, a volcano erupted. The nearby volcano Puyehue blasted ash and steam into the air for weeks afterwards, showing the intense effects of the movement within the depths of the earth.

The Valdivia earthquake demonstrated just how far tsunamis can travel across the world's ocean and how the effects of earthquakes can be felt within a very wide area. This allowed geographers and scientists to better understand the potential dangers and hazards and how to prepare for them. In some places around the world students and residents are taught how to respond in the event of an earthquake or tsunami, including how to seek shelter, avoid risks, and seek to move out of harm's way. Folksongs and tales tell the stories within communities, and decision makers seek to use the geographical information to develop ways to help keep people safe.

Nonetheless, it is impossible to avoid all the dangers of these natural disasters. In March 2011 an earthquake occurred off the coast of the island Honshu in Japan. Known as the Tōhoku earthquake, powerful seismic waves were sent from deep within the Pacific Ocean. The focus of the earthquake was 30 kilometres (16.6 miles) below the ocean floor. The initial earthquake and the aftershocks felt for days afterwards were destructive. The rupture of the earthquake created a series of tsunamis as the energy deep in the ocean displaced huge volumes of water. The waves of the tsunamis were over 3 metres high (11 to 12 feet) and fast moving. This immense wave action flooded and devastated swathes of towns on the coast and even impacted the coast of North America and as far as Antarctica. Along the coast of Honshu, debris and victims were drawn back into the ocean by the waves and the aftermath of this intense natural disaster was immense. Nearly 20,000 people lost their lives because of the Tōhoku earthquake and tsunami. Thousands were injured and many went missing. Homes, schools, shops, and other buildings, roads, railways, water and sewer systems, electricity supply, dams and several nuclear power plants were all affected.

The Tōhoku earthquake and tsunami occurred within the Ring of Fire. Being an area known for frequent seismic activity, scientists track volcanic and earthquake disturbances. While dormant and active volcanoes are monitored for activity to determine potential threats, allowing scientists to predict an eruption within a short-term window, earthquakes can be measured but not predicted. Scientists are unable to say where or when an earthquake may occur, and they cannot know how big it might be either.

Instead, scientists focus on the probability of an earthquake occurring within a certain area. This allows them to develop guidelines to manage potential hazards due to earthquakes, such as rules about how to construct buildings that can better respond to shaking ground within areas that are more prone to earthquakes. Some building designs and materials withstand the shaking better than others. Using deep-ocean buoys and a system of monitors, tsunami warning systems also serve to alert authorities about the risk of increased wave action due to earthquakes. While tsunamis are relatively rare events, they are calamitous. Public education about how to respond to earthquakes and tsunamis is important, as is being prepared and heeding the emergency warnings issued. Would you know what to do if either struck?

Knowing the geography of earthquakes and tsunamis also helps land-use planners to make informed decisions about where to build and where to avoid due to potential disaster. In this way, geography straddles both the need to understand the physical aspects of our world and consider the human dimension too. The dynamic processes of our planet influence people in many ways, particularly communities that live within regions directly impacted by plate tectonics and the active movement of Earth.

CHAPTER 33

Climate Change and Biodiversity

Our vibrant earth is ever-changing and sometimes these transformations are impossible to overlook. Consider how land splits open during an earthquake, a hillside is reshaped through a landslide, or the towering walls of water that surge within a tsunami. Yet, at other times, the shifts are small and gradual. They are barely noticeable. As geographers seek to understand our world, they examine changes over time. This might be noticing the widening of a valley, that there are more people living in an area than ever before, or how traffic congestion has increased within a region. Geographers look at trends that occur within spaces, called spatial patterns. They research landscapes and places and the ways people live and use resources, adapting the natural environment.

In recent years it has become apparent that our Earth is changing in new ways, due largely to the effects of human activity. Long-term shifts in climate patterns have been observed as the composition of the Earth's atmosphere is changing and warming. Gases such as water vapour, carbon dioxide, methane, and nitrous oxide have increased. These are called greenhouse gases because, just like a greenhouse traps heat within the glass, these gases keep heat within our atmosphere.

While the heat in a greenhouse helps to grow plants that wouldn't survive in cooler conditions, for our planet this increase in heat presents a danger. This is because the rise in the average global temperatures is changing climate patterns, causing temperature extremes and altered precipitation patterns. Some nations are reporting their highest ever recorded temperatures. Climate scientists predict that there will be more intense heat and drought in some areas and others will receive greater rainfall and snow. Extreme weather events are expected to become more frequent, intense, and prolonged. This includes heatwaves, floods, bushfires (wildfires), hurricanes, and cyclones. Over time, such extreme weather events will impact the types of vegetation and animals that can live in a region.

Earth's oceans reveal a lot about our planet. As average temperatures rise, evidence shows that polar ice caps and glaciers are melting, leading to more fresh water being added to the oceans. Rising sea levels mean that low lying coastal communities and ecosystems may be inundated, affecting where people can live. As land becomes submerged, lost to ocean waters, people will need to find new places to live. Some communities risk losing the traditional lands central to their culture.

Some places are already experiencing the effects of rising sea levels as salty ocean water moves further inland. In the Mekong River Delta in Vietnam, one of the most densely populated regions in Southeast Asia, sea water now encroaches on valuable rice-growing areas. This region has long been considered a "breadbasket" due to its highly productive rice paddy fields. However, freshwater is crucial for growing rice and this is becoming harder to access. Cultivating rice in the region is now more challenging because as salty sea water pushes inland, less freshwater flows from higher regions. Without adequate freshwater, the livelihoods of many farmers are at risk.

Most scientists are increasingly concerned about the ways in which our world is shifting due to climate change. This includes changed weather patterns, rising sea levels, the impact of fossil fuel use, potential loss of land, melting glaciers, and how salty the ocean is. Some look at subtle shifts while others investigate the large challenges parts of our world are facing, seeking solutions. Many monitor the potential loss of species due to changes in the world's environment, including the impact on biological diversity. As temperatures increase, there are concerns that some species will be lost forever. Biodiversity is the variety of all life on Earth. It includes the range of species we have and their habitats. The more species there are in an area, the more biodiverse it is. From earthworms to elephants, this range of species is what establishes the healthy ecosystems of our planet. This is what sustains life on Earth.

One of the most biologically diverse regions on the planet, the Great Barrier Reef lies off the coast of Queensland, Australia. It stretches for 2,300 kilometres (1,300 miles) and is the world's largest reef system.

Being around 350,000 square kilometres (133,000 square miles) in size, the reef is also the world's largest living structure. There are a great number of species living in this part of the Pacific Ocean. There are over 1,500 species of fish, including the Māori wrasse, a large colourful fish, and the famous clownfish with its stripes of orange, black, and white. Over 4,000 types of molluscs are found in these warm waters, along with giant clams, manta rays, sharks, turtles, and whales. It is a huge, colourful biodiverse underwater world!

The Pacific Ocean has about twice as many species of corals compared to the Atlantic Ocean, and the Great Barrier Reef holds the most. Yet, the biodiversity of these spectacular reefs is vulnerable to climate change. This is because corals are sensitive to changes in water temperature. If water temperatures exceed the average summer maximum over a couple of months, or if the water temperatures drop, coral bleaching can occur. Runoff and pollution, low tides, and greater exposure to sunlight can also cause coral bleaching. As the coral responds to such stresses, the algae living within the coral are lost. Its food source gone, this means the vibrant colours of the coral disappear. While not dead, the pale coral is more vulnerable. Scientists monitor coral bleaching within the Great Barrier Reef and other ocean reefs around the world to better understand these ecological changes and many individuals and groups work hard to better understand and solve such issues.

Earth is a unique planet in our solar system, supporting an array of landscapes and landforms. There are millions of species of plants, animals, fungi, and bacteria on Earth. From the coral reefs of the Pacific Ocean to lush rainforests, biological diversity within the spaces and places of the world is the web of life that we rely upon. This diversity gives us food, water, and places to live in. It also offers us numerous goods and services, valuable resources, medicines, and trade opportunities. Our dependence on nature is unmistakable.

When considering how important biodiversity is across our world, mangroves are fascinating. These areas were once dismissed as being useless swampy areas, but today many scientists consider mangroves to be the quiet superstars in facing biodiversity, conservation, and climate change. With their intricately woven root systems and dense foliage, mangrove forests represent the first line of defence against coastal flooding and property damage due to storm events. These root systems break the energy of waves hitting the shore as they stand between land and ocean. The trees and shrubs that grow along these coastlines withstand the constant tides and salty sea water. Mangroves species thrive in areas where many could not survive and support an abundance of wildlife.

Mangrove forests are located within tropical and subtropical areas, offering a diverse habitat for numerous species. Insects, reptiles, birds, and animals like monkeys and tigers are found within mangrove forests. In the shallow pools within the tightly coiled tree roots lie many species of fish, crustaceans, and molluscs. They serve as a safe nursery; a refuge to hatch and raise young. They also provide shelter for corals at risk of coral bleaching. Scientists in the US Virgin Islands National Park have found just as many coral species in mangrove forests as in nearby coral reefs.

As a transition zone between land and sea, mangroves play a key role. They trap and retain pollutants in their muddy soils and absorb nutrients carried by runoff from inland areas. In this way, they act as a buffer and protect oceans. Mangroves support biological diversity and can mitigate climate change. This means that the mangrove forests around the world are important to us all. While it seems unusual for trees to be able to

A dry river bed in Italy

grow in water, let alone salt water, mangroves do exactly this, and many are optimistic for the future of these vital coastal zones around the world.

As we learn more about issues like climate change, the importance of biodiversity, and the conservation of mangroves, geographers work to understand these challenges and solve problems in different parts of the world. By being aware of these issues, you too can discover more on this topic and take steps to help, both big and small.

Questions on Chapters 32 and 33

For answers see page 214

1. What scale is used to measure earthquakes?
2. Name two of the major greenhouse gases.
3. What is the major crop grown in the Mekong River Delta in Vietnam?
4. Is it true that the Great Barrier Reef is the world's largest reef system?
5. Mangrove forests are located in coastal areas within tropical and sub-tropical regions. They are made up of trees with twisted and coiled roots that provide an important habitat for a range of animal species. Name some of the animals you might find in mangrove forests.

Map Questions on Chapters 32 and 33

For answers see page 215

1. Please examine a map of the tectonic plates and name four of the major plates.
2. The Great Chilean Earthquake triggered a tsunami which was felt across the Pacific Ocean, devastating parts of Japan, Hawai'i and the Philippines. Find the capital city of the Philippines on a map.
3. The Sundarbans are the world's largest mangrove forests, within the Ganges-Brahmaputra delta, in Bay of Bengal within India and Bangladesh. Find the Bay of Bengal and name the ocean it is connected to.

CHAPTER 34

Political and Physical Maps

To examine a globe of Earth is to examine our planet in miniature. You can see the blue waters of the oceans and seas, the continents, frozen landscapes of Antarctica and the Arctic at the South and North Poles, and many island nations. Around the horizontal centre the equator is shown, and you can find the country where you live, along with those you are learning more about. Some globes depict the countries as being shades of green, gold, and brown, while others show countries in pink, yellow, orange, and purple colours. Those in vibrant, varied colours show countries of the world, while the greens, golds, and browns reflect the lay of the land. These show the physical attributes of places, including the mountains, hills, plains, and deserts.

Globes and maps visually represent and share information about places on Earth. Globes show a huge area, capturing the whole world, as do world maps. Other maps may cover just a small area, perhaps a country, state, or region, providing detail so map readers can know that place more intimately. Geographers produce many different maps to serve a variety of purposes. To look at a map is to view part of our Earth and learn about it from a picture, not just words. Maps capture a place by sharing data and information, presenting facts in a format that you can print on paper, fold into your pocket, or check on your smartphone.

In classrooms and homeschools around the world maps are used to teach students about places, including those they are yet to visit and some they may never see in real life. Maps are often used when studying geography, with students completing map exercises so they know where fascinating places are across the world. But maps are used in other subjects too. They are particularly helpful for history. Perhaps you have read about the astonishing journey Sir Ernest Shackleton and his crew made in the early 1900's through the Southern Ocean while World War I raged on. You can use a map to trace their journey from Antarctica to Elephant Island and then over to South Georgia Island. Looking at a map helps to appreciate just how amazing their journey was given the distances they travelled and the harsh conditions they experienced.

Maps are important for navigation. They help a traveller find their way from one place to another. Without a map, how might a tourist in Hong Kong explore from Kowloon over to Victoria Peak on Hong Kong Island? A map shows that Hong Kong is made up of a few islands, where the major centres are, and how to get there. Travellers can see distances, in which direction major features lie, where the important landmarks are, and can plan a route. A lot of information can be crammed into a well-designed map, or they can be pared right back. For instance, a basic tourist map for a city might only show some famous landmarks, bus stops, and street names to help a traveller find their way. Likewise, the famous London Underground map designed by Harry Beck is quick and efficient to use. Whether on a screen or a large-scale wall map, travellers can trace a route across the city or find the stop they need while using the Tube.

Stories of history are peppered with tales of a navigator poring over maps to ensure they are moving in the right direction, and of explorers creating maps as they discovered new places. Maps continue to be storehouses of information. Geographers use maps to share and analyse spatial information, that is, trends and patterns that are based around places. They use maps that include data about physical attributes, such as showing where a river runs and the floodplain associated with it. Such mapping data can show where, in the event of heavy rains, flooding might occur so decisions can be made as to whether to allow development in areas which could potentially be flooded. Geographers also use maps that include social information, such as population density, showing just how many people live within a certain area.

Depending on the purpose for which they have been created and their intended audience, maps can be quite complex and convey a range of details. Whether a simple tourist map or a complex topographical map used by a hiker, maps serve multiple purposes and act as a powerful communication and learning tool. For example, a topographical map is a valuable part of an explorer's backpack. It includes many details on the terrain; vegetation types; the location of rivers, streams, and lakes; where tracks and roads are located; and even where to find a picnic spot or hut, welcome information for those taking a long hike over unfamiliar territory. Importantly, topographical maps also indicate the distance on the ground through a scale. The map shows precisely how close or far away features and places are from one another and also the lay of the landscape. These maps show a three-dimensional landscape on paper. A topographical map uses lines to show the gradient and slopes of the area. Lines close together show the land rising to a steep and dramatic slope, while those far apart indicate flatter areas. By reading the map and noticing these lines, you can visualise the actual landscape of the area.

Compared to these specialist maps, an atlas generally shows two main types of maps: physical and political. Sometimes these are even offered side by side so a reader can understand both together. A political map will show national and state boundaries and the location of major cities and towns. Often different countries are shown through an array of colours to allow readers to easily discern one country from another. These maps help us to understand the political geography of a region, showing the jurisdiction and territorial claims of each nation. By looking at a political map we can identify which nations control certain regions. For instance, a political map of the Pacific Ocean will indicate external territories of independent nations. It shows that the island of Rapa Nui (Easter Island) is part of Chile, Guam is a territory of the United States of America, and that the Galápagos Islands are governed by Ecuador. Political maps help a user to see government boundaries to better understand the political geography of an area.

This is different to maps showing physical features. A physical map shows the natural features of the Earth. Landforms, water bodies, mountains, plains, and deserts are included on physical maps. Using earthy colours, shading, and symbols, these features of the landscape are shown to help a viewer understand the natural conditions of that geographical area. Ice-capped mountains are featured in white or light-grey, while rivers, wide or narrow, are shown through blue lines and the location of cities or towns is with black dots. Generally, more populated places have larger dots to show more people live there, while a small dot is used to show the location of small towns and villages. A bold red dot or a star within a black circle usually indicates the capital city of a nation or state. However, the best way to be sure what each symbol means is to check the legend or key for the atlas or map. This is because mapping conventions do vary.

To look at a map is to see a part of the world. Over the course of history maps have been drawn on cave walls, clay tablets, mammoth tusks, parchment, paper, and they are now instantly available on touchscreens. Yet, not all maps are two-dimensional or graphical. Indigenous Australians used songlines as maps. These maps were vocal and a key part of cultural life, more akin to folk tales. Singing them in the correct order, these song-maps shared landmarks, trading routes, and ancient pathways, as well as cultural laws and myths. To sing about the land and their place within country helped First Australians to develop a spatial understanding beyond a physical chart or map.

Maps help us to visualise and better understand places, both faraway and those close to us. To look at early maps that are missing country boundaries reminds us of the work navigators completed to help shape our image of the world. Examining modern maps gives us details we may miss when simply relying on text. Using maps helps to develop important spatial skills: this is why map questions are included within these lessons. Learning to use maps helps to visualise where one place is in relation to another, but also to build connections and spatial awareness. When using a map, you can see how far or close one place may be to another. A well-designed map will help you better understand spaces and places across our world, no matter where they are located.

CHAPTER 35

Making Maps

Years ago, if you stepped into a map maker's office, you would have seen an array of paint pots, paint brushes in all varieties, felt-tip pens in a range of colours (including plenty of black ones in different thicknesses), pencils, erasers, and many types of rulers. That is because cartographers would create maps by hand, drawing and painting them manually. They would painstakingly draw the details of the place onto the paper, ensuring the proportions and boundaries were accurate and that the map clearly reflected what was on the ground. Once the lines were in place, it would then be coloured using paint and felt-tip pens. The completed map could be copied to make more such maps available, taking great care to conserve the original so carefully created by the cartographer. Today, most maps are made using specialised mapping software on computers. It still takes skill, time, accuracy, and attention to detail, but there is no need for actual rulers, pencils, brushes, and paint pots any longer. Instead, high resolution screens, graphics memory, and powerful processing speeds are key.

The making of maps is referred to as cartography. A cartographer is a person who creates maps. Making a map requires making a range of decisions long before grabbing a piece of paper or pulling up to a computer screen. Knowing the reason for creating the map, the cartographer first determines the area to be included. Knowing both the subject area and the purpose helps them to choose what information and data to include on the map.

The cartographer may also need to decide which map projection they will use. A map projection is a mathematical transformation used to flatten out the curved surface of the Earth. This is important because fitting our three-dimensional world onto a flat piece of paper isn't easy!

Map projections seek to minimise the distortion of shape, area, and direction that can happen when converting three dimensions to two. Some map projections can give the impression that a country is much larger than it actually is, while others can make one continent appear further away from another, all because of the method used to represent our three-dimensional Earth on a flat surface. So, a cartographer needs to decide which is the best projection to use. The Mercator projection is popular among cartographers, including digital maps, because it preserves accurate direction. This makes it useful for navigation, but it does have some distortion, warping land near the North and South Poles. The Mercator projection shows Greenland as being nearly the same size as South America, even though South America is more than eight times the size of Greenland. Using distorted map projections can give us an inaccurate mental map of the world so it is important to develop an understanding of how big countries actually are.

Since 1995 the National Geographical Society has used the Winkel Tripel Projection as the standard map projection. The Winkel Tripel Projection has reduced distortion in terms of shape, distance, and areas. It also avoids stretching and enlarging the size of land near the poles. This makes it a good choice when using a map. Being aware of the cartographer's choice with the projection is important because it helps to inform a map reader. You can check the printed or digital publication details to determine which map projection was used. It will be noted on the map itself or at the beginning of an atlas.

Along with selecting the region, purpose, and map projection, a cartographer also needs to make careful decisions about the level of detail to include on the map. How much information is layered onto a map is directly related to the map's purpose and its intended audience. For example, a cartographer making a regional map may choose not to show every single town and village in an area nor to include every bend (meander) in the river. Instead, they may just focus on the major settlements and the general course of the river to provide a broad picture of the flow of the river through the area. In making this decision one critical element is selecting the most appropriate map scale. The choice of scale determines just how much detail can be represented on one map.

Scale is fundamental to geography and cartography. Scale indicates the relationship between the actual distances on the Earth's surface and the distance used on the map. A map with a scale of 1:1000 means that one unit of measurement on the map is the same as 1000 of that same unit of measurement on the ground. This ensures map users can trust the relative distances shown.

Geographers often refer to maps as being either small or large scale. A small scale allows the cartographer to include a big area on the map, while a large scale is appropriate for a smaller region. This means that a small scale is required for a large area. A world map uses a small scale. To show the entire world on one piece of paper requires hundreds of kilometres of land to be captured in just a fraction of an inch. However, when the purpose of the map is to show intricate details of an area then a large scale is used. For instance, a map providing information on a city block might include the boundaries of every individual block of land and the location of all the infrastructure services, such as water and sewage pipes, telecommunications connections, and electricity and gas supply. In this case, a large scale is used for the map because a large scale map can show all such details for a space.

Once these decisions have been made, a cartographer begins to layer the data and information to be included on the map. Traditionally, a cartographer would start to draw the area on their paper, using pencil and then ink. Today, this process starts with a base map in digital format. Much like the outline a cartographer would draw with black ink on paper, the base map is the beginning of the map itself. Once the base map is selected and constructed, the cartographer then selects the best colours to use. They will also decide upon the most suitable patterns and symbols to show the various elements to be included on the map. For instance, they may choose to show a church with a little cross symbol and decide just how thick the black lines should be to show roads.

Modern cartographers use Geographical Information Systems to create maps. Referred to as GIS for short, it is a computer-based mapping system designed to capture, store, manage, analyse, and present geographical spatial data. Cartographers utilise GIS tools, as do geographers, planners, scientists, and other people involved in making decisions relating to spatial issues. Not only does GIS software provide them with the tools they need to create maps, but it also allows users to analyse the patterns, trends, and relationships shown in that geographic data. It is a powerful tool and draws on huge amounts of data about the world around us. When using GIS to create a map, cartographers select how the data will be layered onto the map. Many decisions are made about how best to present the information, ensuring it is both accurate and clear to readers. Talented cartographers anticipate how intended users will read and interpret the information. An array of maps can be created using GIS, from the simple to the complex.

It only takes a quick look online or in an atlas to appreciate just how many different types of maps there are to read and use. Most atlases generally feature various political and physical maps of the continents and countries around the world, but there are many other types of maps available, including statistical and thematic maps. While statistics are often presented through tables and graphs, they can also be included on a map. For example, the population of cities is statistical data that can be mapped, often using dots to show how populated cities are. Larger dots show more populated areas, while smaller ones mean fewer people live within those areas. This is a simple but effective way to show this geographic information, making it easy for the reader to interpret the data.

Thematic maps are straightforward to read and useful for sharing information on a particular theme or topic. They might show different biomes or climatic zones of a region, vegetation types, or various soil types found there. A range of colours and shades are commonly used for thematic maps. A map reader examines the various colours shown to understand the map. A wealth of information can be conveyed through statistical and thematic maps, allowing map viewers to gain comprehensive insights about a location.

In centuries past, navigational charts were perhaps the most prized category of maps. These maps could safely guide an explorer through treacherous waters and help them plan lucrative trade routes so their voyages would be profitable. In modern times, nautical and aeronautical charts retain their significance even though there are no new islands or lands to discover. Showing more than just shipping routes, such charts reflect the advancements in sea-floor mapping. Exploring and mapping the depths of the sea-floor has been a key advance in modern geography. Compared with the navigational charts of old, modern nautical charts provide greater accuracy and utility, information those explorers could only have dreamed of.

A nautical chart is a large scale map. It indicates the depths of the water in various locations to allow mariners to avoid hazards and obstructions such as rocks, shoals, sandbars, wrecks, and underwater cables. Nautical charts also include information on where to find navigational aids such as buoys, beacons, and lighthouses. This ensures that mariners can accurately determine their position, allowing for safe navigation. Tidal, topographical, and shoreline features are also included on a nautical chart. When navigating areas, fishermen, boaters, and the captains of commercial shipping vessels need to know details about the coastline, cliffs, tidal currents, and where the high and low tide markers are. Nautical charts provide this crucial information.

Cartographers understand the information map viewers seek and determine the most effective method to present it. They layer information, using a range of data in unison to convey more details about a place. Of course, this is the reason behind all maps. The purpose of maps is teach us more about the world. In this way, maps can clearly show the information that helps us to better understand the places and spaces of our world.

Compass and navigational chart

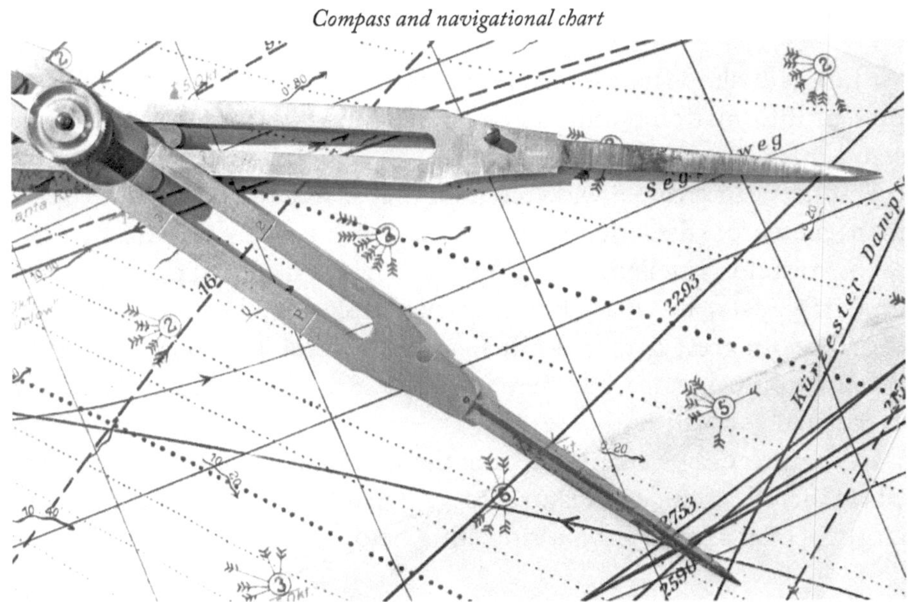

CHAPTER 36

The Elements of a Map

Poet Elizabeth Bishop spent a lot of her childhood in Canada. In 1934 she penned a poem titled *The Map*, capturing the excitement of reading a map and reflecting on what places lay further afield. The third and final stanza of the poem concludes her thoughts on cartography:

> Mapped waters are more quiet than the land is,
> lending the land their waves' own conformation:
> and Norway's hare runs south in agitation,
> profiles investigate the sea, where land is.
> Are they assigned, or can the countries pick their colors?
> What suits the character or the native waters best.
> Topography displays no favorites; North's as near as West.
> More delicate than the historians' are the map-makers' colors.
>
> by Elizabeth Bishop

Just as Bishop shares, cartographers use colours, lines, and skills to present information on maps in a simple way, allowing users to understand this data visually. Working through many different choices, cartographers can create a wide range of maps. This includes the weather maps meteorologists use to forecast the coming weather patterns, road maps to help travellers plan their next trip, rail network maps, and topographical maps that hikers use when exploring, showing the terrain of an area in great detail. While maps vary in the type and amount of information being shared, there are some elements common to nearly every map you will read.

When reading a map, generally the first detail to check is the title. Maps include a range of features to help map viewers, but most importantly, a map should have a title. This helps the map viewer to know what information is included on the map and to help them determine how it is useful. Take a look in an atlas and you are likely to find maps labelled, "Political Map of Australia" or "Physical Map of the United Kingdom". Such titles clearly tell the reader what information the map is sharing, details not to be missed.

Along with a title, a map will share who created it, give a relevant date, and the source data. This information is presented a little differently within an atlas compared to an individual printed map. In an atlas, such details are generally included within the beginning materials. However, on an individual printed map it is likely to be printed close to the legend. This information will generally include a date, the author, and where the data has come from.

It is really useful for a map viewer to know when a map was created so they can see if it is current information or dated. Historical maps, such as one showing the extent of the ancient Roman Empire at a point in history, include a date to indicate that time. Details of the author and the source material will differ within an atlas compared to an individual map, but will include the group, department, or individual that created the map. It will also reference the data they used to create it. Cartographers often use government statistical data to create maps, or they may depict data collected by a different means, such as satellite imagery from an aeronautical company. A map user can check these details to ensure it features information from a trusted source. It also ensures that they can assess the accuracy and objectivity of the information presented.

After checking the title and source material for a map, it is important to check the boundary of the area shown. Each map will include a border. The border of a map is generally chosen early on in the process by the cartographer, determined as they select the reason and purpose for the map. The border information helps to give the context for where the place is. For example, a map of an island will often include some of the surrounding seas and ocean to provide geographical context. A map of a land-locked country is likely to show part of the neighbouring countries, enabling map readers to orient themselves.

The area shown on the map really determines the scale used. The scale of a map represents the relationship between the actual distances on the Earth's surface and the distance used on the map. Maps featuring a large area of the ground use a small scale, while detailed maps of smaller areas are large scale. Expressing this scale on the map can be done in a few different ways. For most maps, the scale of a map is shown with a graphic that looks like a ruler. This is because you need to measure the distances on the map, a task which is generally done using a ruler. This type of graphic is called a "bar scale". Whether it is shown in metres, miles, kilometres, or some other unit, the bar scale is a horizontal line that shows the increments of distance used. Most often it is coloured black and white.

However, there are other ways to show scale, including a representative ratio, which is the most common form used on topographical maps. Topographical maps generally have a scale of 1:25,000. This means that one unit of measurement on the map is the same as 25,000 units of that same measurement on the ground. So, 1cm on the map is the same as 250m on the ground. Whether it is shown using a representative ratio or a bar scale, understanding the scale of the map you are viewing is crucial. It is this measurement that allows you to measure the distance between two places on the map and know the exact distance it would be if you were walking, driving, or flying over that part of land. While on a map of Europe, Paris might be just a couple of centimetres to the south-southwest of Moscow, this distance represents around 2,800 kilometres (over 1,700 miles).

Cartographers use a range of symbols to represent geographic features, such as geopolitical boundaries, capital cities, towns, rivers, highways, and roads. Usually, a map will include a legend or key to help decipher these symbols. The legend will list each of the symbols and colours used in the map and explain what they represent. In an atlas this information is often included within the introductory pages and used consistently throughout the text, while on an individual map it will be placed towards the bottom of the map. Find this and you can decode the map.

Along with scale and symbols, a cartographer may also include grid patterns on a map. These are a series of horizontal and vertical lines. Map readers use these grid lines to help them locate features on a map. Small scale maps of the whole world may use the lines of latitude and longitude to act as gridlines, while large scale maps incorporate lines at intervals most pertinent to the depicted area. Perhaps you have used a map of a town or a historical site, making sure you know where a particular feature is by using the grid lines. Often letters and numbers are used with the grid lines to help with locations: the horizontal lines might be labelled A, B, C, and so on, while numbering from 1, 2, 3… is used for the vertical (generally labelled on the left side). This means you can use the columns and rows to find a landmark that could be shown, say, at C4 on the map. No matter which convention is used, the horizontal grid reference is always provided first and then the vertical. Acting as coordinates, they allow the map viewer to identify an exact location of a place.

Another important tool is provided to help the map reader orient themselves while viewing the information: a compass rose or a simple North arrow. Just as showing surrounding water and land features helps readers with context for the place shown on the map, including orientation direction is key. It was in 1375 that the first compass rose was included on a map, being printed on the Catalan Atlas, and offering valuable orientation information. A compass rose or North arrow informs a map user which direction north is. If just one arrow is shown, it usually points north and includes an upper-case N to indicate this. Doing so allows the map viewer to determine the other directions, while a compass rose shows them all and sometimes is really ornate, decorating the map.

Given all this key information is visual, you may be wondering how maps are made for blind and vision impaired people. If a cartographer has determined that a large part of their audience for a particular map will be blind or vision impaired, they present that information using braille. Generally printed on white paper, these are thermoformed maps, offering the information about the continents, countries, and regions of the world in a tactile form. Some map makers utilise swell paper. This allows them to print maps with black ink which are then placed in a small oven. The heat from the oven activates the special ink, making it expand to a set height. This creates a map that people can feel with their fingertips.

Just as a printed political map may show country and state boundaries, a tactile map can also include this information. Likewise, a physical map will enable map users to trace the mountain ranges, rivers, lakes, and other physical features, such as vegetation types, with their fingertips, reading the information provided. Similar to other printed maps, title, scalebar, and orientation are also provided to guide the map reader and the most appropriate scale is used. However, less information can be held within a tactile map because it is more difficult to layer this type of map. This means cartographers need to be clear about what they want to include on a map and choose symbols which are easy to read with fingertips.

Maps give all users a critical tool to better understand places and spaces in our world. In recent years, significant developments in computer technology have altered the relationship between people and maps. We don't just expect folded paper maps anymore. Users can access and manipulate mapping information through digital screens. Modern satellite communications allow us to pinpoint exact locations of people and places on the entire surface of the Earth using digital locational information that can be mapped with precision. Map readers can select what type of information they want to see on the map with just a few clicks. Tactile and printed maps are important, but so is our access to geographical information systems, which is very exciting! Maps are used every day for learning and exploring.

A globe

CHAPTER 37

Modern Maps

Author Joseph Conrad wrote about his fascination with maps at the beginning of his novel *Heart of Darkness:*

> *Now when I was a little chap I had a passion for maps. I would look for hours at South America, or Africa, or Australia, and lose myself in all the glories of exploration. At that time there were many blank spaces on the earth, and when I saw one that looked particularly inviting on a map (but they all look that) I would put my finger on it and say, "When I grow up I will go there."*

Maps are geographical pictures that reveal the positions of specific features, the distances separating places, and dimensions and configurations of countries. For Conrad, spaces on a map were places he wished to visit and hankered after, particularly those that remained largely blank. His childhood experience was that those blank patches on maps gradually became filled in. Further information about lakes, rivers, and place names was given as explorers discovered the missing pieces. The maps Conrad had a passion for have elements of those we use today, however, modern maps are very different to those he pored over.

Today, a smartphone can provide access to a plethora of maps. These offer a wealth of data and information. A map user is able to manipulate the scale of the map: zoom in for more detail and to access the information on a large scale map, or zoom out and be presented with a smaller scale map. Users can alter the scale at a touch, changing from an entire country to a state, and then are able to target a particular city or suburb, and even focus right into an area so that each street in the neighbourhood is shown in that large scale. A digital map would have been unimaginable to Conrad.

Modern maps not only offer users the ability to view maps of the streets, but also allow them to access satellite and aerial images, blurring the distinction between map and geographical pictures. This technology allows us to see what various regions of the world look like from the air, layering this over a map base. Collaborative efforts between technology giants and organisations like NASA and National Geographic have led to the development of powerful geographic tools. These enable users to view our planet from above through Google Earth. Accessible to all users at no cost, Google Earth is a composite of maps and images, collected from the various groups involved in the project. These are then melded together through complex algorithms to give users an interactive map of planet Earth. An enormous amount of data is represented and offered to users. Billions of images have built this massive digital geospatial database. With this technology you can take a virtual tour of the world without leaving your lounge room.

To provide this service, geobrowsers like Google Earth access a range of information sources. This includes satellite and aerial imagery, topographical data, and ocean bathymetry. Meshing these together, they offer a three-dimensional view of our Earth. This is why they are called "virtual globes". Google Earth isn't really a map at all, but it does contain a wealth of spatial information. Very different to a traditional globe on a stand, viewed on a screen, Google Earth offers dynamic and interactive data about our world. A map viewer can pan out or zoom in; rotate and tilt the view of the Earth; and decide which layers of information they want to see on the map. All this is possible because cameras have travelled the world to capture the imagery used by the platform. While Google Earth is not a true Geographic Information System, it does feature some aspects of GIS. It is a great tool to become familiar with. Users can learn how to manipulate and use information, viewing parts of our world they may not have had the opportunity to visit yet, whether this is Antarctica or an island in the Caribbean Sea with pearl-white sand.

In addition to using aerial and satellite imagery, Google Earth also offers a Street View. This draws on a collection of photographic images of actual streets, allowing a map user to see exactly what an area is like. As its name suggests, the image offered is as though you were standing there on the street yourself. This has been created using a myriad of street photographs which come together to build a comprehensive picture of parts of the world that we live in. While some countries currently have very limited data, in others comprehensive Street Views are offered, allowing a map viewer to see what it would be like to actually walk the streets of particular areas.

Early in 2005, a few months before the launch of Google Earth, Google Maps was released. Appealing to a wide range of users, it has grown to become a globally popular platform. Billions of users access these digital maps every year. Procured and developed by Google, a giant commercially driven technology company, it has changed the way people use maps. While spatially based, Google Maps involves more than just maps. Utilising a range of layers, such as the Street View function of its sister platform, Google Earth, Google Maps essentially serves as a database of place-based information. Stacking information resources, it gives users some choice about how much information they want to access and offers businesses the opportunity to utilise the map to promote themselves. In turn, all the data is held by Google. Holding a huge store of information, Google currently holds a powerful position in shaping the way we think about our world. It even controls the data users can access. Which iteration of Google Maps a user can access changes depending on their geolocation. Facilitated through technology, the ubiquitous Google Maps is accessible through the internet on smartphones, tablets, computers, and used in many cars for maps with real-time traffic information.

Whether digital or printed on paper, data is the fundamental ingredient of a good map. Cartographers and map viewers require accurate information, so maps need to be created using reliable and credible data. This is collected through surveying. Surveyors use a range of instruments to capture and measure features of our landscapes, including compasses and theodolites. A compass measures the orientation, while a theodolite measures the angles within the topography of the land, whether it is hills, mountains, valleys, or beneath a water body. Surveyors also collect data through a method called remote sensing. Remote sensing allows surveyors to use data about a place collected from satellites or high-flying aircraft. They use instruments that detect the amount of light or radiation emitted from places, mounting these on airplanes or space satellites. This allows data to be collected as the plane or satellite moves above the Earth, meaning surveyors can precisely analyse places.

Landsat makes a key contribution to the volume of data collected through remote sensing. Circling Earth more than a dozen times each day, Landsat is a satellite. It collects and transmits masses of data. This is then digitally processed and used to update, expand, correct, or make maps. A joint program between NASA and the US Geological Survey, Landsat was first launched in 1972. This means it has been acquiring images of planet Earth for decades and so offers a comprehensive view of our world and how it has changed over time. The information collected by Landsat enables geographers, planners, leaders, and policy makers to identify trends and changes, facilitating informed decisions.

While this is exciting cutting-edge technology, maps as an information source are older than writing itself. While map images appear on cave walls and on a mammoth tusk uncovered in the Ukraine, historians believe the oldest surviving paper map is one created on Greek papyrus. It shows the geography of the Iberian Peninsula from around 100 BC. Known as the Artemidorus papyrus, it is 3 metres (10 feet) long and many scholars consider it to be an important geographical text, complete with maps (though others suspect it may be a forgery). While questions of its provenance surround it, the document makes one aspect of map making clear: the visual representation of our world is valuable information.

As noted in Chapter 36, current mapping convention is that each map should include date information to indicate when the data was collected. This is particularly important as data collection techniques improve and change. It is useful for a map user to know how recent or dated the information depicted is. However, many online mapping tools offer more than just a static view of a location at a single moment in time. While some maps will indicate the year that the data was collected, others present a timelapse feature. This allows map users to observe changes within a particular location over an extended period. Layering information about the place collected over time, the timelapse feature is a sophisticated aspect of modern digital mapping and has a range of applications in geography. For example, examining the changes in a place over time is particularly useful when assessing the impact of a natural disaster in an area. It can allow geographers to examine how a natural disaster unfolded and assess recovery efforts too. Such maps can also show aspects of coastal retreat, the growth of cities, and the extent of deforestation within an area over time. Previously, several maps would have been viewed and compared, but digital maps can show this ream of data with just a swipe of the cursor.

For the modern geography student, maps offer so much more than the blank spaces Joseph Conrad saw filling in over time. While older maps could depict just a few elements, contemporary digital maps can include layers of up-to-date data. Many old maps were unfinished due to missing information. Others were inaccurate in their distances and details because of the lack of surveying information. However, the technological capacity we have today allows for the efficient and continual collection and analysis of data from multiple sources. High processing speeds provide the means to blend these masses of data together to form a comprehensive view of our world. Our maps are no longer static. Modern digital maps can reflect the dynamic movements and changes in our world. They are a meaningful tool that offer a window into the complexities of our world.

Surveyor

Questions on Chapters 34, 35, 36 and 37

For answers see page 215

1. What is the name given to a map maker?
2. What does GIS stand for and what is it?
3. Cartographers use a scale to ensure consistency and accuracy. Maps are generally described as being large or small scale. Describe what a small scale map would be used for.
4. What is a thermoformed map?
5. What is Landsat?

Map Questions on Chapters 34, 35, 36 and 37

For answers see page 216

1. The following places are external territories in Oceania. Find the place and name which country it is connected to:
   Rapa Nui (also known as Easter Island)
   Guam
   French Polynesia.
2. Please select a printed map and examine it to determine the scale used.
3. Look at the legend or key of a map to see which symbols are used to show key features. This may be dots to show towns and villages, coloured lines to show roads, boundaries, or rivers. Choose at least three different symbols within the legend and find those features on the map.
4. On the same map, please check the title of the map. Also determine whether a date and the source data is provided.
5. Please look at a range of maps to see the differences between them in showing orientation. Some may include a compass rose, while others just use a north point.

CHAPTER 38

Cities and Towns

Cities are one feature included on many maps, commonly marked by black dots. Knowing where people live is a key aspect of understanding places. Showing cities on maps gives important reference markers for users to orient themselves. Today, over half of the world's population live in urban areas. The movement of people from rural and farming areas migrating to cities and towns causes these urban areas to grow and expand in a process called urbanisation. Many people are drawn to cities. They often provide more job opportunities, access to better services, and improved living conditions compared to rural areas. But, as cities expand, environmental and social problems can occur. Natural and rural areas are transformed into urban areas, trying to meet the demands for services, housing, transportation, utilities, and jobs for all. Meanwhile, rural areas essential for food production and other services, become less populated.

On 15 November 2022 the world's population reached 8 billion. Statistics show that around 80 million people are added to the world's population each year, so this number is increasing. Assessing the geographical dimension to population growth is crucial. Geographers want to know which countries and cities are growing and where populations are changing. Population geography focuses specifically on issues relating to population shifts and changes, examining where people live across the world and how this changes over time. It examines factors such as population density (how many people are living within an area), where people live (called distribution), migration patterns, birth and death rates, and the characteristics of a population.

To do this, population geographers analyse demographics, which is statistical data and information about people and places. Population geographers analyse how big populations are in various places, their ethnic diversity, and the structure of the population. They might delve into the educational levels of a particular region, emerging health needs, or determine that an area has an ageing population. Examining the demographics of a region, they seek to understand the people living there. This work includes studying data and layering it into maps to build a social picture of a place. For instance, population geographers may assess how multicultural a place might be, or see that there are more young families in a particular area and so plan to build more schools in the future.

Historically, the Industrial Revolution was a time when many areas experienced increased urban growth. As factories were built in cities there was an increased demand for workers. Millions of people moved away from their farms and rural lifestyles to take jobs in the city. Today, cities remain key centres of economic importance. Cities can offer greater employment opportunities, better pay, as well as social and cultural outlets and industries not always found in rural areas. Compared with towns and agricultural centres, cities also provide more educational choices, whether it is a greater range of schools, tertiary institutions such as colleges and universities, or vocational training in many forms. With their smaller size, towns cannot always offer the same prospects. The sheer number

Tokyo

of people living together in a concentrated urban area leads to a greater variety of services available and enhances diversity within the city limits.

With more people living in urban areas, new technologies and innovations have developed to help fit many people into the one space. This includes the construction of complex transport systems to help move masses of people around the city and also skyscrapers. These tall buildings house more people in a limited footprint and the invention of the elevator supported movement in these tall buildings: they could travel up and down the floors rather than need to climb masses of staircases. Some of the world's tallest residential buildings are found in New York City, in what is dubbed "Billionaires' Row", Dubai in the United Arab Emirates, and Busan, in South Korea. These tower over the city skylines.

London, Paris, Tokyo, and New York City are four places that consistently top the lists of global cities. These are significant international cities historically, economically, and culturally. Their skylines are well known, with landmarks like the Eiffel Tower in Paris, the Empire State Building in New York City, and the Tokyo Skytree. In the east, the cities of Hong Kong, Shanghai, Beijing, Singapore, and Seoul are important Asian trading hubs and home to millions of people. Around half of Asia's population live in cities, with the share of the urban population

South Royalton, Vermont

across this continent expected to continuously increase. These cities are punctuated by their skyscrapers, traffic congestion, pollution, higher populations, and a faster pace. They seem to never sleep and are growing rapidly, forming large scale urban areas across parts of Asia.

While some cities have grown over centuries, others seem to pop up quickly, like Dubai in the United Arab Emirates. Abu Dhabi is the national capital of the United Arab Emirates, but Dubai is its international hub and one of the fastest growing cities in the world. Just a few decades ago it was a small fishing village. Today, it has a population of over 3 million and one of the busiest ports in the Middle East. The discovery of offshore oil in 1966 saw its population skyrocket as it evolved into a strategic global city and key economic hub. Dubai is a thriving metropolis in the desert. Known for the world's largest shopping mall and the world's tallest building, Dubai has developed at a rapid pace. Here, skyscrapers stand tall in stark contrast to the surrounding Arabian desert, the city offering luxurious and lavish living for those who can afford it.

In contrast, such skyscrapers aren't a common sight in towns. Towns are far less crowded and have a low population density. They can offer a close-knit community which fosters a sense of camaraderie and belonging. Lower population densities mean less congestion, so people living in towns, villages, and hamlets generally experience more peaceful living environments, away from the hustle and bustle of city life. The costs of living are often lower in towns compared to cities, making it a more affordable option, particularly for housing. Towns can be located in some very picturesque spots too. They can offer residents a beautiful aesthetic not always available in cities. Many towns and villages around the world are known for their charming main streets, cottages, local shops, landmarks, historic buildings, and serene surroundings. All of these elements create an atmosphere that is quite different to cities. Both visitors and residents can find it refreshing and preferable to city life.

The British educator Charlotte Mason has long been associated with the Lake District within the county of Cumbria, far from the skyscrapers of London. This region is in northwest England, with Scotland bordering to the north. Along with stunning blue lakes, there are forests, mountains, woodlands, and breathtaking coastlines. Known for its natural beauty, the Lake District is dotted with villages and hamlets, such as Ambleside,

Grasmere, Rydal, Keswick, and Windermere. These places inspired the artists JMW Turner and John Constable and numerous authors, including Beatrix Potter, Arthur Ransome, John Ruskin, and Sir Walter Scott. The poet William Wordsworth is closely tied to this part of England, and many of his most famous works were written while he lived within this charming spot. Most of the villages in the Lake District are centred around a focal point, such as a church or the marketplace, and farming plays a key role. These villages and hamlets offer a very different way of life to that in London or Edinburgh.

When comparing urban areas, geographers use the terms towns and cities to differentiate between the size of human settlements. While there isn't one specific definition for each of these terms, most define a town as having between 2,500 and 20,000 residents. Anything less than 2,500 is a village, with hamlets being even smaller. Places with a population of over 20,000 people are classified as cities.

Along with villages, hamlets, towns, and cities, geographers also refer to suburbs. These are urban areas within cities which are less densely populated than the city centres. Unlike the skyscrapers found in city centres to house many residents and workers in one tall building, suburbs are known for the way family homes sprawl across the landscape, along with shops, services, schools, and parks. Suburban homes tend to be larger than those in the city centre and, without all the activity of the city, there is less traffic, congestion, pollution, and noise. Due to the amenities and space available, families may choose to live in the suburbs, with adults needing to commute into the city for work on the train or bus.

Urban geographers study how the growing preference for cities and sprawling suburban development sees the expansion of cities into rural areas, leading to the loss of both farmland and critical environmental zones. The global trend of urbanisation presents complex challenges for our future. As cities grow, rural populations shrink, reducing the number of people in rural areas producing food for the world's growing population. Increasing urbanisation creates demand and pressure for services, infrastructure, jobs, and affordable housing for all residents.

CHAPTER 39

Megacities

Cities are dynamic and exciting places, where life seems to have a faster pace. Newcomers can carve out a new life in a city that just wasn't possible in rural areas. More than ever before, people are moving into cities, attracted by the prospects they can offer. This means that the cities themselves are growing, some developing into megacities. A megacity is a large urban area that is home to over 10 million people. Many of the world's megacities are located within the world's two most populous countries: India and China. These two Asian nations are home to around one-third of the global population and various megacities are found here, including Shanghai, Beijing, Chengdu, Guangzhou, Delhi, and Mumbai.

While cities have developed over the centuries, the emergence of megacities is a relatively recent phenomenon. New York City in the United States of America and Tokyo, Japan were the world's first modern megacities. While in 1975 there were only four megacities – New York City, Tokyo, Mexico City, and São Paolo – since then, dozens more have evolved. Today megacities are found on every continent except Australia and Antarctica. However, trends suggest that more than a dozen new megacities will emerge by 2050 and many of these will be within developing countries. These are places that will experience rapid population growth, changing into key economic locations and major social hubs.

Historically New York City, London, and Paris have been the largest cities in the world, but geographers predict that the continents of Asia and Africa will host the biggest urban populations in the future. Already Kinshasa, the capital of the Democratic Republic of the Congo, Lagos in Nigeria, and Cairo, Egypt's national capital, are huge African cities. Cairo is the largest metropolitan area in the Middle East and Arab world, though other African megacities are arising. These include Dar es Salaam in Tanzania and Luanda in Angola.

However, the substantial urban growth within these cities is largely unplanned. Infrastructure is unable to keep up with the pace of population increases. While these cities of Africa continue to grow, there are major concerns about sustainability due to little forward planning. For example, Lagos, Nigeria is the most populated city on the African continent and one of the most densely populated on the planet. Serving as the commercial capital of Africa's most populous country, Lagos is booming. Every day, hundreds of people arrive in Lagos, seeking new opportunities in the city. This level of migration, along with the existing growth within the city, presents a significant challenge for planners and policy makers. There simply are not enough houses or jobs available, let alone other services and resources, to support the ever-growing population. As a result, slum areas increase as the population grows.

Slums are overcrowded, run-down urban areas. They are defined by substandard housing, poor living conditions, intense poverty, and widespread lack. People living in slum areas do not have enough fresh water, sanitation, or sufficient electricity supply. These areas develop because cities grow so quickly that the city's infrastructure cannot meet the demand of the influx of new residents. Often residents of slums are at risk because these informal housing settlements tend to grow within areas not wanted or used for other purposes. This may include flood-prone or industrial run-off areas, regions within swamps, or those close to rubbish dumping sites. Poor nutrition, unemployment, pollution, inadequate sanitation, traffic congestion, and limited access to health and education services only exacerbate the problems for these citizens. Cities struggle to provide for a population that is increasing rapidly. Urban geographers study cities and the pressures of megacities, seeking solutions to these complex issues.

Some countries recognise the need to invest in the necessary infrastructure for a thriving and growing megacity. China's massive urbanisation project has seen the rollout of substantial road, building, and infrastructure networks in many megacities within its borders, including Chongqing. While established as a locality over 3,000 years ago, Chongqing is a relatively new megacity. It is nestled within the mountains of southwest China and the Yangtze River, on the edge of a booming agricultural industry. The city has become one of the powerhouses of the Chinese economy due to rapid industralisation and strong growth. Trade and commerce are important to the success of the city, including the production of cars, motorcycles, and laptops for the global market.

The success of Chongqing is due in part to the completion of the Three Gorges Dam. Supporting the world's largest hydroelectric power plant, this project dramatically changed the landscape of this region of China. Cargo ships can now travel along the Yangtze River to Chongqing's ports, transporting goods to the world. Supporting this river transport route are extensive railway lines, roads, and two airports. In just over two decades Chongqing has developed to be China's biggest and most populated megacity, surpassing Shanghai in population in 2020. While Beijing, Shanghai, and Guangzhou are all coastal cities in the eastern part of China, Chongqing represents China opening up the western region, showcasing its new and emerging inland megacities.

Along with studying cities and megacities, urban geographers also examine conurbations. Conurbations are the areas that surround a city, including suburbs and other connected cities. Another name for these urban environments is "metropolitan areas", or sometimes they are given the label "greater", such as Greater London and Greater New York. These areas include not only the city itself but also the surrounding area. With substantial growth occurring in these regions, some metropolitan areas can combine into one huge megalopolis or conurbation. It can be hard to discern where one city or towns ends and the next begins. These areas merge to form a continuous urban area.

The megalopolis of Boston, Massachusetts, and Washington DC in the United States of American is often called the Northeast Corridor, or simply "BosWash". There has been so much development within these urban areas that they have joined to create a substantial conurbation. This urban corridor encompasses the major cities of New York City, Philadelphia, Baltimore, and Washington DC. In 2022 it was estimated that this area of the North Atlantic Coast was home to nearly 20% of the total US population. The corridor shows the mass conurbation that can develop when cities develop, grow, and merge into an enormous area.

All cities develop in different ways and at varying speeds, responding to a range of pressures. Tokyo in Japan is one of the world's most populous metropolitan areas. It is a very old city. Located on the island of Honshu, it is the national capital of Japan, previously known as Edo. Tokyo is the largest city in Japan and in Asia. 10% of Japan's total population lives within the metropolis of Tokyo and millions more live within the surrounding cities, including Chiba, Yokohama, and Kawasaki. With so many people passing through this city each day, Tokyo is also home to the world's busiest pedestrian crossing: Shibuya Crossing. Located in the heart of Tokyo's central shopping district, ten lanes of traffic and five major crosswalks converge at this square. Tens of thousands of pedestrians cross it every day in what is called "The Scramble".

While it might sound chaotic with this many people living, working, and moving about the city, Japanese authorities work hard to ensure that this happens as smoothly as possible. To accommodate the millions of residents that live and work in the city, as well as the tourists visiting, Tokyo focuses on strategic planning. They seek to manage and resource the city to support this huge population well. For example, ferrying millions of people around the city each day, Tokyo's trains are well known for being packed during peak times, but also for their cleanliness and precision. They arrive and depart exactly on time. This requires a great deal of work and effort and demonstrates that massive cities can run efficiently with the right planning and resources.

While Tokyo is a megacity in the northern hemisphere, São Paolo in Brazil is the largest city in the southern hemisphere. Around 12 million people reside in the city itself, but over 21 million live within the broader conurbation. This serves as the financial and cultural capital of Brazil. Now dominated by multi-lane highways, the city was first established by coffee plantation owners. The rapid urbanisation of the city attracted people from rural areas and immigrants too. While often called a "concrete jungle" owing to the number and style of buildings in the city, São Paolo boasts one of the largest urban forests in the world: the Parque Estadual da Cantareira. Covering nearly 8,000 hectares, this area of rainforest is an important biosphere reserve and protects water supplies. Showing that even in megacities residents can enjoy nature, it is popular for hikers and the place to see howler monkeys and sloths, and a range of birds, including hummingbirds and toucans. It offers the best panoramic view of São Paolo.

The scale, energy, and vibrancy of megacities are exciting. Successful city leaders and managers work to ensure sufficient housing, transport services, employment opportunities, as well as sanitation, police, rubbish and pollution management, education services, health care, and retail options. They want to provide for everyone, avoid slums, and include green spaces like the Parque Estadual da Cantareira in São Paolo to serve as the lungs of the urban jungle. Urban geographers know that to support millions of people in a megacity requires careful coordination and planning.

Questions on Chapters 38 and 39

For answers see page 217

1. Name one town or village you would find in the Lake District of England.

2. Name two emerging megacities on the continent of Africa.

3. What are some of the differences between living in a city as opposed to a town or village?

4. At what point is a city classified as a megacity?

5. Name the two Asian countries where most of the world's megacities are located.

6. Name four of the megacities within India and China.

7. The national capital of Japan was previously known as Edo. Today it is one of the world's most populous metropolitan areas. What is it called and on which island of Japan is it located?

Map Questions on Chapters 38 and 39

For answers see page 217

1. London, New York City, Paris, and Tokyo are four global cities that have been established for centuries. London and Paris are on the European continent. London is in England and Paris is in France. New York City is on the east coast of the United States of America and Tokyo is in Japan. Please find each of these countries and cities on a map.

2. India and China are the two most populous nations and together represent nearly one-third of the total global population. Please find these nations on a map.

3. Hong Kong, Shanghai, and Beijing are all cities in the People's Republic of China. Beijing is the national capital of China and is located inland. Shanghai and Hong Kong are both coastal cities. Please find these three cities on a map.

4. Singapore is both a city and a nation. It is in Southeast Asia. On a map, find the city and name the country that lies directly to the north of Singapore.

5. Using a map of Africa, find the following cities:
   Kinshasa, in the Democratic Republic of the Congo
   Cairo, Egypt's national capital
   Dar es Salaam in Tanzania
   Luanda in Angola
   Lagos in Nigeria.

CHAPTER 40

Social Geography

While this book is a modern offering of Charlotte Mason's predominantly physical geography content, contemporary geography goes beyond learning only about the physical features of our Earth and finding these on a map. Today geographers explore how different cultures and societies are connected to the land. They observe how they affect the world around them, wanting to understand how the environment influences the way people live, as well as how people use and change places. To do this, geographers use technology like satellite imagery and GIS to analyse processes and patterns. They examine data, maps, undertake surveys and fieldwork to learn more about communities, social networks, migration, politics, and the environmental challenges of the 21st Century. Understanding the social and human dimension of our physical environment is key.

Human geography is the study of how people live around the world, including how they shape the places in which they live. It looks at where people build cities, how they travel, where and how they grow food, and their cultural differences. Human geographers ask questions like, "Why do people live in some areas and not others?" and, "How do cultures and traditions influence where people build homes?" They are interested in how people interact with the environment, including facing the challenges it brings. Human geography tells the story of how people and places are connected.

For centuries, people have worked to shape the land around them just as the landscapes have affected how they live and work. The Inuit living in the Arctic region have a different way of life to that of the Torres Strait Islander peoples of Australia, yet both respond to the environment around them. Geographers study the people and the environments in which they live, along with their communities, cultures, and economies. They seek to understand how societies develop and work and seek to solve complex issues like sustainability and biodiversity conservation.

Geographers study issues such as poverty, inequality, cultural diversity, social change, economic development, transport, and traffic management. Some specialise in the area of urbanisation, examining how megacities have developed in our world. Others pursue economic geography, examining how trade connects people and places. In a world where the population is ever increasing, one important area of social geography is population geography. Population geographers study where people live, how populations grow, and how people move from one place to another. They assess why some areas might have small populations and the reasons people migrate to another region, city, or country. By looking at both physical and social elements, geographers develop a fuller picture of space and place. Studying the human dimension within physical environments helps us to better understand places.

In January 2010 a massive earthquake hit Haiti, a nation on the island of Hispaniola in the Caribbean Sea. The epicentre wasn't far from Port-au-Prince, Haiti's national capital. Stress had built up between the Caribbean plate and the North American plate, which was released through a 7.1 magnitude earthquake just south of the capital city. The loss of life from the earthquake was immense. Over 220,000 people were killed and 300,000 were injured. Thousands of buildings were destroyed by the major earthquake and the many aftershocks that followed, resulting in over one million people becoming homeless.

The aftermath of the earthquake was intense. Search and rescue teams worked to dig people out of the rubble and move residents away from unsafe areas. In Port-au-Prince 19 million cubic metres of debris needed to be cleared away and essential services restored. The destructive physical forces had a huge toll on the Haiti's population. An estimated two million residents were left without food or water. The earthquake severely damaged infrastructure, including drinking water supplies, and many residents that survived the earthquake became sick after consuming polluted water. As people moved into temporary shelters, unable to live in their own homes due to the destruction, crime rates increased. Looting and violence became social problems. Many countries tried to assist the relief efforts, but help was slow to arrive due to the damage sustained at the port and the single runway of the only airport in Haiti. It was difficult to send aid workers and supplies as international rescue teams didn't have the access they needed. When food, water, and other essential supplies did arrive, it was challenging to make logistical arrangements for these to be distributed to those in need.

The experience of Haiti highlights various elements of both social and physical geography. Geographers aren't interested in analysing just the depth of the earthquake, but also the associated factors and issues that added to the complexity of this natural disaster. Before the earthquake, over three-quarters of the population of Port-au-Prince were living in slum conditions and only one-third of the population had access to tap water. As one of the poorest and least developed countries in the world, the buildings of Haiti were not in a good condition. Unlike buildings in Japan, where volcanic activity is a known risk and mitigated by building regulations and good design elements, they were not designed nor constructed to resist the effects of earthquakes. These were densely populated areas of poorly built homes. The city had been unable to keep up with the pace of urbanisation. These factors exacerbated the effects of the natural disaster. The country was poorly placed to respond to such a shock. It was a long and slow road to recovery.

In the years since the tragedy, geographers have analysed the competing issues around the catastrophe in Haiti to learn how to respond better to help people and address the vulnerabilities experienced in parts of the world. This helps to avoid them in the future. These are the types of challenges and projects where geographical skills offer a unique perspective to problem solving. Geographers examine both the physical constraints and issues, but also assess the human dimension, considering how best to work and respond within the cultural and physical landscapes. This means they can offer their skills to a range of important social issues in our world.

Population geography is part of modern social geography. With a global population of 8 billion that continues to rise, knowing where people live and how this is shifting is crucial information. The movement of people from one place to another, called migration, is a massive phenomenon for society today. As people move from one place to another, they share parts of their culture in the new place, thus, migration spreads goods and services across the world, as well as social values, cultural practices, knowledge, and information. People moving around the world has occurred for centuries, however, today it occurs on a much larger scale. In 2024 it was estimated that there were over 280 million international migrants and millions more required international humanitarian aid and support. Given the intense need, this is a critical field of study involving geographers.

People may need to flee their homes for a number of reasons, seeking a new region or country to live in. Migration can be caused by conflict, weather-related events, environmental degradation, or the cascading effects of climate change. Some regions of the world experience the intense pressures of migration. For instance, conflict in Ukraine, Syria, and Afghanistan saw more people fleeing their homes and needing help. Once on the move, migrants are vulnerable. Smuggling, human traf-ficking, violence, abuse, exploitation, and modern slavery are all dangers for migrants. Equipped with data and information on the pressures and trends in migration across regions, geographers try to offer workable solutions to help these difficult situations. Some countries in Africa are

Refugees fleeing the war in Ukraine

trying to address crisis conditions for migrants and refugees, relying on geographical knowledge to assist.

Africa is the world's second-largest continent and almost equally divided in half by the equator. The history of the continent has been shaped by migration. Between the 15th and 19th Centuries, millions of Africans were transported from their home nations and shipped across the Atlantic Ocean. Taken mainly from within the central interior, they were sold as slaves in North and South America. Millions more were transported within the African continent. They experienced brutal conditions and those who remained at home felt the widespread impacts. It had a devastating effect on the population of the continent. Today, Africa is home to more countries than any other continent, with hundreds of native languages and indigenous groups represented. Parts of Africa are still affected by mass migration. For example, conflict in the Dafur region of Sudan between people from different cultural and religious backgrounds has caused millions of people to flee their homes to live in camps. This is a conflict between nomadic and sedentary tribes. Fighting over access to grazing land and water, their cultural, religious, and economic differences have led to violence, war, hunger, disease, and the migration of millions of people trying to escape the conflict. Leaving their homes to seek safety, many people have been displaced.

These complex social geography issues not only impact landscapes, societies, politics, and economics, but also dramatically alter the lives of the millions of people involved. Social geographers examine these challenging issues, working with others as they seek to solve these problems. Addressing the challenges of hunger and poverty, helping to ensure that all children can receive an education, and working to improve health conditions are just some of the pressing issues geographers can work on. This is another reason why understanding geography can make a huge difference in our world.

CHAPTER 41

Geography for our Future

While serving as the 44th President of the United States of America, Barack Obama spoke about the importance of geography today:

> *The study of geography is about more than just memorising places on a map. It's about understanding the complexity of our world, appreciating the diversity of cultures that exists across continents. And in the end, it's about using all that knowledge to help bridge divides and bring people together.*

To study geography is to learn about the places that create the beauty and diversity of this planet. Geography helps us to understand the dynamic systems of Earth, including its physical features and environments, but also the people who live within those places. Being able to locate the Empty Quarter of the Arabian Desert or Mount Kilimanjaro on a map of Africa is great, but knowing about those places and the people within that region is better. This is why geographers study landforms, climates, ecosystems, and natural hazards, as well as diverse cultures and societies, social and economic issues, and sustainability. Learning about geography means finding out how to navigate some of the most complex issues and challenges of our world.

There are a range of physical systems that affect the everyday life of all people. Geography helps us understand these. Knowing how the water cycle works, about the movement of ocean waters through various currents, reading weather systems, or understanding why towns, cities, and megacities were established in certain locations, are all aspects of geography. By seeking to understand our environment, geography students can work within a range of jobs, such as environmental management, land surveying, climate change, cartography, nature conservation, meteorology, and town planning. Ultimately, geographers are problem solvers. By examining places, scale, and trends, they identify where and when problems might arise and look for solutions to these.

Delving into different places all around the world, we are offered a passport when we study geography. People, places, cultures, international development, and stewarding global citizenship are just some of the themes that fascinate students, piquing their curiosity about the world and the people that live within it. As President Obama noted, it is far more than just memorising places on a map. Rather, it is reading and translating maps, interpreting data, information, and trends, and appreciating what that might represent on the ground. It is about how and why places are connected and this knowledge helps to make sense of the world in different ways.

Some of the world's biggest companies understand the power of high-quality geographical knowledge. Many use geographical location technology, particularly when selling goods. Geospatial location tools allow customers to track their online purchases across the world. Trackers can show each step of the journey from the moment you click "buy" on a website. A customer can see if the item they want is in stock, when the item leaves the warehouse, the route it takes to arrive at their home, and what time it is expected to be delivered to their front doorstep. Online tools and apps show exact geolocations, drawing on geographical information. Analysing this data can help companies to identify more efficient delivery routes. After all, reducing travel time and costs can mean greater profit for companies, so knowing geography is valuable. For example, a delivery company that examines transport trends within their logistics can learn how to go with the flow of traffic, rather than work against it. Likewise, online accommodation companies rely on geographical data to help match prospective guests with available properties, just as meal-ordering services connect restaurants and cafés with hungry diners wanting food to arrive directly to their door. This is all done through the power of geography.

While you don't necessarily find jobs listed for "geographers" as such, students of geography can find themselves working in a range of different fields, and it isn't all about reading and creating maps. Helping to develop policies that affect people and the environment, undertaking research to better understand aspects of our world, tracking parts of our food systems, or analysing our weather patterns are just some of the many jobs students of geography can do. There are a range of diverse jobs and, in this modern era, some in areas you may not expect. For example, today some geography graduates are employed by game design companies. They are involved in creating the world of a game play, ensuring that elements like the environment, climate, and topography are realistic. Understanding geography ensures that these designers and creators know that the worlds they invent are believable and sensitive to the cultures and peoples that are portrayed.

Studying geography can shift the scale of how you consider place, people, issues, and opportunities. It can broaden your horizon. In 1968 Bill Anders, Frank Borman, and Jim Lovell completed the Apollo 8 mission. They travelled around the far side of the moon and achieved significant firsts that would lead to Neil Armstrong being able to be the first man to step onto the moon. As they circled around the moon, Earth came into their view from space making them the first men to see Earth as a whole planet. The trio saw the rising of their home planet. They escaped the gravitational pull of Earth and re-entered it, but also experienced a different pull that our planet had upon millions. Bill Anders captured some photographs of Earth from space, including an image which is now known as "Earthrise". This picture sparked a new awareness not just of space and the moon, but of our own planet. It helped people to understand that we have one planet as our home in the vast solar system. In understanding this, people also realised how important it was to protect and conserve our planet.

Today, "Earthrise" still allows us to see world geography in a new way. As poet Archibald MacLeish wrote when Anders' photograph was published:

> *To see the Earth as it truly is, small and blue and beautiful in that eternal silence where it floats, is to see ourselves as riders on the Earth together, brothers on that bright loveliness in the eternal cold.*

In modern society we often hear people talking about how important it is that we care for the environment. Yet, sometimes what is missing is knowing about places first, because, when we know about them, we do feel that pull to care for them, for ourselves and for future generations. When taught well, geography can awaken curiosity and interest in the places and people of our world, offering a perspective to better understand our planet, so we want to conserve it.

Throughout these chapters you have read about the world around you and places further afield. You now understand about different countries and continents, our oceans, lakes, and rivers, and a range of other geographical concepts. However, this is just the beginning! There is so much more to read, learn, and discover about geography now you've started on your own journey of exploration. As you continue your geography studies, I hope you will appreciate with reverence the immense beauty and diversity of our planet Earth.

Earthrise

150 Years of Modern Geography

In the 150 years since Charlotte Mason first wrote *Elementary Geography* a lot has changed in the field of geography. This epilogue highlights some of the key progressions relating to geography to help you see how much has changed in that time. It is by no means an exhaustive list, rather, it pinpoints some important advances and shifts in this discipline of study since Charlotte's book was released and why a modern version was needed.

In 1915 Alfred Wegener's book, *The Origin of Continents and Oceans*, was published. Describing what he called "continental drift", Wegener put forward the idea that the continents of the world are slowly moving. Fifty years later those ideas developed into the modern theory of plate tectonics. The continents of the world rest on these massive slabs of rock and are indeed, aways moving. From this, scientists came to better understand the Ring of Fire in the Pacific Ocean, largely through the work of John Tuzo-Wilson. In the 1960's, Tuzo-Wilson identified a type of tectonic plate boundary not previously known. This introduced the concept of hot spots within the mantle, such as those within the Ring of Fire and the famous San Andreas Fault. It served to explain an important geological concept integral to physical geography. The Wilson Mountains in Antarctica were named in honour of his contribution to geophysics.

After World War II, advances in astronomy and space travel accelerated, changing our geographical perspective of the world and Earth's place in the universe. In the 1920's Edwin Hubble discovered there was a universe beyond our own Milky Way, expanding our view of space and time. From his work at the Mount Wilson Observatory in California, America, Hubble showed that our universe was much larger than presumed. It sparked other to build research on this revelation. Beginning in the 1950's, the Space Race was held against the backdrop of the Cold War, with the United States of America and the Union of Soviet Socialist Republics competing, each wanting to be the first to conquer space. In July 1969, American astronaut Neil Armstrong became the first man to walk on the moon. Travelling into space and landing on the moon led to advances in aeronautical technology and changed our view of the universe.

In the 1960's the Canada Land Inventory was developed by Roger Tomlinson. This inventory is recognised as being the beginnings of Geographical Information Systems (GIS) and so Tomlinson is known as the "Father of GIS". Surveying all the land within the nation of Canada, the inventory provided information to help make better plans for the future, identifying regions for parks and reserves, farming, the expansion of towns and cities, and other types of land uses. What was different about this survey was that it was the first to use computers. The result was a powerful tool processing masses of data to generate maps. The inventory demonstrated how computers could process statistical and spatial data. GIS allows geographers to record more data on digital maps.

Along with GIS, Global Positioning Systems (GPS) has revolutionised modern geography. During the Cold War era the United States Navy began conducting experiments in satellite navigation, tracking submarines carrying nuclear missiles. Orbiting satellites could track the shifts in the radio signal known as the Doppler Effect, allowing them to pinpoint the location of submarines. Called NavSTAR, the Navigation System with Timing and Ranging was launched by the US Department of Defence in 1978. This satellite system formed the foundation for GPS, which, when it achieved full global coverage, meant that the position of any object around the world could be reported. Over time, this space-based radionavigation system has developed and progressed, incorporating accurate atomic clocks from Nobel-prize winning physics and creative engineering.

This technology paved the way for in-car navigation options and the "you are here" dots that feature on modern digital maps. In 2000 US President Clinton made the decision to allow more worldwide utility of GPS. Prior to this, it was used predominantly by the US Government.

Unscrambling the GPS signal allowed more users to access this information. This saw GPS receivers being used more and rapid technological advances. It also ushered in a new era of mapping practices. From this, global mapping technology started to develop, including the location trackers on your cellphone or smartwatch, or those on a train, plane, or ship. Whether you are hailing a taxi, checking a flight, tracking an online order, looking for somewhere to eat while travelling, or tracking your fitness on a wearable device, GPS can give important location-based data to help.

The invention of GIS and geospatial technology is one of the revolutionary dimensions of contemporary geography. Satellite imagery, remote sensing, GIS, and GPS have transformed how we view and study our Earth. In 1995 the United Kingdom became the first country to complete a large-scale electronic mapping program, holding a huge GIS database of digital information. While the UK Ordnance Survey had first started in 1791, it became a world leader in mapping and GIS. Today, GIS is an industry worth billions of dollars. Hundreds of thousands of organisations access the digital information held within these systems. It has dramatically reduced our reliance on printed paper maps, and the power of GIS technology was highlighted during the Covid-19 pandemic when it was used to provide a digital resource to monitor the global health crisis. Maps can be generated far quicker than they could in the past. For instance, Google Maps estimates that it can currently map as many buildings in one year that used to take a decade to map. Thousands of street names, addresses, and businesses can now be added at a rapid pace.

It was the motorcar that first helped to drive the printing of paper maps. Car manufacturing is one of the world's largest industries and is a universal symbol of modern technology. The advent of the car meant that people no longer travelled by horse and cart and an extensive road network developed. Modern life became reliant on cars and drivers needed directional information. This meant paper maps. The founders of Michelin, brothers Andre and Edouard Michelin, first compiled the *Michelin Guide* in 1900 to help motorists travel around France. For no charge, motorists could pick up the Guide which included maps of the country, along with a list of restaurants, hotels, mechanics, and fuel stations, and instructions on how to repair and change tyres. The maps and information were designed to encourage motorists to venture further afield (to help support their tyre business). It quickly became popular. Soon, the Michelin Guide became available in Europe and Northern Africa. Today, the Guide covers countries across Europe, Asia, North America, and South America. However, now the focus is on identifying the best restaurants, as few people use paper motoring guides compared to digital map options.

One of the most popular digital map platforms used today is Google Maps. Along with the sister program, Google Earth, this was launched in 2005, allowing everyone to use GIS technology and updated mapping data. The release of these facilitated the use of GIS technology within our everyday lives. In 2007 the Apple iPhone was released, revealing the capacity of this spatial data. The first smartphone, the iPhone allowed users to hold not only a phone to make calls, but also served as a computer and mobile GPS device, collecting and transmitting data. It meant that GIS could be used by anyone anywhere.

A smartphone has access to a huge amount of information, including digital maps that are in a constant state of change. Advancing technology and additional data means they are becoming more detailed over time. Once constrained by printing technology and lack of data, now maps are informed by aerial photography, satellite imagery, and remote

Phone maps

sensing, and generated by massive location-based data sets. The rise of digital maps is reshaping our understanding about what maps are for, such that the word "map" hardly seems to cover the geo-spatial technology we have. The main tool of a geographer, the map, was forever altered.

On 3 May 2000 the first geocache was hidden in Oregon, USA. A modern, digital version of a treasure hunt, geocaching involves finding small boxes hidden across nearly every country in the world. It is estimated that there are over 3 million geocaches, most of which contain a notebook, tokens, and a scroll of paper. All are assigned coordinates and often clues are given about their location. Enthusiastic geocachers decipher the clues to seek these treasures and have the thrill of finding something hidden in plain sight. Seekers hide the treasures, recording their location and exchange the details with others. They take care to carefully hide the geocache again and replace the trinkets they find within these small treasure chests. All these details are carefully logged and recorded so all participants know the information around the geocaches. This is community problem solving and treasure hunting on a map base.

A sensational new mapping based augmented reality mobile game was unleashed in July 2016: Pokémon Go. Overlaying virtual Pokémon (pocket monsters) on an accurate digital map, players can use their smartphone or tablet to hunt down and collect Pokémon, then use them to battle opponents. Like geocaching, it is based on a mapping culture.

A child finds a geocache

Players try to collect items and individuals and groups will even gather in certain spots in a modern geography-based game. Both geocaching and Pokémon Go reflect the emerging trend of digital data representing a huge and valuable market in contemporary society.

Data is a foundational element of the modern economy and the way humans work and interact in the world. The ever-increasing amount of data also changes the way our maps work. While traditionally paper maps were updated and reprinted infrequently, the digital capabilities we have today mean that constant updates are built into the design of maps. This also means that the map we accessed last time may be different to the one we see the next time we check it. Updates can be made every second of every day, raising some concerns about how these maps are authored and how reliable they are.

The end of World War II heralded many changes across the world including within the field of geography. Since this time geography as a discipline has expanded and changed considerably. This is why many of the chapters Charlotte originally wrote could not simply be updated for the modern geography student. The approach and curriculum for teaching geography changed dramatically after World War II. What had been a subject that described faraway places to students in Charlotte's day, became a complex study in not just physical geography, but also economics, politics and citizenship, national identity, social and human geography, the growth of cities, and research on how the environment works. A contemporary student of geography covers a range of topics Charlotte Mason could not have anticipated. We now have digital tools, like geo-visualisations of three-dimensional maps, that she would not have imagined. It is an exciting field of study and gives much scope for the intrepid traveller and emerging global citizen. Many new developments and innovations are continuing, making it an exciting choice of study. I trust this book has helped you to see what a wonderful subject geography is and that you are eager to read and learn more!

ANSWER KEY

Questions on Chapters 1 and 2

1. Which planet is closest to the sun? *Mercury is closest to the sun.*

2. Which planet is furthest from the sun? *Neptune is the furthest most planet in our solar system.*

3. How many planets are there in our solar system? *There are eight planets in our solar system. In order from the closest to the sun these are Mercury, Venus, Earth, Mars, Jupiter, Saturn, Uranus, and Neptune.*

4. Why do planets shine rather than twinkle like stars? *Unlike stars, planets do not generate their own light; they reflect the light of the sun. This is why their light appears more constant in the sky rather than twinkling.*

5. What is the name of the path that planets take around the sun? *An orbit.*

6. How many days does it take Earth to orbit the sun? *One year, or 365¼ days.*

7. What are the five layers of the Earth called? *The innermost core, inner core, outer core, mantle, and crust.*

8. Is the inner core solid or liquid? *The inner core is solid. It is the outer core that is molten.*

9. What is the study of rocks and the form of our Earth called? *Geology.*

Questions on Chapters 3, 4 and 5

1. What are the main components of our atmosphere? *Nitrogen and oxygen are the two main gases in our atmosphere. There are also trace gases, water vapour and dust.*

2. What is the first layer of Earth's atmosphere called? *The troposphere.*

3. In which layer of the atmosphere is the ozone layer found? *The ozone layer is found in the stratosphere.*

4. List some of the colours of auroras. *Auroras can be green, yellow, red, pink, purple, and even blue.*

5. What does a barometer measure? *Air pressure, which is the weight and pressure of air pressing down on a particular point on our Earth.*

6. What type of weather does a low-pressure system bring? *Wind, clouds, and often rain too.*

7. Clear skies, warmer and drier conditions are associated with what type of atmospheric pressure system? *A high-pressure system.*

8. What is the name of the instrument that measures wind speed? *An anemometer.*

9. Describe what a weather forecaster or meteorologist does? *They examine the air pressure, temperature, humidity, wind speed, and wind direction to determine what the weather will be like to help people be prepared.*

Questions on Chapters 6 and 7

1. What geographic line marks the horizontal centre of the surface of Earth? *The equator.*

2. Do you live in the southern or the northern hemisphere? *Answers will vary depending on your location, so please guide your child accordingly as to whether you are north or south of the equator.*

3. What are lines of latitude often called? *Parallels.*

4. What are lines of longitude called? *Meridians.*

5. What is the line of longitude at 0° called? *The Prime Meridian.*

6. Name three countries that the Tropic of Capricorn passes through. *Australia, Namibia, Brazil, Madagascar, Chile, Argentina, South Africa, Paraguay, French Polynesia, Mozambique, and Botswana are all correct answers.*

7. Is the Antarctic Circle located in the northern or southern hemisphere? *The Antarctic Circle is within the southern hemisphere.*

8. The Tropic of Cancer is 23.5° North of the equator. How many degrees north is the North Pole? *The North Pole is at 90° North.*

Questions on Chapters 8 and 9

1. Name the four cardinal points you would see on a compass rose. *North, east, south, west are the cardinal points.*

2. Name the four ordinal points. *These are northeast, southeast, southwest, and northwest are the four ordinal (or intercardinal points).*

3. Using four simple compass arrows on a piece of paper, draw the four cardinal points. *In checking your child's answer, please ensure that north is the arrow pointing directly upwards and south points straight down. East*

will be the horizontal line pointing to the right of their page, while west is the horizontal line to the left.

4. Please point to the east. *Answers will vary, so help guide your child, looking to where the sun rises. You can also use a compass or compass app for accuracy.*

5. Please point to the west. *Again, answers will vary, but look to the direction in which the sun sets, or use a compass or compass app.*

6. What does GPS stand for? *Global Positioning System.*

7. Describe one way that you might use GPS technology. *Answers will vary, but options include watching for a home delivery, tracking a flight or bus through an app or online platform, using a smartphone to gain directions, geocaching, or playing location-specific games, such as Pokémon GO.*

Questions on Chapters 10 and 11

1. What is the Earth's axis? *It is a line on which the Earth spins. The tilt of the axis creates the seasons of the year.*

2. Why don't countries along the equator experience seasonal differences in the amount of sunlight? *This is due to them receiving equal amounts of sunlight and darkness all through the year because of their location at the middle of planet Earth.*

3. If it is summertime at the North Pole, what season would it be at the South Pole? *Winter.*

4. What is the North Pole Star called? *Polaris.*

5. What is the longest day of the year called? *The Summer Solstice.*

6. When people in the southern hemisphere are celebrating the Summer Solstice, what day is marked in the northern hemisphere? *Winter Solstice.*

7. On what two days of the year is there roughly equal amounts of both sunlight and darkness over the whole Earth? *The Spring Equinox (or Vernal Equinox) and the Autumn Equinox.*

Questions on Chapter 12

1. Why does latitude help define climatic zones? *The latitude of a place shows how close to, or far away, a place is from the Equator. Places further away from the equator have less direct sunlight which affects the average temperature of these places and the type of vegetation that can grow in these areas.*

2. Name two of the five Köppen climate classifications. *Answers will include tropical, arid, temperate, continental, or polar zones.*

3. Looking at a map, name the climatic zone you live in. *Answers will vary, but guide your child to use a map and find the zone where you live.*

4. What type of trees are found within the boreal or taiga forest? *Conifers or "pine trees".*

5. In which Köppen Classification zone is the Sahara Desert located? *The arid zone.*

6. In which Köppen Classification zone is the South Pole located? *The polar zone.*

7. Looking at a map, name three countries that lie within the tropical zone. *Most common answers will include the following: Indonesia, the Maldives, Mexico, Fiji, the Seychelles, Mauritius, Singapore, Maldives, Venezuela, Colombia, Cuba, or the Philippines; but there are other nations in this zone.*

Questions on Chapters 13, 14 and 15

1. What is the largest continent on Earth? *Asia.*

2. In which ocean would you find Sri Lanka? *Located in the Indian Ocean, Sri Lanka forms part of the Asian continent. It was formerly known as Ceylon.*

3. Which three countries are represented on the island of Borneo? *Indonesia, Malaysia, and the Sultanate of Brunei.*

4. What ocean surrounds Antarctica? *The Southern Ocean, also sometimes called the Great Southern Ocean.*

5. Name the seas and oceans surrounding Africa. *Indian Ocean, Red Sea, Atlantic Ocean, and Mediterranean Sea.*

6. The world's longest river is in Africa. Which river is it? *The Nile River.*

7. Describe what an oasis is. *An oasis is a body of water in the desert. They may be natural springs, wells, or irrigation systems.*

8. What are some animals you might see in the grasslands of Africa? *Given the text, answers are likely to include elephants, giraffes, lions, hyena, wildebeest, and zebras.*

9. What is the largest lake in Africa? *Lake Victoria.*

Map Questions on Chapters 13, 14 and 15

1. Name the oceans and seas bordering the continent of Africa. *The Mediterranean Sea is the north, the Red Sea is the east and the Indian Ocean is along the southeast border. The Atlantic Ocean washes the western shores of Africa.*

2. Name the two continents located south of Asia. *Australia (or Oceania) and Antarctica are south of Asia. Both are within the southern hemisphere.*

3. The equator passes through thirteen countries, including seven in Africa. Name the African countries that the equator passes through. *In Africa the equator passes through Gabon, Congo, Democratic Republic of the Congo, Uganda, Kenya, and Somalia. It also passes through the island nation of São Tomé and Príncipe.*

4. Find the South Orkney, South Shetland, and South Georgia Islands on a map of Antarctic waters.

5. Find and name two of the four main seas surrounding Antarctica. *The Weddell, Bellingshausen, Amundsen, and Ross Sea are all acceptable answers.*

Questions on Chapters 16 and 17

1. The equator passes through which three South American countries? *Brazil, Ecuador and Columbia.*

2. Name two of the seven countries the Andes Mountains pass through. *Answers will include Venezuela, Colombia, Ecuador, Peru, Bolivia, Chile, and Argentina.*

3. What is the highest city in the world? *La Paz in Bolivia.*

4. Which highway passes through both North and South America? *The Pan-America Highway.*

5. What are the two largest countries in North America? *Canada and the United States of America.*

6. Describe what a cay is and how it is formed. *Cays are small sand islands that form on the surface of coral reefs. These are formed as ocean currents deposit sediment, including sand, on a part of the coral reef. Over time this builds up, creating a small, low island fringed by coral reefs.*

7. What is the tallest peak in North America? *Denali, or Mount McKinley, located in Alaska.*

8. What is the north face of Denali called? *Wickersham Wall.*

9. What is a Continental Divide? *A Continental Divide is a physical*

boundary that creates a division in a river system. Continental Divides are found on every continent on Earth. Each river feeds into a specific bay, sea, or ocean basin and Divides create the drainage systems for this to occur as they form a living barrier running through the continent.

Map Questions on Chapters 16 and 17

1. Darien Gap covers 96 kilometres (60 miles) of treacherous land between the countries of Panama and Columbia, with dense rainforest, high, steep mountains, and swampy ground. The southwest coast of Darien Gap is the Pacific Ocean and the Gulf of Uraba is to the northeast. Please find both water features on a map.

2. The Equator passes through the countries of Brazil, Ecuador, and Columbia. Find the capital cities of each nation. *Brasília is the capital of Brazil; Quito is the capital of Ecuador; and the national capital of Columbia is Bogotá.*

3. Find the Andes Mountains on a map and name the seven countries they pass through. *Venezuela, Colombia, Ecuador, Peru, Bolivia, Chile, and Argentina.*

4. The Galápagos Islands are an archipelago of islands in the Pacific Ocean and a part of Ecuador. In which direction do they lie from the South American continent? *The Galápagos Islands lie to the west of South America.*

5. Find the national capital of Greenland. *Nuuk is the national capital and is located on the southwest coast.*

6. San Francisco, New York City, and Chicago are some of the biggest cities in the United States of America. Find each city and note which state it is located in. *San Francisco is within the state of California; New York City is within New York state; and Chicago is in Illinois.*

7. Nassau is the national capital of the Bahamas, a country made up of more than 3,000 islands and cays. Which country lies directly south of the Bahamas? *Cuba.*

8. The Pacific Ocean washes against the eastern shores of the United States of America while the Atlantic Ocean borders the west. Name three states on the west coast. *Answers will include Washington, Oregon, and California, but Alaska and Hawai'i are acceptable too.*

Questions on Chapters 18 and 19

1. What are the three regions of the Pacific Ocean? *Polynesia, Micronesia, and Melanesia.*

2. Name four islands found in Polynesia. *Based on the text, answers are likely to include Samoa, Tonga, Tuvalu, the Cook Islands, French Polynesia, the Pitcairn Islands, Rapa Nui (Easter Island) and Hawai'i, but please check a map if others are offered.*

3. What is the national capital of Australia? *Canberra.*

4. Which ocean borders the west coast of Australia? *The Indian Ocean.*

5. Which ocean borders the east coast of Australia? *The Pacific Ocean.*

6. What is the southern-most state of Australia? *Tasmania.*

7. Name two of the six regions of the Asian continent. *Answers will include Southeast Asia, Southern Asia (or the Indian subcontinent), the Middle East, Northern Asia ("Asian Russia"), Central Asia, and Eastern Asia.*

8. Singapore, Indonesia, the Philippines, Vietnam, Laos, Cambodia, and Thailand are part of which region of Asia? *Southeast Asia.*

9. Name one sea found in the Middle East. *The Mediterranean, Aegean, Caspian, Black, Red, and Arabian Seas are all correct answers.*

10. Name one river found in Asia. *Based on the text, answers are likely to include the Ganges, Yangtze, Yellow, and Mekong Rivers, but please check a map if others are offered.*

11. What is the highest point on Earth? *Mount Everest, within the Himalayas.*

Map Questions on Chapters 18 and 19

1. Which key line of latitude passes through Australia? *The Tropic of Capricorn.*

2. Name the water body that lies between the mainland of Australia and the state of Tasmania. *The Bass Strait.*

3. Tahiti is part of French Polynesia and is located east of the Cook Islands. Name two main islands that lie to the west of the Cook Islands. *Answers are likely to include Samoa, Tonga and Fiji, but please check a map if others are offered.*

4. What is the national capital of New Zealand | Aotearoa? *Wellington, Te Ara.*

5. Thailand is located in Southeast Asia. Which countries border Thailand?

In the east and northeast Thailand is bordered by Cambodia and Laos, while Myanmar is to the northwest, and Malaysia to the south.

6. Kazakhstan is the ninth largest country in the world and home to the Baykonur Cosmodrome spaceport. Which country borders Kazakhstan to the north? *Russia.*

7. The national capital of Turkmenistan boasts the honour of being the only place to have an indoor ferris wheel. Name the capital of Turkmenistan. *Ashgabat.*

8. Name the seven countries that make up the Arabian Peninsula. *A peninsula is a piece of land almost surrounded by water and the Arabian Peninsula is made up of Saudi Arabia, Yemen, Oman, Bahrain, Qatar, Kuwait, and the United Arab Emirates.*

9. Shanghai and Beijing are two megacities in China. Find them on a map and name which is the national capital. *Beijing is the national capital of China.*

Questions on Chapter 20

1. What is the smallest nation in Europe and the world? *Vatican City.*

2. Moscow is the capital city of which nation? *Russia.*

3. Name the highest peak in Europe. *Mount Elbrus in Russia is the highest peak on the European continent. It is located within the Caucasus Mountains.*

4. Which river flows through Paris? *The Seine River.*

5. Name the three Baltic States. *Estonia, Latvia, and Lithuania.*

6. Portugal and Spain are located on which peninsula? *The Iberian Peninsula.*

7. Name three Scandinavian countries. *Sweden, Norway, Denmark, and Finland are all correct answers. While Finland is not one of the Scandinavian peninsulas, politically and culturally it is considered to be part of Scandinavia.*

Map Questions on Chapter 20

1. Vatican City is the world's smallest independent state. It is entirely landlocked by one nation. Name that country. *Italy.*

2. The water bodies surrounding the European peninsula include two oceans and three seas. Please find the Arctic Ocean to the north of

Europe and the Atlantic Ocean in the west. Then find the Mediterranean, Black, and Caspian Seas, which are located to the south.

3. Find the capital city of England and note whether it is located in the east or west of the country. *London is the national capital and is found in the southeast, on the Thames River.*

4. The national capital of France, Paris, is situated on the Seine River. The river runs in a northwesterly direction and at the port city of Le Havre it flows into which major water body? *The Seine River flows into the English Channel.*

5. Germany shares its borders with nine countries. Name these countries. *Denmark to the north, Switzerland to the south, and Austria to the southeast. Poland and the Czech Republic lie to the east, while France, Luxembourg, Belgium, and Netherlands are to the west.*

Questions on Chapters 21 and 22

1. Which continent does the Southern Ocean encircle? *Antarctica.*

2. What is the smallest ocean on Earth? *The Arctic Ocean.*

3. Challenger Deep, the deepest sea-trench on Earth in the Mariana Trench, is located in which ocean? *It is found within the Pacific Ocean.*

4. What work are bathymetric scientists involved in? *Mapping the sea floor and charting the topography of our oceans.*

5. What branch of science studies the features of oceans? *Oceanography.*

6. Which ocean is the Caribbean Sea a division of? *The Atlantic Ocean.*

7. Which warm ocean current of the Atlantic Ocean originates from the Gulf of Mexico? *The Gulf Stream.*

8. How is a bay different to a gulf? *A bay is a large coastal landform, generally in a curved shape. Like a gulf, the waters within a bay are partially enclosed by land. Bays are smaller than gulfs and have a wider mouth. Gulfs are larger and deeper, but have a narrower and deeper mouth compared to a bay.*

Map Questions on Chapters 21 and 22

1. Find all five oceans on the map and name them. *The five oceans of the world are the Pacific, Indian, Atlantic, Arctic, and Southern Oceans.*

2. The Black Sea is an inland sea in Europe. Which ocean is it a division of and how are they connected? *The Black Sea is a division of the Atlantic Ocean. It is connected through the Bosporus Strait (in the southwestern*

corner), the Sea of Marmara, the Dardanelles, the Aegean Sea, and the Mediterranean Sea. Additionally, the Black Sea is connected to the Sea of Azoz through the Kerch Strait.

3. There are over twenty islands located within the Caribbean Sea, but Cuba and Jamaica are two main islands. On a map, find the capital cities of both Cuba and Jamaica. *Havana is the capital of Cuba and the main seaport for the nation. Kingston is the capital city of Jamaica and Kingston Harbour is one of the world's biggest natural harbours.*

4. The island city of Singapore dominates the Strait of Malacca. The Strait of Malacca connects the Indian Ocean to what sea and ocean? *The South China Sea (one of the largest seas in the world) and the Pacific Ocean.*

5. McMurdo Sound borders the Antarctic continent. It is a large bay within the Southern Ocean and this icy body of water is the location for a large research station. Which sea is to the north of McMurdo Sound? *The Ross Sea is north of McMurdo Sound.*

Questions on Chapters 23, 24 and 25

1. Please name the three processes of the water cycle and briefly describe each. *The three key processes are evaporation, condensation, and precipitation. Evaporation is when water turns into vapour and rises into the warm air. Condensation sees water change to liquid form due to cooler air temperatures. Precipitation is the part of the water cycle when the water falls back onto the surface of the Earth. This may be liquid as raindrops, but it could be in a solid state, frozen as hail, sleet, or snowflakes.*

2. Name two rivers found on the South and North American continents. *Answers based on the text are likely to include the St Lawrence, Mississippi, Colorado, Amazon, Paraná, and Orinoco Rivers.*

3. Are alluvial fans found on land or at sea? *Alluvial fans are found on land. They are triangular-shaped areas where alluvium has been deposited by the flowing water onto the land.*

4. The Yangtze Delta is formed where the Yangtze River meets which sea? *The East China Sea.*

5. Name the world's largest lake. *The Caspian Sea.*

6. What is the capital city of Australia and the name of the lake that was created for the capital? *Canberra is Australia's capital city, and Lake Burley Griffin is the lake created to frame the Parliamentary Area.*

7. How is a dam different to a lake? *A dam is a constructed feature in the*

landscape that diverts and restricts the flow of water to create an altered waterbody.

8. In which country and continent do you find the Okavango Delta? *Within the country of Botswana, on the continent of Africa.*

Map Questions on Chapters 23, 24 and 25

1. Which five countries border the Caspian Sea? *Azerbaijan, Iran, Turkmenistan, Kazakhstan, and Russia.*

2. Lake Eyre | Kati Thanda is a lake located within Central Australia. The country of Australia is made up of six states and two territories. Using a map, list the names of the states and territories of Australia. *The states of Australia are Western Australia, South Australia, Tasmania, Victoria, Queensland, and New South Wales. The two territories are the Northern Territory and Australian Capital Territory.*

3. Follow the path of the Danube River in Europe and note which countries it passes through. *The Danube River passes through Germany, Austria, Slovakia, Hungary, Croatia, Serbia, Romania, Bulgaria, Moldova, and Ukraine.*

4. The Amazon River ends at the Atlantic Ocean, where the Amazon Delta is located. Name the bay that the Amazon flows into. *The Amazon River flows into Marajó Bay.*

5. The powerful Dettifloss waterfalls are found on Iceland as the Jökulsá á Fjöllum River flows from the Vatnajökull glacier to the Greenland Sea. Name the national capital of Iceland. *Reykjavík is the national capital of Iceland.*

6. The world-famous Kew Gardens are an important part of the Royal Botanic Gardens in England and feature some beautiful ponds. The Kew Garden are in southwest London. Name the river that passes through London. *The Thames.*

7. Find Botswana on a map of Africa and list which countries border it. *The countries of Namibia, Zambia, Zimbabwe, and South Africa all border Botswana.*

Questions on Chapter 26 and 27

1. On which continents can glaciers be found? *Glaciers can be found in Antarctica, North America, South America, Africa, Asia, and Europe. Every continent except Australia has glaciers.*

2. What is the difference between an ice sheet and an ice cap? *An ice sheet covers a greater area (more than 50,000 square kilometres or 19,000 square miles) and is flatter in shape. In contrast, an ice cap is smaller and is shaped more like a dome, being taller in the centre and spreading out to the edges.*

3. In which national park is Old Faithful located? *Yellowstone National Park in Wyoming, United States of America.*

4. Name two countries where hot springs can be found. *Based on the text, answers will include Australia, Chile, Greece, Iceland, Japan, and Türkiye, but New Zealand, Spain, Italy, Indonesia and the United States of America are correct too.*

5. Do stalagmites grow upwards from the floor of a cave or down from the ceiling? *Stalagmites grow upwards from the cave floor while stalactites hang tight to the ceiling and grow in a downwards process.*

Map Questions on Chapters 26 and 27

1. Fjords are found mainly in Norway, Chile, New Zealand, Canada, Greenland, and the American state of Alaska. Find these five countries and the state of Alaska on a map.

2. Many glaciers and fjords are found in Scandinavia. Which countries form Scandinavia and what are the major water bodies in this region? *Most geographers consider Sweden, Norway, Denmark and Finland to make up Scandinavia. The major water bodies surrounding Scandinavia are the Atlantic Ocean, Norwegian Sea, North Sea and Baltic Sea, the Gulf of Bothnia and the Gulf of Finland. Students may also identify Skagerrak and Kattegat.*

3. Locate Milford Sound | Piopiotahi on a map of New Zealand. *It is found in Fiordland, in the southwest of the New Zealand's South Island.*

4. Find the Outer Hebrides of the west coast of Scotland. This is an archipelago, made up of islands and skerries. Name the ocean it lies within. *The Atlantic Ocean.*

5. Hot springs with bathing facilities and traditional inns, known as onsens (温泉), are popular in Japan. Find Japan on a map and name the four main large islands. *While Japan is made up of many islands, the four main ones are Honshu, Hokkaido, Shikoku, and Kyushu.*

6. Name the ocean and four seas that surround Japan. *The Pacific Ocean, the Sea of Okhotsk, the Sea of Japan, the East China Sea and the Philippine Sea.*

Questions on Chapter 28

1. Which body of water does the White Cliffs of Dover look out upon? *The English Channel.*

2. Coastal landforms are created through both erosion and depositional processes. Name two depositional landforms found in coastal zones. *Sand dunes, sand bars, spits, and tombolos are all coastal landforms that are created by depositional processes.*

3. Name at least one feature of a coastal zone that is created by erosional processes. *Cliffs, sea arches, sea caves, and sea stacks are all created through erosion.*

4. A tombolo is a type of spit. Please describe it. *A tombolo connects an island to the shore, acting as a type of sandy land bridge between the mainland and island, reshaping the coastline.*

5. In which country do you find Ha Long Bay and the Gulf of Tonkin? *Vietnam.*

Map Questions on Chapter 28

1. Sugarloaf Mountain is in Rio di Janeiro in Brazil. On a map, find the capital city of Brazil and name the ocean that runs along the east coast of this country. *While São Paulo is the largest city in Brazil, Brasilia is the national capital. The ocean along the east coast of the country is the Atlantic Ocean.*

2. Find the Gulf of Tonkin and identify which countries and sea border Vietnam. *The Gulf of Tonkin is in northern Vietnam. The bordering countries are China (to the north), Laos and Cambodia (to the west). The South China Sea is the waterbody along the east coast of Vietnam.*

3. The more densely populated parts of Hong Kong are Hong Kong Island and Kowloon Peninsula. Victoria Harbour lies between the two. In which direction from Hong Kong Island does Lamma Island lie? *Lamma Island lies to the southwest of Hong Kong Island.*

4. The Skeleton Coast is in Namibia, Africa. Which ocean adjoins this coastline? *The Atlantic Ocean.*

Questions on Chapter 29

1. What is the highest peak on Earth and within which mountain range is it found? *Mount Everest is the highest peak and it is part of the Himalayan Mountain Range.*

2. In the United Kingdom many mountains are named "Ben" after the Scottish Gaelic word, Beinn, which means "mountain". What is the name of the tallest mountain in the United Kingdom? *The tallest mountain in the United Kingdom is Ben Nevis, which is located in Scotland.*

3. Sir Edmund Hillary and Tenzing Norgay were the first to summit Mount Everest in 1953. Which mountain in New Zealand is also associated with Sir Edmund Hillary? *Mount Cook | Aoraki, was a mountaineering challenge for Hillary in New Zealand's South Island. It is the highest mountain in the Southern Alps mountain range and in New Zealand.*

4. Which landform is referred to as "the roof of the world"? *The Tibetan Plateau.*

5. What is the highest point of a mountain called? *The summit. This is different to a peak, which is a pointed top. A mountain may have many peaks but only one summit.*

6. In which biome are mesas and buttes located? *Both are found in arid or semi-arid regions.*

7. In which American state is the Grand Mesa located? *The state of Colorado.*

8. How does a butte differ to a mesa? *Many buttes were first plateaus or mesas, but over time have eroded. A butte is often taller than a mesa. Also, a butte is taller than it is wide, while mesas can be very large or small.*

Map Questions on Chapter 29

1. Mount Rainer is found in the North American continent. It is located in the state of Washington, in the United States of America. On a map find Washington state and list the bordering states, country, and ocean. *The state of Idaho is to the east and Oregon is in the south. The bordering country to the north is Canada, and the ocean on the west coast is the Pacific Ocean.*

2. Mount Kilimanjaro and Table Mountain are both found on the African continent. Identify which countries they are located in. *Mount Kilimanjaro is found in Tanzania and Table Mountain is in South Africa.*

3. On a map of Europe find the countries that the Alps stretch across. *The Alps are in the nations of France, Italy, Switzerland, Germany, Austria, Lichtenstein, and Slovenia.*

4. On a map please find a mountain range within the continent that

you live in. *Answers will vary, but Australians may wish to locate the Great Dividing Range, while the Rocky Mountains or the Appalachians might be chosen by those families in North America. Students in Asia may wish to choose from the Himalayas, Annapurna Mountain Range, or the Zagros Mountains.*

5. Please find the Himalayan Mountain Range and the Tibetan Plateau on a map. Name two of the countries within this part of Asia. *Nepal, Tibet, China, India, and Bhutan are all acceptable answers.*

6. Monument Valley is found in Utah. On a map, find the states that border Utah. *To the north is the state of Idaho, while Arizona is to the south. Nevada is to the west of Utah and Colorado to the east. The northeastern corner of Utah borders with Wyoming, and at the Four Corners Monument, Utah borders with the corner of New Mexico. This Four Corners Monument is important because it is the only point in the United States of America that is shared by four states (Utah, Arizona, Colorado, and New Mexico).*

Questions on Chapters 30 and 31

1. On which mountain is the Khumbu Icefall located? *The Khumbu Icefall is close to Base Camp on Mount Everest.*

2. How is a crevice different to a crevasse? *They are different in size. While a crevice is a little crack in a rock, a crevasse is a deep, narrow crack in a rock or glacier.*

3. Why are seracs dangerous? *Seracs are large pillars of ice and can suddenly fall due to ice release. They can block areas or cause avalanches.*

4. How is a gorge different to a canyon? *Both are deep valleys, but canyons are wider than gorges, encompassing a greater area.*

5. Which canyon is deeper: the Grand Canyon in the United States of America or the Yarlung Zangbo Grand Canyon? *The Yarlung Zangbo Grand Canyon is deeper.*

6. In which country is the Blyde River Canyon Nature Reserve located? *South Africa.*

7. Volcanoes are classified into three categories, one of which is active. What are the other two categories? *Volcanoes can also be categorised as dormant or extinct.*

8. Which is the largest active volcano in the world? *Mauna Loa in Hawai'i.*

9. There are three main different types of volcanoes. Name the three types.

There are stratovolcanoes, or composite volcanoes, like Mount Vesuvius in Italy. There are also shield volcanoes, like Mauna Loa; and Cinder Cones.

Map Questions on Chapters 30 and 31

1. The Grand Canyon National Park is found in the state of Arizona. Name the country and American states bordering Arizona. *The country of Mexico borders Arizona in the south. The state of Nevada is located to the northwest and Utah to the north. The state of New Mexico is to the east and California to the west. The state of Colorado meets the northeastern tip of Arizona, so these two states meet at the Four Corners, the quadripoint where the boundaries of Arizona, Utah, New Mexico and Colorado all meet.*

2. The Drakensberg Mountain Range is located within both the countries of South Africa and the Kingdom of Lesotho. Find the capital city of Lesotho. *Maseru is the national capital of Lesotho and located on the western border of the country.*

3. Mount Fuji is a volcano on the Japanese island of Honshu. Find the island of Honshu on a map and also Okinawa, another Japanese island. *Students will find these islands in the Pacific Ocean. Okinawa is south of Honshu.*

4. The Ring of Fire is an area of seismic activity around the Pacific Ocean. Find the Ring of Fire on a map, tracing around its location. *The Ring of Fire is one of the most geologically active areas on Earth. It extends from Mount Erebus, the southernmost active volcano in Antarctica, along the western coast of South and North America across to Alaska, across the Bering Strait, and through to Japan, the Philippines, and south to New Zealand.*

5. Mauna Loa is an active volcano in the American state of Hawai'i. Name the capital of the Hawaiian Islands and find it on a map. *Honolulu is the capital of Hawai'i and is located on the south shore of the island of Oahu.*

6. In which country is Eyjafjallajökull found? *Iceland.*

7. Name the ocean that surrounds Iceland and list the closest countries. *Iceland is found within the Atlantic Ocean, close to the North, Norwegian and Greenland Seas. Nearby countries include Greenland (a part of Denmark), Ireland, the United Kingdom, and Norway.*

Questions on Chapters 32 and 33

1. What scale is used to measure earthquakes? *While the Richter scale was*

previously used, earthquakes are now measured by magnitude, in a scale called the Moment Magnitude scale.

2. Name two of the major greenhouse gases. *The major greenhouse gases are water vapour, carbon dioxide, methane, and nitrous oxide.*

3. What is the major crop grown in the Mekong River Delta in Vietnam? *Rice is grown throughout this region.*

4. Is it true that the Great Barrier Reef is the world's largest reef system? *Yes, it is true. Made up of over 3,000 individual reefs and 900 islands, it is a massive reef.*

5. Mangrove forests are located in coastal areas within tropical and sub-tropical regions. They are made up of trees with twisted and coiled roots that provide an important habitat for a range of animal species. Name some of the animals you might find in mangrove forests. *Answers may vary, but based on text answers are likely to include insects, reptiles, birds, and animals such as monkeys and tigers, as well as many species of fish, crustaceans, and molluscs.*

Map Questions on Chapters 32 and 33

1. Please examine a map of the tectonic plates and name four of the major plates. *By convention there are seven main, or "primary", tectonic plates identified: the African, Antarctic, Eurasian, Indo-Australian, North American, Pacific, and South American Plates.*

2. The Great Chilean Earthquake triggered a tsunami which was felt across the Pacific Ocean, devastating parts of Japan, Hawai'i and the Philippines. Find the capital city of the Philippines on a map. *Manila is the national capital of Philippines. It is on the island of Luzon.*

3. The Sundarbans are the world's largest mangrove forests, within the Ganges-Brahmaputra delta, in Bay of Bengal within India and Bangladesh. Find the Bay of Bengal and name the ocean it is connected to. *The Bay of Bengal is within the northeastern Indian Ocean. The nations of India, Bangladesh, Sri Lanka, and Myanmar all border the Bay of Bengal.*

Questions on Chapters 34, 35, 36 and 37

1. What is the name given to a map maker? *A map maker is called a cartographer.*

2. What does GIS stand for and what is it? *GIS is the acronym for Geographical Information Systems. This is a computer-based mapping system*

designed to capture, store, manage, analyse, and present geographical spatial data. Cartographers use GIS to make maps.

3. Cartographers use a scale to ensure consistency and accuracy. Maps are generally described as being large or small scale. Describe what a small scale map would be used for. *A small scale is used for maps showing a large area. A world map is a small scale map. This is because to show the entire world on one piece of paper requires hundreds of kilometres of land to be captured in just a few millimetres.*

4. What is a thermoformed map? *A thermoformed map is essentially a braille map, created to help blind and vision impaired map users by offering spatial information in a tactile form.*

5. What is Landsat? *Landsat is a satellite that circles Earth more than a dozen times each day. It collects and transmits masses of data which is then processed through computers for mapping purposes. Landsat was first launched in 1972 as a joint program between NASA and the US Geological Survey.*

Map Questions on Chapters 34, 35, 36 and 37

1. The following places are external territories in Oceania. Find the place and name which country it is connected to:
   Rapa Nui (also known as Easter Island);
   Guam;
   French Polynesia.
   Rapa Nui is part of Chile. Guam, is a territory of the United States of America. French Polynesia is an overseas country of France.

2. Please select a printed map and examine it to determine the scale used. *Answers will vary depending on the map chosen, but the scale will be expressed in a bar scale or a representative ratio, such as 1:10,000 and is likely to be included within the legend.*

3. Look at the legend or key of a map to see which symbols are used to show key features. This may be dots to show towns and villages, coloured lines to show roads, boundaries, or rivers. Choose at least three different symbols within the legend and find those features on the map. *Answers will vary as the children work from different maps, but please guide them to look for the most common features on the map they are using.*

4. On the same map, please check the title of the map. Also determine whether a date and the source data is provided. *Again, answers will vary, but guide your child to find where to find this information on at least one map.*

5. Please look at a range of maps to see the differences between them in

showing orientation. Some may include a compass rose, while others just use a north point.

Questions on Chapters 38 and 39

1. Name one town or village you would find in the Lake District of England. *Based on the text, answers will include Ambleside, Grasmere, Rydal, Keswick, or Windermere.*

2. Name two emerging megacities on the continent of Africa. *Based on the text, answers will include: Kinshasa, in the Democratic Republic of the Congo; Cairo, Egypt's national capital; Dar es Salaam in Tanzania; Luanda in Angola; and Lagos in Nigeria.*

3. What are some of the differences between living in a city as opposed to a town or village? *Answers will vary, but students should note the greater population size of a city compared with a town. Many are likely to observe the increased opportunities and variety of services, social activities, and cultural events available in a city that towns may not have. This includes schools, universities, employment, shops and markets, health facilities, transportation options, art galleries, museums, concert halls, and much more. Students may include that living in a town can mean closer community connections, lower population density, less traffic and congestion, and possibly a more picturesque landscape.*

4. At what point is a city classified as a megacity? *Based on population, once a city reaches 10 million people it is a megacity.*

5. Name the two Asian countries where most of the world's megacities are located. *India and China.*

6. Name four of the megacities within India and China. *Based on the text, answers will include Shanghai, Beijing, Chengdu, Guangzhou, Chongqing, Delhi, and Mumbai.*

7. The national capital of Japan was previously known as Edo. Today it is one of the world's most populous metropolitan areas. What is it called and on which island of Japan is it located? *Tokyo is the capital city of Japan and is located on the island of Honshu.*

Map Questions on Chapters 38 and 39

1. London, New York City, Paris, and Tokyo are four global cities that have been established for centuries. London and Paris are on the European continent. London is in England and Paris is in France. New York

City is on the east coast of the United States of America and Tokyo is in Japan. Please find each of these countries and cities on a map.

2. India and China are the two most populous nations and together represent nearly one-third of the total global population. Please find these nations on a map.

3. Hong Kong, Shanghai, and Beijing are all cities in the People's Republic of China. Beijing is the national capital of China and is located inland. Shanghai and Hong Kong are both coastal cities. Please find these three cities on a map.

4. Singapore is both a city and a nation. It is in Southeast Asia. On a map, find the city and name the country that lies directly to the north of Singapore. *Malaysia is the country that is north of Singapore.*

5. Using a map of Africa, find the following cities: *Kinshasa, in the Democratic Republic of the Congo, Cairo, Egypt's national capital; Dar es Salaam in Tanzania, Luanda in Angola, Lagos in Nigeria.*

Thank you for choosing Modern Elementary Geography by Jo Lloyd, brought to you by Living Book Press.

Three Sisters, Blue Mountains, Australia